Praise for Jonathan Carroll

"Jonathan Carroll is as scary as Hitchcock, when he isn't being as funny as Jim Carrey. If you've never read this wonderful fantasist, buy this book. You'll stay up all night and thank me in the morning."

—Stephen King

"Wonderful insights and poetic phrases . . . Poetic and magical, dense with a wonderful strangeness reminiscent of Fellini and urgent with inklings of horror around the corner . . . Carroll often startles with the deftness of his insights, both personal and metaphysical, and there are lines that, for their poetry, one wants to cut out and frame. . . . Beauty and wisdom reside here."

—Publishers Weekly

"He's a born writer, a writer of impulse, instinct, and personality in the way the old Hollywood stars were actors. His likes, dislikes, and ingenuous charm shimmer through his extraordinary prose, most specifically for all things childlike. No one in this field has set off sparks in quite the same way since Ray Bradbury. When Jonathan Carroll is on the page, you have to watch him."

—Philadelphia Inquirer

"If you haven't discovered the lyrical, twisted, fantastical, and entertaining novels of Jonathan Carroll, then it's time you did. His books fit very well on the shelf alongside Graham Joyce, Peter S. Beagle, and Charles de Lint, all masters of style and language."

—The Davis Enterprise

"His style is a kind of hybrid of Hermann Hesse and D. M. Thomas. . . . Taking the reader far beyond comic book sorcery and the world of the one-dimensional, love-crossed hero, Carroll achieves that rarest of literary triumphs: bold adult fantasy that shimmers with both invention and feeling."

—Booklist

"The narrator, Miranda Romanac, a Manhattan rare-book dealer, goes to a high school reunion and a dinner party. This is normal reality. . . . The transition to fantasy is adroitly handled. Miranda meets two crucial characters, Hugh Oakley and Frances Hatch, the elderly former lover of many great twentieth-century artists. Miranda's love affair with the married Hugh is brisk and engaging. The salad of mythologies, involving predestination, alternative realities, and reincarnation, works surprisingly well. The unfolding of the plot pulls the reader through a succession of strikingly bizarre incidents which are recounted in a languid prose style . . . that suggests a delicate and distant irony."

—Times Literary Supplement

"The author of *Bones of the Moon* evokes an eerie world of hidden meanings in this compelling tale of a woman's journey to the edge of reality. Carroll writes with a stark elegance that infuses the everyday world with a hint of surrealism and a taste of the unreal. Highly recommended for fantasy and general fiction collections."

—Library Journal

Books by Jonathan Carroll

The Land of Laughs

Voice of Our Shadow

Bones of the Moon

Sleeping in Flame

A Child Across the Sky

Black Cocktail

Outside the Dog Museum

After Silence

From the Teeth of Angels

The Panic Hand

Kissing the Beehive

The Marriage of Sticks

The Wooden Sea

TOR®

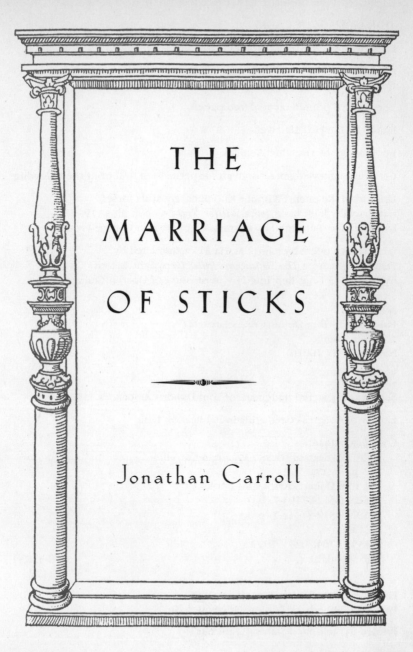

THE
MARRIAGE
OF STICKS

Jonathan Carroll

THE MARRIAGE OF STICKS

Copyright © 1999 by Jonathan Carroll

Edited by David G. Hartwell

Book design by Gretchen Achilles

Grateful acknowledgment is given for permission to reprint the following:

Lines from the poem "Without Knocking" by Attila József,
translated by John Bátki, from *Winter Night*. Copyright © 1997
by John Bátki. Reprinted by permission of Oberlin College Press.

Lines from a poem by Rainer Maria Rilke, translated by
Franz Wright, from *The Unknown Rilke*. Copyright © 1990
by Oberlin College. Reprinted by permission of Oberlin College Press.

A Tor Book
Published by Tom Doherty Associates, LLC
175 Fifth Avenue
New York, NY 10010

www.tor.com

Tor ® is a registered trademark of Tom Doherty Associates, LLC.

Library of Congress Cataloging-in-Publication Data

Carroll, Jonathan.
    The marriage of sticks / Jonathan Carroll.
        p.   cm.
    "A Tom Doherty Associates book."
    ISBN 0-312-87193-7 (hc)
    ISBN 0-312-87243-7 (pbk)
    I. Title.
PS3553.A7646M37   1999
813'.54—dc21   99-33233
                                                          CIP

First Hardcover Edition: September 1999
First Trade Paperback Edition: November 2000

Printed in the United States of America

0 9 8 7 6 5 4 3 2 1

To

IFAH

ROGER PEYTON

ELLEN DATLOW

WENDY SCHMALZ

PATRICIA POWELL

What would I do without you?

Bend your back to it, sir: for it will snow all night.
—THOMAS LUX, *Old Man Shoveling Snow*

PART

ONE

THE DOG MAKES
THE BED

IN THE END, each of us has only one story to tell. Yet despite having lived that story, most people have neither the courage nor any idea of how to tell it.

I did not live this long so that now, when I am finally able to talk about my life, I will lie about it. What's the point? There is no one left to impress. Those who once loved or hated me are gone or have barely enough energy left to breathe. Except for one.

There is little else to do now but remember. I am an old old woman with a head full of memories, fragile as eggs. Yet the memories remain loud and demanding. "Remember me!" they shout. Or "Remember the dog that spoke." I say, "Tell the truth! Are you sure? Or are you making up more convenient history just to make me feel better?"

It is too easy to turn your best profile to history's mirror. But history doesn't care. I have learned that.

Mirrors and treasure maps. X marks the spot not where a life begins, but where it begins to matter. Forget who your parents were, what you learned, what you did, gained, or lost. Where did the trip *begin*? When did you know you were walking through the departure gate?

My story, the X on my map, began in a Santa Monica hotel with the dog that made the bed.

WE'D MET RIGHT after college. For a while, for a year and a half, both of us truly believed this would be the great love of both our lives. We lived together, visited Europe for the first time together, talked shyly about marriage and what we would name our children. We bought things we knew would live in a great old house we'd have someday by an ocean. He was the best lover I ever had.

What ruined us was simple: at twenty-one you're too damned optimistic. Too sure life has so many wonderful things in store that you can afford to be careless. We treated our relationship like a dependable car that would always start and run, no matter how cold or bad the weather. We were wrong.

Things got bad very quickly. We were unprepared for failure and each other's dumb cruelty. When you're that young, it is easy to go from lovers to enemies in a couple of breaths. I began calling him Dog. He called me Bitch. We deserved the names.

So why, twelve years later, was that very same Dog sitting in an expensive hotel room when I came out of the shower, wet hair wrapped in a towel and pleased to see he'd made the bed? A bed we'd shared for the last ten hours with as great a relish as always between us? Because you take what you can get. Women love to talk. If you find a man who loves to listen *and* who happens to be a great lover, damn the rest. You're the one who has to live inside your skin and conscience. If you can visit an old lover and still revel in whatever things you once had between you, then they are still yours if you want them. Is it right to do? I only know that life is a series of diminishing returns, ending with too many days in a chair, staring. I always sensed it would be that way. I wanted to be an old woman remembering, not complaining or fretting until death rang the dinner bell.

Over the years Dog and I had met when it was convenient. Almost always it was a joyous, selfish few days together. Both of us left those meetings replenished. His word, and it fit.

He'd made the bed and straightened the room. But that was Doug Auerbach: an organized man and a successful one too, up to a point. I admired him but was glad we had never married.

The place looked exactly as it had the day before when we'd walked in. He was sitting with his hands in his lap, watching a game show on television. The oohs and aahs of the audience sounded sad in that cavernous lilac room. I stood looking at him, toweling my hair, wondering when we'd meet again.

Without taking his eyes from the set, he said he'd been thinking about me. I asked in what way. He said he'd been married and divorced, had only sort of succeeded at what he'd wanted to do with his life, and generally regretted more than he was proud of. He saw me as just the opposite. When I protested, he looked up and said, "Please don't!" As if I was about to do something terrible to him.

Then he turned off the television and asked if I would do him a big favor. Across the street from our hotel was a large drugstore. He wanted me to go there with him while he bought a razor and some shampoo. He knew I had lots to do before my plane left for New York that evening, but there was no leeway in his tone of voice.

I hurriedly dressed while he sat and watched me hustle around the room. What could be so important about a trip to the drugstore? I was annoyed, but also felt there was something both pathetic and urgent about his request.

The store was one of those large discount places that sold thirty kinds of toothpaste, and all the customers seemed to be moving down the aisles in a stupor.

Like the others, we grazed the razor and shampoo shelves. It was clear he was in no hurry to find what he wanted.

"What's going on, Doug?"

He turned to me and slowly smiled. "Hmm?"

"Why do you need me around to buy soap?"

He didn't say anything for a moment, only looked at me and seemed to consider the question. "I've been wanting to do this ever since I heard we were going to meet. More than the talk, the sex, more than anything. I just wanted to go into a store with you and walk around, making believe we were husband and wife. Just out for a few minutes to buy some aspirin and a *TV Guide,* maybe a couple of ice-cream cones. It would've been better really late, but I didn't want to say anything last night.

"I've always been jealous when I go into an all-night drugstore or market and see couples shopping together. I look in their baskets to see what they're buying."

"Didn't you ever do that with your wife?" I wanted to touch his arm but held back.

"Sure, but I didn't *know* I was doing it then. Now I do. Know what I mean? Then it was just a drag, something necessary. With you, I knew it would be a little adventure and we'd know we were having fun while we did it. Even if we didn't buy anything, it'd be . . ."

He looked at me but didn't say anything more. The worst part was, I knew exactly what he was saying, and was sorry. Yet there were other things to do and they were more important to me than this. I wanted to comfort him but wanted to leave just as much. It meant so much more to him than to me.

We bought his stuff, went back to the hotel, and checked out. Waiting for my cab out on the street, we hugged. I told him we'd see each other in New York at the end of the summer.

When the cab arrived he said, "You know there's a famous rap singer now named Dog. Snoop Doggy Dogg."

"Doesn't matter. You're the only Dog Man I'll ever love."

He nodded. "Thanks for the drugstore."

THAT SHOULD HAVE been reason enough to tell me that there was more in the air then than oxygen. Why does it take a lifetime to realize that premonitions are as numerous as birds in a cherry tree? During the cab ride to the airport I saw something else that, in retrospect, *certainly* should have told me to think hard about what was going on rather than just look at my watch and hope I didn't miss the plane.

The driver was a big old man who wore a San Diego Padres baseball cap and didn't utter a sound other than a resentful grunt when he banged my suitcase into the trunk of his car. That was fine because I sat in the back with a cell phone and returned calls to people I'd avoided while in L.A. I had the practice down to an art— call someone and tell her you're on your way to the airport but just had to touch base with her before you left. Then she told you everything in a five-minute chat she would have taken two hours to tell over an expensive dinner. Who said patience came as you grew older? I had less and less and was proud of it. Whatever success I had was due to keeping things short and sweet, and expecting the same of others.

In the middle of my last call I had my eyes closed and didn't register what the driver said until a moment later. When I opened them we were passing an astonishing sight: there by the side of the freeway was a woman in a wheelchair.

It must have been eight at night and there were no streetlamps, only the stab and drift of headlights across the Los Angeles darkness. Only a moment to glimpse her and then we were gone. But for that moment there she was, illuminated by the car in front and then us: a woman sitting in a wheelchair on the shoulder of a superhighway out in the middle of nowhere.

"Nuts. L.A. is full of nuts!"

I looked in the rearview mirror. The driver was staring at me, waiting for me to agree.

"Maybe she's not nuts. Maybe she's stuck there, or something has happened to her."

He shook his head slowly. "No way. Driving a cab, you see things like that four times a day. You want to see how crazy the world is, drive a cab."

But that didn't satisfy me and I called 911 to report it. I had to ask the driver exactly where we'd been on the road. He answered in a curt voice. The operator asked if there were any more details. I could only say no, there's a woman in a wheelchair on the side of the road and something's wrong with that, you know?

The whole flight to New York I kept thinking about that half hour in the drugstore and then the woman in the wheelchair. Both made me uneasy. But then we landed and there were so many things to do that week before I met up with Zoe.

Even the idea of seeing my old best friend and doing what we'd planned made some part of my heart nervous. We were going to our high school class's fifteen-year reunion.

Events like that always sounded great months before they happened. Then as the time closed in, my enthusiasm began to curdle like bad milk. With this reunion, part of me wanted to know what had happened to certain classmates after all those years. The other part was both petrified and appalled to be seen by people who'd owned my life when I was eighteen years old.

Now I am unconcerned by my past, but at thirty-three I wasn't. Back then, embarrassment still arrived in capital letters. I cared very much what most people thought of me. Even fifteen years after high school, I wanted to walk into the reunion sure that most of my old classmates would be pleased, impressed, or jealous—and not necessarily in that order.

Zoe was different. Compared to my life since high school, Zoe Holland's had been a shooting gallery, with her as the target. She dropped out of college freshman year and married when she found out she was pregnant. The culprit was a vain little scorpion named Andy Holland who, three months after they were married, started sleeping around with whomever he could find. Why he wanted to be married neither Zoe nor I could ever figure out. They had two children in quick succession.

Then, out of the blue, Andy announced one day that he was leaving. Zoe was suddenly on her own with two babies and no prospects. The fact that she prevailed was inspiring because nothing she had done before prepared her for it.

She had been one of the queens of our high school class—high grades, lots of friends, and the captain of the high school football team, Kevin Hamilton, was her love. Everyone looked at Zoe and sighed. But she was such a nice person that almost no one resented her good fortune.

She was an optimist and, even in the midst of her later torment, believed if she worked hard and remained kind, things would improve.

She took a couple of part-time jobs and struggled through. When her kids were old enough to go to school, she enrolled in community college. There she met the next disaster in her life, a handsome guy who began beating her up a few months after he moved in.

Suffice it to say, Zoe's philosophy wasn't correct and throughout the ensuing years more bad happened to her than good. By the time the class reunion rolled around, she was living in a sad little house in our old hometown; one of her children did serious drugs and the other didn't have much to say for himself.

I TOOK THE train up from Manhattan. Since my parents moved to California, I hadn't been back to Connecticut in a decade. The ride that hot Friday afternoon was the beginning of a trip to the past I was ambivalent about making.

I hadn't seen Zoe for years, although we spoke on the phone now and then. She was waiting for me at the station looking happy and exhausted in equal measure. She had put on weight, but what really struck me was how large her breasts were. In high school one of our constant running jokes was how neither of us had much in that department. Now there she was in a black polo shirt that stretched in ways that said it all. I must have been pretty unsubtle in my staring because after we hugged, she stood back, put her hands on her hips and asked in a proud voice "Well, what do you think?"

There were people walking by so I didn't want to say anything too obvious. I shook my head and said, "Impressive!"

She hugged herself a moment and grinned. "Aren't they great?"

We got into her old Subaru station wagon and drove through town. All the way to her house she rhapsodized about new boyfriend Hector, who was the greatest thing to happen to her since she didn't know when. The only problem was, Hector was married and had four children. But his wife didn't understand him and . . . You can take it from there.

She had the look of a saint in a religious painting. I kept looking from her face to those movie-star breasts and didn't know what to say or think. Married Hector held her life in his hands but she seemed thrilled. From the sound of it, she was just happy someone was interested enough to *want* to hold her life, take the weight from her while she rested up.

Her house was so small that it didn't have a driveway, so we parked on the street in front. At first glimpse, it was the kind of house you see in biographies of famous people as the home where they were raised, or the first one they owned when they were starting out, poor but enthusiastic.

She had arranged for her kids to be away for the weekend so we could have the place to ourselves and not worry about them.

As she fumbled through her keys searching for the one to the front door, I felt a momentary squirt of fear go up me. Suddenly I didn't *want* to go into this house. Didn't want to see what was there. Didn't want to see the concrete results of my friend's life on the mantelpiece, the walls, the coffee table. Things like photographs of kids gone bad, souvenirs from places where she'd been happy for a few days, a cheap couch that had known a million hours of unmoving asses watching TV with no real interest.

But I was completely wrong and that broke my heart even more. Zoe had a wonderful home. Somehow she had distilled all of her love and care into those few small rooms. Walking through them, admiring her taste, sense of humor, and talent for putting the right things in exactly the right places, I kept wondering, Why *hasn't* it worked for her? Why has everything gone so wrong for such a good person?

There was a small backyard that she'd saved for last to show me because there sat the surprise. Pitched in the middle of it was a familiar brown tent that made me laugh loudly as soon as I saw it.

"Is that *it*?"

Zoe was beaming. "The exact same one! I've saved it all these years. Tonight we're going to camp out again!"

When we were teens, our weekend ritual in the summer was always the same: set up this tent, stock it with junk food and fashion magazines, then spend the night inside gabbing and dreaming out loud. Our houses belonged to our parents, but this old Boy Scout tent in Zoe's backyard was ours alone. Her brothers were banned from it and we took swift action when they tried to invade. What we talked about in there all those nights was as secret and important as the blood moving through our veins.

I walked over and touched the tent flap. As I held it between my fingers, the rough familiar cloth was an instant tactile reminder of a time when life still made sense, limits were for old people, and James Stillman was the most important person on earth for me.

"Look inside."

I bent down and peeked into the tent. Two sleeping bags lay on the floor with a Coleman lamp between them. There was a box of Zagnut candy bars.

"Zagnuts! My God, Zoe, you've thought of everything!"

"I know! Do you believe they still make them? Oh, Miranda, I have so many things to tell you!"

We went back into the house. She showed me to her daughter's room, where I changed into cooler clothes. Afterwards she suggested we take a drive around town before dinner and have a look at our old stomping grounds.

Far more disturbing than any spook house at an amusement park is a ride through the old hometown if you've been away for years. What do you expect to see? What do you want to see? Having been away so long, you know it'll be different. Still, seeing the inevitable changes makes quick deep slashes across your soul. Loss, loss. Where are all those places I once was?

Iansiti's Pizza Parlor was gone, replaced by a store with a post-modern facade that sold CDs. There were only records when I lived here. LPs, *not* CDs. I thought about all the slices of pizza with extra cheese and pepperoni we'd eaten in Iansiti's, all the dreams and teen-age hormones that once filled that dumpy place with its stained menus and bunch of fat-bellied Italian cousins in T-shirts eyeing us from behind the counter.

"Sometimes when I'm driving down these streets, looking at our old hangouts, I think I see myself inside them." Zoe chuckled and slowed for a yellow light in front of the bank where James's mother had worked.

I turned to her. "But *which* you? The one you were, or the you now?"

"Oh, the one I was! I always think of myself as seventeen here. I've never gotten over the fact I'm twice that age but still living in this town."

"Don't you feel strange going by the old places? Like your parents' house?"

"Very. But when they died, so did it. A house is the people who live there, not the building. I just wish I hadn't sold it when the market was so bad. The story of my life."

We drove by the high school, which despite some new buildings still looked as glum as ever. Past the town park, where, one fifteen-year-old summer night, I almost lost my virginity. Then down the Post Road to the Carvel ice cream stand where James and I sat on the hood of his old green Saab and ate vanilla cones dipped in heated chocolate.

Until that moment, I hadn't been able to get up the nerve to ask Zoe *the* question, but seeing that cherished Carvel stand was a sign it was time. As casually as possible I asked, "Is James coming to the reunion?"

Zoe looked at her watch and dramatically blew out a breath like she'd been holding it for minutes. "Phew! You went a full hour without asking. I don't know, Miranda. I asked around, but no one knew. I'm sure he knows about it."

"I didn't realize till we started driving around that this whole *town* is haunted by him." I turned to her. "I didn't know how I'd react coming back, but more than anything it's James everywhere! I keep seeing places where we were together. Where we were happy."

"Miranda, he was the love of your life."

"When I was eighteen! I *have* done other things since then." The tone of my voice was stiff, prissy. I sounded too much on the defensive.

"Not as much as you think." She grinned and threw me a quick look. "High school is a terminal disease. It either kills you while you're there, or waits inside your soul for years and then comes back to get you."

"Come on, Zoe, you don't believe that! You had a wonderful time in high school."

"Exactly! And that's what killed *me*. Nothing was ever better than high school."

"You sound so cheerful about it."

She chuckled. "Right now I'm looking forward to the reunion because in those people's eyes, no matter what's happened to me in the last fifteen years, I'll always be Zoe the golden girl. The cheerleader with the great grades and the boyfriend who was captain of the football team. And you'll always be Miranda Romanac, the good girl who shocked everyone senior year by going out with the baddest boy in school." She slapped my knee.

In a bad Irish accent I said, "Aye, and God bless the boy!"

She raised a hand as if it held a glass and she was offering a toast. "And God bless Kevin. I'm also looking forward to this because I hope he'll be there. And he'll be absolutely wonderful, sweep me off my feet and save me from the rest of my life."

My heart filled so quickly that I couldn't catch my breath. It was exactly the way I had been thinking for weeks.

I MET JAMES Stillman in geometry class. God knows, I knew *about* him before; he had a reputation fifteen miles long. He mesmerized innocent girls into his bed. He'd once stolen a pair of skis from the town sport shop, then had the chutzpah to return there the next day to have the edges sharpened. He and his friends were reputed to have burned down the abandoned Brody house during one of their infamous parties there. All told, James was not interested in being a solid citizen.

A group of typical thugs had usually slouched around our school halls wearing gaudy leather jackets and intricately piled hairdos that looked like hood ornaments, but James Stillman's brand of bad was planets away from those human clichés. What fascinated me was his great, singular style when I didn't even really know what that word meant yet. Despite his reputation, he dressed like a preppy, in tweed jackets, khakis, and loafers. He listened to European rock groups— Spliff and Guesch Patti—and was even rumored to love cooking. When he was going out with Claudia Beechman, he had a bouquet of yellow roses delivered to her in gym class on her birthday. Like most of the girls in the high school, I watched him from afar, wondering if all the things said about him were true. What *would* it be like to know him, date, kiss him? But that was academic because I knew the thought of someone as colorless and well behaved as me would never even cross his mind.

"What'd he say?"

Only after a *thud* inside my brain did I realize that James Stillman had asked *me* a question. He sat behind me in geometry class but only because seating was alphabetical. Before I had a chance to digest what had happened, he repeated the question, this time adding my name to it.

"Miranda? What'd he say?"

He knew me. He knew who I *was*.

The teacher had said the earth was an oblate spheroid, as I dutifully noted in my book. I turned and said, "He said the earth's an oblate spheroid."

James watched me intently, as if whatever I said he'd been waiting all morning to hear.

"A what?"

"Uh, an oblate spheroid."

"What's that?"

I was about to say, "Like an egg that's been leaned on," but something inside said shut up. I shrugged instead.

A small slow grin moved his mouth up. "You know, but you're not admitting it."

I panicked. Did he know I was playing dumb just for him?

"It's okay to know things. I just know different stuff." He smiled mysteriously, looked away.

After class I kept my eyes down and gathered my books as slowly as possible. That way there would be no chance of walking out of the room at the same time he did.

"I'm sorry."

I stood still and closed my eyes. He was behind me. I didn't know what to say. I didn't need to because he came around and stood in front of me.

"Sorry about what?" I couldn't look at him.

"About what I said. Do you think you'd ever want to go out with me?"

All I remember about that moment was I could actually *feel* fate's wheels turning inside me. In the split second before I answered, I knew everything would now change, no matter what.

"You want to go out with *me*?" I tried to make it light and sarcastic so I would be in on his joke if there were one.

His face was expressionless. "Yes. You don't know how much I've been wanting to talk to you."

WE WERE INSEPARABLE for the rest of the year. He was everything I wasn't. For the first time in my life, I learned with increasing joy that *different* could be *complementary*. We had worlds we wanted the other to see. Somehow those very different worlds fit together.

Remarkably, we never slept together, which was one of the great mistakes of my life. James was the first man I ever loved with an adult heart. To this day I still wish he'd been my first lover instead of a handsome forgettable goof I said yes to a month after I got to college.

I never asked about other girls before me, but contrary to his reputation, James never did anything I didn't want. He was gentle, loving, and respectful. A sheep in wolf's clothes. On top of that, he was a wickedly good kisser. Don't get me wrong—just because we never did *it* doesn't preclude a few thousand delicious hours horizontal, hot, and hungry.

Because we were such different souls, he seemed delighted by my prim, skirt-down-over-the-knee worldview. He knew I wanted to be a virgin when I married and never tried to force the issue or change my mind. Maybe because he was so used to girls saying yes to everything he wanted, I was like an alien to him—something peculiar, worth studying.

As is so often the case, our relationship ended when we went off to different colleges in different states. Those first months apart, I wrote him furious, impassioned letters. He responded with only stupid two-line postcards now and then, which was perfectly in keeping with his bad-James part. Gradually college and its different faces, as well as the rest of my new life's diversions, slowed my letters to a trickle. When we saw each other again that first Christmas vacation home, it was warm and tender, but both of us had new lives elsewhere. Our reunion was more nostalgia than building toward any kind of future.

Over the next years I'd heard things about James from different sources, but never knew which were true and which third-hand information. Someone said he worked in a boatyard, another that he'd finished college and gone to law school. If the last was true, he became a very different J. Stillman from the one I had known. They said he lived in Colorado, then Philadelphia; he was married, he wasn't. Sometimes when I was restless in bed at night, or low, or just dreaming about what might have been, I thought about my old love and wondered what had happened to him. The first thing that came to mind on reading the invitation to our class reunion was *James Stillman.*

FOR OLD TIMES' sake, Zoe and I had dinner at Chuck's Steak House. We'd worked there together as waitresses one summer and walked home late all those warm nights with nice tips in our pockets, feeling very adult. Chuck had died years before, but his son took over and kept the place looking exactly the same.

Earlier, Zoe had said she had many things to tell me, but since that afternoon a kind of delicious time warp had set in. Both of us were content inside it talking mostly about *then* and little about now. A half hour sufficed for catching up on where we were in our lives. This was to be a weekend for memories, photo albums, "Whatever happened to . . .?" and the sighs that come with remembering who you were. At dinner neither of us expressed much interest in talking about what we'd become or where we hoped to go with our lives. Perhaps that would have come after the reunion—a natural summing up after seeing old classmates and putting the weekend and the experiences into context. But as things turned out, that summing up was done for us.

After Chuck's, we returned to Zoe's house. Both of us were dying to get into the tent, our old mood, those times. We hurriedly washed, changed into our pajamas, and by the hissing light of the Coleman lamp, talked until two.

The next morning she got up before I did. The first thing I remember about that momentous day was a violent tugging on my arm. Not knowing what was happening, I tried to clear my head and sit up at the same time. I forgot I wasn't in a bed but wrapped in the cocoon of a sleeping bag. Held on all sides, I started thrashing around, which only tightened the bag around me. By the time I extricated myself, my hair was standing out from my head, my face was heated to two hundred degrees, my pajama top was wide open.

"Miranda!"

"*What?* What's the matter?"

"Are you all right?"

Early as it was, I went instantly on the defensive. "What do you mean?"

"You know exactly what I mean. The way you were thrashing around. And everything you talked about last night, the way you see things now. . . . You have such a good life. You're successful and you said it yourself; things've worked out. But you're not happy. The way you talk—"

"How *do* I talk, Zoe?"

"Like you're old. Like you don't expect anything better to happen because you've lived too long and seen too much to have any more hope. I'm luckier than you. I don't think life's very friendly either, but I know we *can* control hope. You can turn it on and off like a spigot. I try to keep mine on full blast."

"That *sounds* good, but what happens when things go wrong? What happens when you're disappointed time after time?"

"It kills you! But you go on and when you've got the strength, you start hoping again. It's our choice." She reached over and took my hand. It made me very uncomfortable.

"Maybe I've just learned to be careful."

"Would *careful* you have the guts to fall in love with a James Stillman today?"

The question was so accurate, so right into my bull's-eye, that I started crying. Zoe squeezed my hand tighter but didn't move.

"I saw a woman last week in a wheelchair by the side of a road. Right there on the side of the L.A. freeway with all these cars zooming by. I was so frightened for her. Out in the middle of nowhere. What was she doing? How did it happen? I haven't been able to stop thinking about her and I didn't know why until right now.

"It was me, Zoe."

"You? How?"

"I don't know. Her helplessness, the danger, the *wrongness* of her being there. The longer I live, the more careful I get. It's like you stop using certain limbs because you don't need them, or because you only used them as a kid to swing on trees. Then one day you realize you can't even *move* that leg anymore—"

"And you end up in a wheelchair."

"Right, but even that's okay because everyone else around you is in one too. Nobody we know climbs trees anymore. But sooner or later we come to the freeway and we're alone; no one to help and we've *got* to get to the other side. We're stuck, and it's dangerous."

"So you're stuck?"

"Worse; I'm *careful* and I don't know how to stop it. I wouldn't fall in love with James now. I'd get one sniff of what he's like and run away. Or push my wheelchair as fast as I could to get out of there. He's too dangerous."

" 'Cause he *has* legs?"

"And arms and . . . a tail! He could swing from trees with it. That's what was so wonderful about him, what was so wonderful about those days—I was using all my arms and legs and loved it. Today I'd be too scared of the risk. I wish I knew the flavor of my happiness."

She looked at me while I continued to cry. Life had come to a stop on a nice summer's day in my oldest friend's backyard. I had no desire to go to the reunion now, even if James was there. Seeing him would only make things worse.

WHAT THE DEAD
TALK ABOUT

"DO YOU EVER wonder what the dead talk about?"

We stood elbow to elbow in front of the mirror in her tiny bathroom, putting the final touches on our makeup.

"What do you mean?"

She turned to me. One of her eyes was perfectly done, the other bare and young-looking. Made up or not, her eyes were too small to contain the amount of life behind them. In a corner of the room a small radio played Billy Idol's "White Wedding."

"I was just thinking about my parents—"

"No, go back to what you said: what the dead talk about."

She pointed her mascara stick at me. "Well, I believe in an afterlife. I don't know what kind, but I'm sure something's waiting. So if there *is,* is it one big place? Do you get to be with people you knew? Assume for a minute that you do. I was thinking about my parents. What if they could see us now, getting ready to go out to-night? What would they say?"

"They'd say it was cute."

"Maybe. But now they know so much more than we do. Whenever I see a hearse go by or hear someone's died, that's the first thing that comes to mind: Now they *know*. Always, the first thing. Now they know."

"Hmm."

"Even the smallest, most forgettable little . . . termite of a person. Some guy who sat on the street in Calcutta all his life, begging, dies and suddenly knows the biggest answer of all."

"A lot of good it does him when he's dead. Why are we having this conversation, Zoe? Are you trying to get us in the mood for the reunion?"

"I'm thinking out loud to my oldest friend."

It was my turn to stop. "Do you have a lot of friends? The kind you can really talk to, cover a lot of ground with?"

"No. It gets harder the older you get. You're less patient. You need so much patience for a good friendship."

"All right, you're the optimist: What *does* get better as we get older? You get wrinkles, you're less patient, you're supposed to know more, but that's not true. At least not as far as important things are concerned."

She didn't hesitate a second. "Appreciation. I appreciate things much more. My kids when they're around. Or sitting with Hector in a bar that smells musty and old . . . things like that. I was never aware of what things *smelled* like when we were kids, you know? Too busy wondering if I looked right or what was going to happen next. Now I'm just happy if the minute is right. When there's peace in the air and I don't want to be anywhere else in the world. I always wanted to be somewhere else—even when I was having a good time. I was always sure there had to be better."

We looked at each other and, as if on cue, slowly shook our heads.

"Don't you wish you could go back and tell yourself what you know now? Say, 'Zoe, it doesn't get any better than this so *enjoy* it, for God's sake.' "

"It wouldn't make any difference. I tell that to my kids all the time but they look at me like I'm nuts."

Finished with the makeup, we carefully looked each other up and down.

"Why are we so worried about how we look?" she asked. "All the men will be wearing plaid pants and white loafers."

In as deep a Lauren Bacall voice as I could find, I said, "James Stillman would never wear white shoes." Then I added, "*I'm* not worried about tonight: twelfth-grade me is."

"Bullshit!" We both laughed. "Let's go."

Even though it was evening, her car had been sitting in the sun all day and it felt as if we were riding inside a deep fryer. Neither of us said much because we were trying to steel ourselves for whatever was coming.

THE PARKING LOT at the country club was full of cars, but not so full that it didn't send a chill up my spine.

"What if we're the only ones who came?"

"No way. Look at all the cars."

"But Zoe, there aren't many! What if only Bob Zartell and Stephanie Olinka come?"

Just saying the names of the two most awful people in our class made me laugh. It was terrible, but I couldn't help it.

"Bob Zartell is worth a zillion dollars."

"Get out!"

"Really! He owns a huge condom company."

"Condoms? That adds new meaning to the word *dickhead.*"

We parked and got out. I was already so sweaty that I had to peel the dress off my back. A bunch of dark sweat patches would make my grand entrance complete. Why hadn't I gotten tan before tonight? Or worn more of a power outfit, one that radiated money and cool?

Before I had a chance to think more such happy thoughts, Zoe put her arm through mine. "Let's go."

The only other time I had been to Spence Hill Country Club was in tenth grade when a girl invited me to spend a summer afternoon there. She had a face the color of wet cement and a personality to match. After a few hours, I got so tired hearing about how she hated everything that I excused myself early and went home. What I remember most about that day was arriving home so happy to be there that I sat in the kitchen and talked with my mother till dinner.

"Here we go, Miranda."

"I have to go to the bathroom."

"Zoe? Zoe Holland?"

We turned and there was Henry Ballard, the nicest person in our class, looking exactly as he had fifteen years before.

"And Miranda! Both of you. How great!"

It was the best way to begin the evening. Henry, like Zoe, had been everyone's favorite. In a moment, we were all gabbing away while people walked around us into the building. Some said hello, others smiled, some we even recognized. For the first time all day I felt relaxed. Maybe everything was going to be all right.

"I guess we'd better go in?"

He nodded, but turned and looked behind. "I'm just waiting—ah, there he is!"

A nondescript guy in a beautiful blue suit waved and hurried toward us. Zoe and I exchanged glances but neither could place him.

"Sorry I'm late. I dropped the car keys; they hit my knee and slid *under* the car." The man smiled and their look said everything.

Why did it jolt me? Because Henry had played football and dated sexy Erma Bridges? Because I'd once made out with him at a movie and could still remember how gently he kissed? Or because some obnoxious part of me couldn't accept he'd lived a life where he'd learned he liked men and ended up kissing them the same tender way we'd once kissed?

"Zoe, Miranda, this is Russell Lowry."

We shook his hand and talked as we moved slowly toward the door. Henry kept touching Russell in the way one does when a relationship is new and still sending off sparks. I've never been able to figure out if those touches are to reassure yourself the person is still there, or just the delight of knowing they're close enough *to* touch whenever you like.

"Henry told me about you. He made sure I was well prepped on who's who tonight so I don't make any serious faux pas."

I stopped and asked, "What'd he say about me?"

Russell narrowed his eyes and pretended to be scrolling through a mental file. "Miranda Romanac. Smart, attractive rather than pretty. Big crush on her in tenth and eleventh grades. Several serious make-out sessions. Most of all, Henry said you were the first girl he ever wanted to hang around with."

"Wow! That's a compliment."

"That's what he said."

Suddenly I was overwhelmed by familiar faces that shot a cannonful of fifteen-year-old memories at me. I was looking for James among them.

Some looked good, some terrible; some were impossible to recognize unless they introduced themselves or were pointed out as so-and-so. We entered the ballroom and the four of us beelined for the bar. We stood with big drinks, wearing the kind of tight, phony smiles North Korean diplomats use.

There was no way I was going to circulate, at least not until I got the lay of the land. Surveying the room, I was amazed to remember how much of an affect some of these people had once had on me. There was beautiful Melinda Szep, who'd saved my life in Algebra 2 by letting me cheat off her tests. Linda Olson, who one night in tenth grade had the kindness to explain and answer a hundred questions about what really happened in bed with a man. It was a turning point because hearing what she said allowed me to relax. Then there was Steve Solomon, who'd been the first person on earth to put his hand on me *down there*.

Even seeing classmates I'd never had much contact with filled me with a delightful warmth and nostalgia. At a table in one corner were Terry West and Eric Maxwell, class party boys, dumb and sweet as cows. Both were fat and red-cheeked now. They looked so happy to be together again. Had they kept up over the years? Had their lives been good?

Only a few couples were dancing. It was still too early in this dangerous evening. Like us, most people were smiling uneasily or trying to remain invisible until they got their balance.

"Is that Mike Sesich and Kathy Aroli?"

"Yup."

"He looks so *old*. Do we look that bad?"

"I hope not. But she looks good. Too good."

I finished my drink and ordered another. Were we going to spend the whole evening like this, figuring out who people were and then either envying them or feeling aghast?

Henry and Russell excused themselves and went off to mingle.

"Just because they're happy doesn't mean they can abandon us!"

"What do you think? Henry and Russell?"

"Adorable, but I keep remembering the time we made out at the movies. It's strange."

"I'm just having trouble adjusting my gyroscope. I'm okay, but I have to go to the bathroom. Don't move. Stay right here."

I nodded and watched her walk away. Brandon Brind came to the bar and ordered a drink. Here was a guy I'd always liked. After a hesitant greeting, we fell into easy conversation. He'd done all right. From the way he spoke about his life, he sounded happy and sane and looking forward to what tomorrow had to offer.

We talked a long time. I didn't realize how long until Zoe came back from the bathroom, looking very shaken. She was pleasant to Brandon and asked several questions, but it was plain she needed to tell me something. I excused myself and we took off.

"Look at us, running off to the bathroom to talk. What? What happened?"

"Oh, Miranda, you can't believe—"

"What, what's the matter?"

As we were about to enter the bathroom, from out of nowhere came one of the eeriest human voices I have ever heard. Hearing a voice like that, you instinctively know something is terribly wrong with whoever owns it. A midget's voice? No, it was higher. I wondered if it was a joke, a gag recording. It came from behind me, so I didn't have a chance to turn before seeing Zoe's expression freeze, then melt to pure dread.

"What, going to the bathroom *again*? What's wrong with your bladder? What's the matter with you, Zoe?" It started out playful but ended aggressive.

Then I heard, "Hello, Miranda."

I turned, and the first thing that registered was his haircut. It was the worst haircut in the world. Not even in Ulan Bator could a man get worse. Thick and unkempt in some places, it was much too short in others. It looked like someone had randomly hacked away at his hair with a pair of scissors, then grown tired and simply stopped.

Then I recognized his face, the eyes particularly because they still contained some of the same jollity they'd once had. But now there were other things in them too—lunacy, anger, and confusion like no other. You could not look for long.

And you didn't want to look because everything there was wrong, *off*: his expression, the way his eyes wouldn't stay on you for more than a second before sliding away then back, then away. . . .

"Kevin?"

He smiled and twisted his head to the side, like a dog when it's confused. Kevin Hamilton, Zoe's beloved Kevin. Captain of the football team, Dartmouth College, the halest fellow you ever met. Now he was so bizarre that my mind flooded and all its circuits shorted out.

"Aha! I *knew* you'd be here! I told Zoe when I saw her, I bet Miranda Romanac's here. And I was right. I was right."

I was speechless. I looked at Zoe. She stared at him horrified, fascinated.

"I came back to town just for the reunion. We live in Orange now. Know where that is? In New Jersey. We have ever since my dad died. But I forgot your telephone number, Zoe, so I couldn't call to tell you I'd arrived. My sister said I shouldn't call, but I said, 'Look, we were going *out* for years. . . .' "

He went on and on like that in a high-pitched, weirdly sonorous, disconnected ramble about himself, the reunion, Zoe, his "research." I was glad because it allowed me to absorb the shock and watch him closely without seeming rude.

Within seconds you knew he was mad, but what species of madness was hard to say. Although he spoke strangely, much of what he said was coherent, even intelligent. Seeing him this way, I had to keep reminding myself that Kevin Hamilton had been one of our class scholars. We were sure he would do great things. I had heard almost nothing about him except that he had graduated from Dartmouth and gone to Wharton School of Business, but that was expected. Even at eighteen, you knew you'd see him interviewed a decade later on TV or read about him in *Time* magazine.

Apparently others at the reunion knew about Kevin, because no one got near us while we stood with him. A couple of times I saw others I recognized and smiled. They smiled back and started over, but on seeing him they quickly veered away. He kept talking.

Gradually what had happened came out. He was the oldest of four children. His father, with whom he was very close, died suddenly when Kevin was in graduate school. Kevin had had to quit and come home to take care of the others. Somewhere along the line, the pressure sent cracks up and down his psyche and he simply fell apart. He was institutionalized and since then had been on heavy medication. He spent his days in the library researching things, but when I asked what, he looked at me suspiciously and changed the subject.

I could not imagine how Zoe was feeling. Whatever she had brought with her to this night—dreams, expectations—had been met at the door by this human nightmare of everything gone wrong, all hope abandoned. Once again my poor friend had lost.

"Excuse me, Kevin, but we have to go." I didn't care if I hurt his feelings. I took her by the arm and we fled into the ladies' room. He was still talking when the door whooshed shut behind us.

Luckily no one else was in there. Speechless, we stared at each other. It was as if a beautiful piece of crystal had dropped and shattered on the floor. Of course you sweep it up, but first you must accept the fact that it is gone forever.

Zoe went to the sink and turned on both spigots. She lowered her head and cupping handful after handful, threw water on her face. Then she squirted out a handful of bright green hand soap from the dispenser and thoroughly washed her face clean of all the makeup she'd so carefully applied an hour before.

I wanted to be so much smarter than I was, able to come up with something right to say that, even for a moment, might fill the black space I knew was in her heart and would be for a long time.

"Where did I learn my clichés?" She was looking in the mirror. Her face was blank and shone from water.

"What do you mean?"

"Love never dies. Hope springs eternal. The one thing we should have learned by now is to put a seat belt around our heart. The road is dangerous but we never put the damned seat belt on."

"Zoe—"

"He said something to me once I'll never forget. He said, 'We'll start to reminisce when we're a hundred and four because till then we'll be too busy.' I was going to bring Hector tonight. He could have come. But I thought about Kevin, you know, and maybe there was a chance that something might happen . . . so I didn't."

Where was my wisdom? I kept licking my lips and scouring my brain but nothing came. She continued to look blankly in the mirror, as if seeing her face for the first time.

The door opened and Kathy Herlth sauntered in. She was as gorgeous as ever but still carried the icy wind of disdain for everything on earth that froze the rest of us humanity to death.

"God, did you see Kevin Hamilton? He's got to change his lobotomist! He's standing out there talking like a Klingon. Sort of looks like one too."

It was so cruel and true that Zoe coughed out a huge laugh. I did too.

Kathy shrugged. "I knew I shouldn't have come to this. It's so depressing. *You* two have sure come full circle tonight. Kevin's mad and James is dead. That ends that chapter, huh?"

"What?" The word came out much slower than I wanted. My hand froze as I was about to wipe tears of laughter off my cheek. I looked at my hand when she spoke again. It had already made a fist. I didn't feel it. I didn't feel anything.

She looked surprised. "What do you mean? About what?"

"About James."

"James? What about him? Oh God, Miranda, didn't you *know*? He's *dead*. He died three years ago. In a car crash."

Everything was so clear, incredibly sharp and accentuated: Zoe's gasp, the sound of water hissing in the sink, Kathy's high-heel scrape across the tile floor. Their faces—Kathy's cool but interested, Zoe shocked beyond her own new trauma. These things were clear, but some essential part of me had already left. Something left my body and floating high above the room looked down, taking one last glimpse before leaving forever.

The part that had loved James Stillman with the energy and abandon only beginners have. The part that had smoked twenty delicious cigarettes a day, laughed too loud, didn't worry about dangerous things. The part that wondered what sex would be like and who would be the first. The part that looked too long in mirrors at the only flawless face I would ever see there.

Fearless teenage me, so sure one day I'd find a partner with whom my heart would rest happily ever after. A man I would put on like lotion. James taught me that, showed me great happiness was possible right from the beginning. He was dead.

"Jesus, Miranda, I thought you *knew*. It happened so long ago."

"How—" I stopped to swallow. My throat was dry as cork. "Um, how did it happen?"

"I don't know. Diana Wise told me. But she's here tonight! You can ask. I saw her before."

Without another word, I walked out of the room. Zoe said something but I kept going. I needed to find Diana Wise immediately. Without the facts, a precise description, James Stillman's death would stay liquid in my brain and it had to be solid, real.

Hadn't the ballroom been billiard-chalk blue before I'd gone into the bathroom? Blue with white borders? I could have sworn it was; yet now it was a weak ocher, the color of young carrots. Even the colors had changed with the terrible news.

People mulled around talking, laughing, and dancing. Tonight they could be eighteen *and* thirty-three at the same time. It was wonderful. Mouths were full of teeth and shiny tongues. Words surrounded me as I moved. I felt like a visitor from another planet.

"They moved to Dobbs Ferry—"

"I haven't seen *him* since, Jesus, I don't know—"

"The whole house was carpeted with the most ugly brown shag—"

When we were eighteen, people still listened to records. There were three speeds on a record player: 33⅓, 45, and 78. The only time you ever used 78 was when you wanted to laugh. You turned it up there and played 45s on it. Hearing familiar voices transformed to a high silly chirp was always good for a laugh. As I walked more and more quickly through the room searching for Diana, thinking about James, thinking about him dead, the world around me switched to 78. Voices became a speeded-up muddle. This whizzing chaos became so strong that I had to stop and close my eyes. I breathed deeply a few times, telling myself not to panic. When I opened my eyes, Zoe was standing in front of me.

"Are you okay?"

"No. Have you seen Diana? I can't find her."

"We will. Come on, she's got to be here." She took my hand and we walked together. Later, when my mind cleared, I thought, How kind of her. Zoe had had her own nightmare only minutes before. Yet here she was, holding my hand and helping when she could just as well have been shut off in her own pain from meeting Kevin Hamilton.

"There! Over there."

Unlike so many others at the reunion, Diana Wise looked almost exactly as she had when we were in school. Interesting face, long black hair, the sexy smile of an Italian movie star. We had been almost-friends in high school, but she was so much maturer than we that we had always held her in awe.

"Diana?" She was talking to a man I didn't recognize. Hearing her name, she turned and saw me. Touching the guy on the hand as a good-bye, she took me by the arm.

"Miranda. I've been looking for you." Her voice was strong and assured. The expression on her face said she knew what I needed. I was grateful not to have to ask the question. Not to have to say the words out loud, into the world: Is it true? Is he really dead?

The three of us walked through the lobby back out into the summer evening. It was warm and beautiful, the air still heavy from the day and full of the voluptuous smell of honeysuckle. I was empty and scared. I knew what was coming. Even though answers were what I wanted, I knew that when I heard them there would be no way back to a part of my life that, until a few hours before, was still intact.

"Diana, what happened to James? How did it . . ." I couldn't say any more.

She put a hand into her long black hair and drew it slowly away from her face. "I bumped into him a few years ago in Philadelphia. He was working for a company that had something to do with art— selling it, dealing it? I don't really remember. Maybe it was an auction house, like Sotheby's. Anyway, we ran into each other on the street. He loved what he was doing. He was so revved up. Remember how excited he could get about things?"

I wanted to tell her how I'd seen that excitement, seen his whole being glow about something that had grabbed his attention.

"We were both in a rush and only able to have a quick cup of coffee together. He sounded wonderful, Miranda. Said for the first time in his life he felt like he was on the right track. Things were where he wanted them. He had a girlfriend. He was absolutely *up,* you know?"

"How did he look?" I wanted a picture, an image of him grown up I could hold on to.

"Older of course, thinner than he was in school, but still those great eyes and smile." She paused. "He looked like James."

I began to weep. Those words held everything I did and did not want to hear. Zoe put her arms around me. The three of us stood on the lawn, a few feet—and light-years away from all the happiness and goodwill inside the building.

When my storm had mostly passed, I asked Diana to go on.

"We exchanged numbers and promised to stay in touch. We called a couple of times but I didn't go back to Philadelphia, and who ever comes to Kalamazoo?

"One night three years ago, very late, I got a call. A woman asked for me two times. She was so upset that I had to *convince* her who I was. She said she knew I was a good friend of James's and wanted me to know he'd been killed in a car accident.

"He'd been in New York and gotten a call from his girlfriend in Philadelphia. She wanted to break up with him because she'd met someone else. Apparently she was that cold—wanted out and there was nothing more to talk about.

"As soon as he got off the phone, James jumped in his car and drove straight down there. It was very icy and the roads were bad. He made it to Philadelphia but was driving too fast. When he tried to get off the turnpike, the car skidded and went off the road. She said he died instantly."

"Instantly?"

"That's what the woman said."

"Who was she?"

"I don't know. She wouldn't give a name, even when I asked. I bet it was the girlfriend.

"He asked about you, Miranda. When we had coffee, he asked if I had heard anything about you."

My heart lurched. "Really?"

"Yes. He was disappointed when I didn't know."

We were silent while music from the reunion filled the air around us.

"Is there anything else?"

"No. I told you I asked the woman for her name but she wouldn't say. She hung up right after that."

Zoe sighed and looked at the ground. It was such a final, nothing-left sigh.

"Thank you, Diana. It makes it clearer."

We hugged. She stepped back, hands on my elbows, and looked at me a moment more. Then she turned and started for the building.

"Diana?"

"Yes?"

"Really, he was happy?"

She only nodded. Which was better than any words. It allowed me my own vocabulary for his happiness.

"Thank you."

She reached into her handbag, took out a card, and handed it to me. "Call if you want to talk, or if you're ever in Kalamazoo, Michigan."

Zoe and I stood in silence in the middle of the lawn. After time had passed I said, "I don't want to go back in there. I'll call a cab. Could you give me a key to your house?"

"Let's go someplace and drink a lot."

Instead we ended up driving around again. Past the same places we'd seen that afternoon, which now felt like a million years ago. I turned on the radio and, as if they knew our mood, all the stations seemed to be playing only songs we'd loved when we were young. Which was all right because we finished being young that night and it was right to be immersed in it one last time.

I hadn't been paying attention to where she was going, and realized where we were only when she slowed and turned into the parking lot of the Carvel ice cream stand.

"Good idea!"

"If we're not going to get drunk, we'll get fat."

We ordered the old usual—vanilla cones dipped in heated chocolate—and went back to her car. In our party dresses we sat on the hood and ate.

"They're still delicious."

"I haven't had one in years. I used to bring the kids when they were young, but they wouldn't be caught dead with me in public these days."

We watched people come and go. Back at the country club, our classmates were dancing and reliving happy times. But Kevin was back there too and so was James.

"Zoe, what do we do now?"

"Hope, honey. Same thing as I said before."

"Not much hope in Mudville tonight."

"Did I ever tell you about the time I found Andy's gun?"

That stopped me. "You're kidding! Andy, your slimy ex-husband?"

"Yup. It was the first year we were married. I was putting away clean underwear in his drawer. Sitting on top of his Fruit Of The Looms was a gun."

"Why'd *he* have it?"

"The most interesting thing was, the moment I found it, the only thing that went through my mind *wasn't* 'He's got a gun!' What hit me was, 'The world is an amazing place.' You know how it is when you're first with someone and love him: you think you know everything about him. Then you open a drawer one day and there's something—an old love letter, a diary, a gun. It's impossible to connect with the person you thought you knew.

"It was kind of wonderful, Miranda. I knew no matter what happened, life was always going to be interesting."

"Because you found a gun?"

"No! Because it was part of Andy too. I really didn't know him and that excited me. There were all these new things to discover. In the end we divorced, but back then, life was still opening up. It excited me. It still excites me. You should let it do that. You should let that happen."

A YOGURT TRILOGY

"YOU'RE A THIEF, Miranda."

I rolled my eyes. "Yes, Jaco."

Sniffing the air as if something stunk in the room, he went on as if I hadn't spoken. "Perhaps the most unscrupulous I have ever done business with."

I tapped my front tooth with a fingernail. "Jaco, we've had this conversation before. You always say the same thing: I'm a crook, a bitch . . . always the same spring rolls. But I find the books you want. You wanted a signed first edition of *The Gallery*; I got it for you. You wanted a letter from Eliot, I found it for you—"

"True, but then you charge so much that I have no money left!"

"You'd have to live another four hundred years before you ran out of money. Don't buy it! You know Dagmar will if you don't." It was a rotten thing to say, but I was so disgusted with him at the moment I couldn't resist.

As usual, her detested name straightened his back and narrowed his greedy eyes.

Dagmar Breece. Jaco Breece's nemesis. All I had to do was wave her name in front of him and the mean old man started snorting like Ferdinand the Bull.

Dagmar and Jaco Breece had two passions: cashmere and twentieth-century authors. That was great when they were married and ran a sweater company together for four decades. The business was successful, they had a couple of nice children who grew up and away, they shared a passion for collecting. Then when she was sixty years old, Dagmar fell in love with another man and promptly moved out on her husband. Good riddance.

What galled Jaco more than losing her, however, was her saying he could keep the rare book and manuscript collection they'd spent years amassing. She would start another with the help of her rich new boyfriend.

That's how I came to know them. Several years before, when they were still together, Dagmar came into the store and bought an Edward Dahlberg manuscript I had listed in a catalog. After that, I found a number of things for them, both when they were married and after she left. I liked Dagmar but not Jaco. Not one bit.

Standing there watching him fume, I wondered how he would have reacted if he'd known I was going to a dinner party at her apartment that night.

"What else do you have that's new?"

"Some Rilke letters—"

"Everyone has Rilke letters. He wrote too many."

"Jaco, you asked what's new. I have some letters—Noooo, wait! I have something else that'll interest you!"

My store is small, so it was only three steps to the sideboard. I disliked the whole pompous leather-and-dark-oak look of most rare book dealers' stores, so mine was furnished with 1950s Heywood

Wakefield blond wood furniture and a very warm red-and-white Chinese rug. Together they made the room light, slightly odd, and, I hoped, welcoming. I loved books and everything about them. I wanted customers to know that when they walked in.

The difference between my business and the business of other book and manuscript dealers was that I sold anything else I fancied too.

Opening a drawer, I took out the long thin case made of crocodile skin. It looked like the kind Victorian gentlemen used for carrying cigars. What I had inside was much better than that. Opening it, I put it down on the counter in front of Jaco, knowing he would go into cardiac arrest when he realized what it was.

"I don't collect fountain pens, Miranda."

"It's not a pen. It's a Mabie Todd."

"Then maybe Todd would like it."

"Very funny. Look at the barrel."

He looked at me like I was trying to pull a fast one but in the end he picked up the largest fountain pen I'd ever seen.

"So? It's a pen."

"Jaco, turn it around. Look closely."

He turned till he saw the name engraved in gold lettering on the black barrel. When he spoke again, his voice was almost a whisper, as if his tongue had grown too big for his throat. "No! Is it?"

I nodded. "I have authentication."

"How did you—"

"At a Sotheby's auction last week. I saw it in their catalog. I think it came from Lord Esher's estate."

"Rolfe." He read the name reverently. "I remember from the Symons biography, he was supposed to have always written with a huge fountain pen."

"That's right."

Exasperated and smiling for the first time, he shook his head.

"Miranda, how do you find these things? How did you find Frederick Rolfe's fountain pen?"

"Because I love what I'm doing. Hunting for things, having them in my hand for a while. I love selling them to people like you who care."

"But you never keep anything for yourself?"

"Never. You have to decide whether you're going to collect or sell. Collecting would exhaust me. I'd never be happy with what I owned. I would always want more. This way, I can enjoy things for a while and then sell them to the right people."

"Like Dagmar?"

"Like Dagmar, *and* you. Do you want this?"

"Of course I want it!"

I WAITED A good half hour after he left before I made the call. Jaco had the disconcerting habit of returning in a rage to demand a better price for something he had just bought. In the beginning I'd been cowed by his fury, but not anymore.

"Hello?" Her voice was soft and elegant, as sexy a woman's voice as I knew.

"Dagmar? It's Miranda. Jaco was just here. He bought the pen."

"Of course he did, darling. It's exactly what he would want. That's why I bought it. It's a fabulous piece."

"But why sell it to him? Didn't you want it for your collection?"

"Yes, but he would love it more. Baron Corvo is one of his few heroes."

"I don't understand. You finally left him after all those years of unhappiness, but you're still giving him things?"

"Not giving, *selling*. Loving Jaco was like sitting on a cold stone: you give it all your heat but it gives none back. You end up with a chill in your behind. I couldn't take it anymore. But leaving doesn't erase most of my adult life. I still love him for a few things and always will. Not that I necessarily want to. Sometimes you can't control who you love."

"But you're happy you left?"

"Blissfully. The only time I look back is to check to make sure I locked the door. Tell me how Jaco reacted when he saw the pen." I could almost hear her smile through the telephone.

"He flipped. He was in heaven."

"No doubt. *Hadrian the Seventh* is his favorite book. No wonder—the story of a miserable, undeserving person who's chosen to be pope. Jaco identifies totally."

"I'll bring you a check tonight."

"No hurry. Today I'm beyond madness anyway. The caterer called and said he won't be able to make the yogurt trilogy for dessert, which essentially ruins the dinner. But we have to be strong."

"Yogurt trilogy?"

"Don't be cynical, Miranda. One taste and you'd be a believer. Plus our apartment smells like a wet washcloth, *and* I have to go have my hair done. Sometimes it would be nice being a man. For them, a haircut is nine dollars. For a woman it's a religious experience. So I have to go, sweetie. If I live through today, I'll be immortal. Be here at seven. I've invited three Scud missiles for dinner and told each you're the catch of the century."

"That's tough to live up to."

"But you are!"

FEW PEOPLE CAME into my store to browse. For the most part, the clientele knew exactly what they wanted. I lived a good deal of the time on the road, tracking down their specific and often expensive desires. You could page me on my wristwatch or call me on the smallest portable telephone I could find. I was happy when I could spend even a few weeks at a time in the store straightening things up, paying bills, reading catalogs and faxes. Yet I was also happy in airports, hotel rooms, restaurants that served regional dishes I had never heard of. There was no man in my life. I was free to come and go as I pleased.

In college I had majored in sociology, but realized junior year how unsatisfying demographic charts and terms like *gemeinschaft* and *gesellschaft* were. For extra money I found a job at a used book store and was lucky enough to be there the day a man came in with two cardboard boxes of books to sell. Among them was a signed limited edition of Faulkner's *The Hamlet,* which happened to be on the reading list of a course I was taking. Knowing it was valuable, I showed it to the owner of the store. He said I could keep it because I'd been honest and was a good worker. I took the book to class to show the professor. His eyes widened and he asked if I would sell it to him for a hundred dollars. There was something in his tone that made me suspicious. I looked up the telephone numbers of several rare book dealers and called to ask what the book was worth.

Nothing is permanent, but books are one of the few things that come close. Hearing how valuable the Faulkner was, I realized I had been made privy to one of life's small secrets, which was that there are objects that mean nothing to most people, but everything to some. What's more, if you knew anything about the subject, you quickly discovered collecting books was one of the last real treasure hunts possible in this age. There are old books everywhere and most people don't care about them. The few who do will go to remarkable lengths to possess them.

As I continued, I realized I was good at the job—this in itself is a great reward. I loved my customers' excitement and delight with what I found. I loved the serendipity of the hunt. My heart still pounded on seeing something unique or important in a junk store, second-hand shop, a Salvation Army bin in the bad section of some downtown. Slowly reaching out, I would take it in my hand, knowing one of the greatest pleasures of all was here. Opening the book, I would check the first pages to make sure it was what I thought. Yes, there was the proof if you knew what to look for—the letter *A*, or the even more obvious *first edition*. Other indications, emblems, marks . . . the secret alphabet and language of book collectors. On the inside front cover someone would have carelessly written in pencil, *$1* or *50¢*. I paid ten cents in Louisville for the most beautiful first edition of *The Great Gatsby* I've ever seen. Five dollars for *The Enormous Room*. I couldn't understand why more people weren't doing this. Even if you knew only a little about the subject, it was like looking for gold everywhere you went.

After reading the journals of Edward Weston and Paul Strand, I became interested in photography. That opened up an altogether new world, not to mention business opportunity. On a trip to Los Angeles, I discovered a large box of photographs at a yard sale. Most were of strangers, but some subjects were famous movie stars of the 1930s and '40s. What struck me was how beautifully the pictures were lit and how naturally the people had been posed. On the back of each was a stamp with the photographer's name, Hurrell, and address. I bought them and never forgot the look on the woman's face as I handed her money: it said I was a sucker and she was the winner. But even then, without ever having heard of the great photographer George Hurrell, I knew she was wrong.

"Miranda?"

I came out of a daze to see one of my favorite people in the world standing at the door.

"Clayton! I'm sorry, I was daydreaming."

"The sign of all great minds. Give your old boss a hug."

We embraced and, as usual, he had on another mysteriously beautiful cologne that made me swoon.

"What are you wearing today?"

"Something French. Called Diptyque, which I think is appropriate for a bookseller, wouldn't you say?"

"Absolutely. Where have you been, Clayton? I haven't heard a word from you in months." I took his hand and led him to a chair. He sat down and looked slowly around before speaking. He must have been sixty, but looked years younger. A full head of hair—and the wrinkles on his face came mostly from smiling. I had gone to work for him in New York after college. He had shown me everything he knew about the rare book business. Enthusiasm and generosity were at the heart of his personality. When I left to open my own store, he lent me ten thousand dollars to get started.

"Do you still have that nice Stevens? I have a buyer. A Scientologist from Utah."

"A Scientologist who reads Wallace Stevens?"

"Exactly. I've been out west, drumming up business. Bumped into some very interesting people. One man lived on a strict carrot diet and collected nothing but Wyndham Lewis. That's why I haven't been around. I don't know about you, but books haven't been flying off my shelves recently. That's why I've been traveling. How are things for you?"

"So-so. They go in waves. I sold a bunch of Robert Duncan in L.A. a couple of months ago. That put me back on track. Do you know who I saw when I was out there? Doug Auerbach."

"Ah, the Dog. What's he been doing?"

"Making commercials. He makes a load of money."

"But you said he wanted to be Ingmar Bergman. I can't imagine making dog food ads satisfies that desire. Does he still miss you?"

"I guess. I think he misses the time when his life had more possibilities."

"Don't we all? Well, Miranda, I've come to see you, but I've also come on a mission. Have you heard of Frances Hatch?"

"Am I going to be embarrassed saying no?"

"Not really. She's a well-kept secret to all but a few. Frances Hatch was a kind of Jill of all trades, mistress of none, in the twenties and thirties. Although she *was* mistress to an amazing number of famous people. She was a sort of lunatic combination of Alma Mahler, Caresse Crosby, and Lee Miller.

"She came from big money in St. Louis but rebelled and ran away to Prague. She went at the right time to the wrong city. Things *were* going on there, as in the rest of Europe in the twenties, but it was nowhere near as interesting as Berlin or Paris. She stayed a year studying photography, then moved to Bucharest with a Romanian ventriloquist. His stage name was 'The Enormous Shumda.' "

"To Bucharest with The Enormous Shumda? I love her already."

"I know—a strange choice of geography. But she was always being towed somewhere by one man or another and willingly went along for the ride. Anyway, she left after a short time and ended up in Paris, alone."

"Not for long, right?"

"Right. Women like Frances never stay alone long." He opened his briefcase and took out a photograph. "Here's a self-portrait she took around that time."

I looked at the picture. It was a beautiful black-and-white shot, reminiscent of the work of Walter Peterhans or Lyonel Feininger: angular, stark, very Germanic. I laughed. "This is a joke. You're joking, right, Clayton?" I looked again. I didn't know what to say. "It's a self-portrait? It's wonderful. From the way you described her, I thought she'd just be a ditz. I'd never have imagined she was so talented."

"And?" He pointed to the picture and, eyes twinkling, started to smile.

"And, she looks like a schnauzer."

"My first thought was an emu."

"What's that?"

"They look like ostriches."

"You're telling me this emu was the lover to famous people? She is ugly, Clayton. Look at that nose!"

"Have you heard the French phrase *belle laide*?"

"No."

"It means ugly enough to be desirable. The ugliness adds to the sexiness."

"This woman is not *belle* anything."

"Maybe she was great in bed."

"She'd have to be. I can't believe it, Clayton. Part of me thinks you're bullshitting. Who was she with?"

"Kazantzákis, Giacometti. Her best friend was Charlotte Perriand. Others. She lived a fascinating life." He took the photo from me. After glancing at it once more, he put it back in his briefcase. "And she's still alive! Lives on 112th Street."

"How old is she?"

"Got to be way up in the nineties."

"How do you know her?"

"Frances Hatch is rumored to have letters, drawings, and books from these people and others, the likes of which would make any dealer weep. Very important stuff, Miranda, just sitting there growing yellow. For years she made noise about wanting to sell, but never did till now. Her companion died a few months ago and she's afraid of being alone. Wants to move into an expensive nursing home in Briarcliff but doesn't have the money."

"It sounds great if you can get her to sell you the stuff. But why tell me?"

"Because at age ninety-whatever, Frances no longer likes men. She had some kind of late-life revelation and became a lesbian. With the exception of her lawyer, she deals only with women. I've known her for years and she says she's really willing to sell now, but only if it's done through a woman dealer. If she'll sell, I'll go fifty-fifty with you." He made no attempt to hide the desperation in his voice.

"That's not necessary, Clayton. I'm glad to help if I can. Besides, I've always wanted to meet an emu. When would we go?"

He looked at his watch. "Now, this morning, if you'd like."

"Let's go."

BEFORE CATCHING A cab, Clayton said he needed to find a market, but not why. I waited outside. In a few minutes he reemerged with a bag full of serious junk food. Things like pink Hostess Snowballs, fluorescent orange Chee-tos, Twinkies, Ding Dongs, Devil Dogs, Yankee Doodles. . . .

"Those aren't for *you*?"

"It's the only food Frances eats. Anyone who visits her is expected to bring a bag full of this merde."

"No wonder she's ninety! If she ate those all her life she's probably eighty percent chemically preserved. When she dies, her body will have the half-life of plutonium."

He took out a package and looked at it. "When was the last time you ate a Ding Dong? They all sound obscene—Devil Dogs, Ding Dongs. . . ." He tore open the wrapper and we contentedly ate them as we rode uptown.

Ms. Hatch lived in one of those beautiful turn-of-the-century buildings that looked like fortresses. It had outlived its neighborhood but was falling to ruin. There were gargoyles on the front facade and a long courtyard with a fountain in the center that no longer worked. It was the kind of building that deserved quiet and reserve, but as we walked across the courtyard, salsa and rap music swept down from open windows and crashed on top of us. Somewhere a man and woman yelled at each other. The things they said were embarrassing. As often happened in situations like that, it struck me how people feel no shame anymore talking publicly about anything. While riding the subway recently, I'd sat next to two women talking loudly about their periods. Not once did either of them look around to see if people were listening, which they were.

When I mentioned this to Clayton, he said, "No one's concerned with dignity today. People want either to win or to be comfortable." He gestured toward the windows above us. "They don't care if you hear. It's like the TV talk shows: those idiots don't mind your knowing they slept with their mother, or the dog. They think it makes them interesting. Here we are. This is it."

The hallway smelled of old food and wet paper. Illegible graffiti had been spray-painted big and black across the mailboxes. A yellow baby carriage without wheels was pushed against a wall. The elevator didn't work.

"What floor does she live on?"

"Third, but she never goes out. Sometimes I wonder how many old people are prisoners in their apartments in this city. Too scared, or they can't climb the stairs. There's got to be a lot of them."

We climbed in silence. I noticed here and there signs of the one-time beauty of the building. The banister was bird's-eye maple, the ironwork beneath it intricate and pretty. The stairs were made of dark green stone with swirls of black inside, like a frozen cyclone.

There was lots of noise everywhere. Music, people talking, the general white noise from many television sets going full blast. It made me appreciate my own building, where the neighbors were unfriendly but quiet.

On reaching the third floor, we walked down a long hall to the end. Unlike the others, which looked like the police had periodically beaten them in, Frances Hatch's oak door was immaculately preserved. There was a small brass plaque with her name engraved on it. It had recently been polished. Clayton rang the bell. We waited quite a while.

The door opened and I think both of us took a step back in surprise. A short bald man with a moon-round face and no chin, dressed in a dark suit, black tie, and white shirt stood there. His face said seventy or eighty, but he stood so straight that he could have been younger.

"Yes?"

"I'm Clayton Blanchard. Ms. Hatch is expecting me?"

"Come along."

The man turned and walked stiffly back into the apartment, as if rehearsing for the march of the tin soldiers. I looked at Clayton. "I thought you said she only spoke to women?"

Before he had a chance to reply, the soldier called out, "Are you coming?" We scurried in.

I didn't have a chance to look at anything, but my nose noticed how good it smelled in there. "What's that smell?"

"Apples?"

"In here, please."

The man's voice was so commanding that I felt I was back in high school, being summoned to the principal's office.

I saw the light before entering the living room. It was blinding and came through the door in a white flood. We walked in and I was in love before I knew it. Frances Hatch's living room was full of Persian rugs, rare Bauhaus furniture, and the largest cat I had ever seen. The rugs were all varying shades of red—russet, cerise, ruby. Which mixed brilliantly with the stark chrome furniture. It softened the starkness but also made individual pieces stand out in their pure simplicity, almost as if they hovered over the varied redness below. High windows went all the way down the room, taking in as much light as the day had. On the walls were a large number of photographs and paintings. I didn't have a chance to look at them before another imperious voice called out, "Over here, I'm here."

As if it knew what she had said, the cat stood up, stretched languorously, and walked over to where Frances Hatch was sitting. It stood looking up at her, tail swishing.

"How are you, Clayton? Come over here so I can see you."

He walked to her chair and took the large bony hand she held out.

"Cold. Your hands are always cold, Clayton."

"It runs in my family."

"Well, cold hands, warm heart. Who have you brought with you?"

He gestured for me to come over. "Frances, this is my friend Miranda Romanac."

"Hello Miranda. You'll have to come close because I can barely see. Are you pretty?"

"Hello. I'm passable."

"I was always ugly, so there was never any question about that. Ugly people have to work harder to get the world's attention. You have to prove you're worth listening to. Did you meet Irvin?"

I looked at the man with the big voice.

"Irvin Edelstein, these are my friends Clayton and Miranda. Sit down. I can see you better now. Yes. You *do* have red hair! I thought so. Very nice. I love red. Have you noticed my rugs?"

"I did. I love the way you've done this room."

"Thank you. It's my magic carpet. When I'm in here I feel just a little bit above the earth. So you're a friend of Clayton. That's a good sign. What else do you do?"

"I'm a bookseller too."

"Perfect! Because that's what I want to talk about today. Irvin is here to advise me on what I should do. I have very valuable things, Miranda. Do you know why I've decided to sell them? Because all my life I've wanted to be rich. In one month I'll be a hundred. I think it would be very nice to be rich at a hundred."

"What will you do with the money?" It was a rude question to ask, especially after having just been introduced, but I liked Frances already and sensed she had a good sense of humor.

"What will I do? Buy a red Cadillac convertible and drive around, picking up men. God, how long has it been since I was with a man? You know, when you're my age, you think about who you were all those years. If you're lucky, you grow very fond of that person. The men I knew were silly most of the time, but they had nerve. Sometimes they even had the kind of guts you usually only dream of. Guts are what matters, Miranda. That's what Kazantzákis told me. God gave us courage but it is dangerous music to listen to. That man had no fear. Do you know who his hero was? Blondin. The greatest tightrope walker who ever lived. He walked across a rope over Niagara Falls and halfway there stopped to cook and eat an omelette."

"Clayton said you lived enough for three normal lives."

"I did, but that was because I was ugly and had something to prove. I was a great lover and sometimes I had courage. I tried to tell the truth when it was important. Those are the things I'm proud of. Someone wanted me to write my autobiography, but it's my life. I don't want to share it with people who care less about it than I do. Anyway, by then I was too old to remember if I was telling the truth about everything, and that's very important. But Irvin gave me this little gizmo and it's a great comfort." She reached into her lap and held up a small tape recorder. "I sit here and feel the magic carpets under my feet and the light through the window is warm and when an especially nice memory comes, all I have to do is press this button. I tell the machine something I haven't remembered for a long time.

"Just this morning, right before you arrived, I was thinking about a picnic I had with the Hemingways at Auteuil. Lewis Gallantiere, Hemingway, and mad Harry Crosby. Why those two men ever got along was beyond me, but it was a lovely day. We ate Westphalian ham and Harry lost three thousand francs on the horses.

Amazed, I looked at Clayton and silently mouthed, "Hemingway?"

"I think of Hemingway a lot. You know, people never stop talking about him and Giacometti, but they always describe them in such distorted, frenzied ways. People want to believe they were wild and dissolute because it fits a romantic image. But Gallantiere said something before he died that must be remembered: All the great artists put in a good day's work every day of their lives when we were all living in Paris. People want to think those books and paintings arrived out of the ether, whole cloth. But what I remember most is how hard they worked. Giacometti? He would have murdered you if you came to his studio while he was working."

CLAYTON GAVE ME many wonderful things over the years, but the introduction to Frances Hatch was the most important. I will remember that first morning with her as long as I live. Afterwards we met frequently, both to settle the business of her collection and because I loved being in that room with her and her crowded memories. In college I'd read a poem by Whitman about an old man in a boat, fishing. He has lived a full life, but is tired now and waiting peacefully to die. Until then, he's content to sit and fish and remember.

Even as a kid, full of pepper and brass, I was enchanted with the idea of living so fully that at the end you had nothing left you wanted to do and were willing to die.

When we left her apartment that day, I felt like I had been in a room with pure clarity and understanding, if such things are possible. As if they were concrete substances I'd been allowed to hold in my hand awhile and I'd gotten their weight and feel. It proved such things were feasible and it lifted me.

I went back to my store feeling supercharged. I buzzed through the rest of the day wishing only that I had someone important with whom to share the experience. I was glad for the party that night, glad I could mingle and talk and hope for some of the common magic Frances had found all of her life.

I'd been to Dagmar Breece's home for several dinner parties. Frequently they were loaded with both interesting people and strange people. In contrast to Jaco, who didn't like anyone stealing his thunder, Dagmar and her boyfriend Stanley had the modesty and good sense to invite an intriguing crowd and let them steer the evening. What was also nice was that you weren't expected either to dress up or to perform. Showoffs were discouraged, and only if they were engaging were egos permitted to flourish.

I went home at five and changed. The phone rang while I was dressing. It was Zoe, calling to chat. We spoke too long and I barely had time to finish up. Luckily Dagmar and Stan's building was only a few blocks from mine—although in a decidedly nicer neighborhood.

One of the reasons why I liked living in Manhattan was that the city would share your mood the moment you walked out the door. If you were in a hurry, everything else was too, even the pigeons. You shared the same speed and sense of urgency to get wherever you were going.

When you had time to kill, it was happy to give you things to look at and do that easily took up whole days. I didn't agree with people who said Manhattan was a cold, indifferent town. Sure it was gruff, but it was also playful and sometimes very funny.

All the way to Dagmar's the traffic lights were green for me. When I got to her block, I said a little thank-you. Seconds later, a madman pushing a baby carriage heaped with junk wobbled by. Without saying a word, the man smiled and tipped an imaginary hat at me, as if he were the city's spokesman acknowledging my thanks.

On the back wall of the elevator was a large mirror. Riding up, I had a look. My hair was shorter than a month before. Why do women cut their hair shorter the older they get? Because they don't want to be bothered? Because few faces can bear to be framed so luxuriously after a certain age? Looking more closely, I saw a lot more gray in my hair than I had been expecting by age thirty-three. The lines around my mouth were okay, but the beauty creams I used were getting more expensive because they were supposed to work that much harder. I held up both hands and turned them back and forth to see how *they* were doing. The elevator stopped. Dropping my hands, I turned around quickly.

The doors opened and I stepped out into the corridor. To my surprise, Dagmar was standing outside their apartment with a champagne glass in each hand.

"Miranda! There you are."

"What are you doing out here?"

"Hiding from the men. They're in there talking about boxing."

"Aren't there any women?"

"Not yet. Men always come early to parties when they know there are going to be gorgeous women."

"You *did* invite other women, I hope."

"Of course. And couples too. I wouldn't throw you completely to the lions."

"Now I'm nervous."

"Don't be. Just take off your clothes and walk right in. Come on." She handed me a glass and we went in.

Unlike the Hatch apartment, Dagmar and Stan's was very sparsely furnished. Jaco had been there once and spitefully said you could clean the whole place with a fire hose and three Brillo pads. That wasn't true, but it was not cozy and I never understood how two such warm people could be comfortable living in a hi-tech igloo. Walking down the hall to the living room, I heard a bunch of men burst into laughter.

The living room was full of people, but the balance was about half-and-half. Doing a quick scan, I recognized a bunch of them and waved to a few. The unfamiliar men I saw on first glance looked good but not interesting. To a one, they had hair that was either slicked back with gel, gangster style, or falling over their shoulders in the chic of the moment. I knew it was an unfair assessment, but that's how I went about things: Guilty until proven interesting.

Dagmar squeezed my shoulder and went off to talk to the caterer. A man I'd met there some months before came right up and introduced himself. He was a broker who specialized in railroad stocks. For the next few minutes, we chatted about train rides we had known and loved. That was fine because he did most of the talking, which allowed me to continue looking.

A waiter came around with a tray of hors d'oeuvres. Their nice smell reminded me that the only thing I had eaten that day was a Ding Dong and a cup of coffee in the taxi with Clayton. Railroad Man and I took what looked like caviar-and-egg biscuits and popped them into our mouths.

The hors d'oeuvre was so lethally hot and spicy that it exploded on contact. I barely had enough presence of mind to slap a hand across my mouth before squealing like a stabbed rabbit. He did almost exactly the same thing. We stared at each other. It was so unexpected and shocking. Thank God he fumbled in his pocket, brought out a package of tissues, and handed me one. Without a second thought, we spat the bombs into the tissues and wiped our mouths. I think we might have gotten away with it, but some people had seen us and were watching. He looked at me and made the sound of a train whistle: "Woo-OO-Woo!"

I laughed and gave him a push. My eyes were tearing, my mouth was on fire, and I was embarrassed as hell but couldn't stop laughing. "Everyone's staring!"

"So what? My life just passed before my eyes."

Everyone *was* staring, but that made us laugh harder. Stan came over and asked what was wrong. We explained and, sweet man that he is, he ran to stop the waiter from offering the hors d'oeuvres to other people.

Who would have guessed that moment on fire would change everything?

Half an hour later dinner was announced. As we moved into the dining room, a man I didn't know came up and asked if I was all right. In his forties, he had a big thatch of unruly brown hair à la John Kennedy, and the kind of warm broad smile that made you like him right away, whoever he was.

"I'm fine. I just ate an hors d'oeuvre from hell and it paralyzed me."

"You looked like you'd seen a goat."

I stopped. "You mean a ghost?"

There was the smile. "No, like you'd just seen a goat walk into the room! Like this." In an instant, he wore an imbecilic expression that made me giggle.

"*That* bad?"

"No, impressive! I'm Hugh Oakley."

"Miranda Romanac."

"This is my wife, Charlotte."

A knockout, she had the kind of unique beauty that only deepened and became more interesting with age. Her eyes were Prussian blue, the hair as white-blond and swept as a meringue. My first impression was that everything about Charlotte Oakley seemed Nordic and . . . white. Until her mouth, which was thick and sexual. How many men had fantasized about that mouth?

"Hello. We were worried about you."

"I thought I'd eaten a flare."

"Make sure to say a little prayer to Saint Bonaventure of Potenza before going to bed tonight," Hugh Oakley said.

"Excuse me?"

"That's the saint invoked against diseases of the bowels."

"Hugh!" Charlotte pulled his earlobe. But she was smiling, and oh, what a smile! If I'd been a king, I would have traded my kingdom for it. "One of my husband's hobbies is studying the saints."

"My new favorites are Godeleva, who protects against sore throats. Or Homobonus, patron of tailors."

"Come on, Saint Hugh, let's eat."

"Don't forget—Saint Bonaventure of Potenza."

"I'm praying already."

He touched my sleeve and moved away with his wife. We continued to our places at the tables. By coincidence, Hugh and I were seated at the same one, although there were people between us.

Unfortunately, my neighbor took a shine to me and all through the first two courses asked personal questions I didn't want to answer. Sometimes I looked over and saw Hugh Oakley talking with a well-known SoHo gallery owner. They seemed to be having a great time. I wished I were in their conversation and not mine.

Because I wasn't paying attention to what the guy on my right was saying, it didn't register when he began to touch me as he spoke. Nothing bad, just a hand on the arm, then a few sentences later fingers on my elbow to emphasize a point, but I didn't want it. Once when his hand stayed too long on mine, I stared at the hands until he slowly pulled his away.

"*Oops*. Sorry 'bout that."

"That's okay. I'm hungry. Can we eat?"

The silence that followed was welcome. The food was good and my hunger had returned. I dug into the chicken-whatever and was content to eat and let the talk flow in and out of my mind. If it hadn't been for that, I wouldn't have heard what Hugh said.

"James Stillman would have been one of the best! It was a tragedy he died."

"Come on, Hugh, the guy was uncontrollable. Don't forget the Adcock disaster."

Hugh's voice was angry and loud. "That wasn't his fault, Dennis. Adcock's husband had us all fooled."

"Yeah, your friend Stillman most of all."

I leaned so far forward I felt my chest touching the table. "Did you know James Stillman?"

They looked at me. Hugh nodded. The other man snorted dismissively. "Sure, who didn't? Half New York knew him after the Adcock thing."

"What was that?"

"Tell her, Hugh. You're his big defender."

"Damned right I am!" He glared, but when he spoke to me his voice dropped back to normal range. "Do you know of the painter Lolly Adcock?"

"Sure."

"Right. Well, a few years ago her husband said he had ten of her paintings no one had ever seen. He wanted to sell them and contacted Bartholomew's—"

"The auction house?"

"Yes. Adcock wanted them to handle the auction. James worked for Bartholomew's. They thought *very* highly of him, so they sent him to Kansas City to verify if the paintings were real."

The other man shook his head. "And in his great enthusiasm, Mr. Stillman cut a deal with the wily Mr. Adcock, only it turned out the paintings were fakes."

"It was an honest mistake!"

"It was a stupid mistake and you know it, Hugh. You never would have done it that way. Stillman was famous for going off half-cocked. Half-cocked Ad-cocked. I never thought of that. Very fitting."

"Then explain how he found the Messerschmidt head that had been lost for a hundred years."

"Beginner's luck. I need another drink." The man signaled a waiter. While he was giving his order I grabbed my chance.

"Did you know him well?"

"James? Yes, very well."

"Can we—Um, excuse me, would you mind if we switched seats? I'd really like to ask Hugh some questions."

The gallery owner picked up his plate. As we were changing, he asked, "Were you also a Stillman fan?"

"He was my boyfriend in high school."

"Really? I didn't know he *had* a past."

I felt the hair on the back of my neck go up. "He was a good man."

"I wouldn't know. I never cared to spend time with him."

When I sat down I was so angry I couldn't speak. Hugh patted me on the knee. "Don't mind Dennis. He needs Saint Ubald."

"Who's that?"

"Patron saint against rabies. Tell me about you and James."

We talked through the rest of dinner and dessert. I didn't eat a thing.

Hugh Oakley was an art expert. He traveled the world telling people what they owned, or should buy. Listening to him talk, I quickly understood why he looked so young. His enthusiasm for what he did was infectious. His stories about unearthing rare or marvelous things were the tales of a boy with a treasure map and a heart full of hope. He loved his work. I loved hearing him talk about it.

Years before, he had given several lectures at the Tyler School of Art in Philadelphia, and that's where he met James. Hugh described James as a young man who was lost but convinced there was something significant waiting for him. Something that would arrive one day out of the blue and lead him home.

"After my last lecture he came up, looking so bewildered that I was concerned. I asked if he was all right. The only thing he could say was, 'I want to know about this. I *have* to know more about this.' I'd felt that same excitement at Columbia when I heard Federico Zeri speak. Do you know his book *Behind the Image*? You must read it. Let me write the title down." He slipped a hand into his pocket and brought out a Connolly leather notebook and a silver mechanical pencil. He wrote down the title and author's name in distinctive block lettering. It was not till later that I learned it was the typeface known as Bremen. Another of Hugh Oakley's many hobbies was meticulously copying in various faces poems and stories he liked and then, like a monk from the Middle Ages, illuminating them in paints he made from scratch.

I was so absorbed in what he was saying that it took a while to realize I was hogging him from the rest of the party. I worried what his wife would think. Looking around, I was relieved to see her deep in conversation with Dagmar Breece.

Somehow we'd gotten off the subject of James. I needed to know as much as Hugh was willing to tell.

"What exactly *did* happen to James?"

"The idiot heart."

"What do you mean?"

" 'Hope gleams in the idiot heart.' It's a line from a Mayakovski poem. His girlfriend had those words—the idiot heart—tattooed on the inside of her wrist like a bracelet. Can you imagine? But it's the *age* of tattoos, isn't it?

"Her name was Kiera Stewart. She was a graduate student at Temple. Beautiful Scottish girl from Aberdeen. James was nuts over her, but you only had to meet her once to see she was an ocean of bad news. Women like that give you wonderful for the first few months, but then start taking it back bit by bit as the relationship goes on. After a while you're wondering if that great stuff ever really existed at all. But you're so hooked on them by then and the tidbits of delicious they parse out, it's like being addicted to drugs.

"The tragedy was, James was just coming into his own around the time they met. He'd found what he wanted to do with his life. And he was so good at it that the right people were already watching to see what he'd do next.

"The good is always the enemy of the great. From the beginning, he had the rare ability to discern between them. The trouble was, in our business insight often comes slowly and through meticulous detective work. James constantly wanted to achieve right now, this second." Hugh shook his head. "He once said he had a lot to prove but didn't know to whom.

"So everything happened at once. Not many people can handle that. His star was rising, he'd met a wild woman who sent him spinning, and then his bosses sent him to look at the Adcock paintings. James thought he was invincible. For a while it looked like he was.

"Then it all crashed. He made a big mistake. Adcock's husband turned out to be a clever crook, but not clever enough. The deal blew up in James's face. That was bad enough, but then Kiera got wind of what happened. Over the phone she told him their relationship was finished. Over the *phone*. Classy, huh? A platinum bitch. He got in his car in the middle of the night, drove down to Philadelphia to see her but never made it. That's the story, Miranda. I'm sorry I can't tell you more. He was a great favorite of mine."

"You haven't *touched* your desserts!"

Startled, I felt a firm hand on my shoulder and looked up to see Dagmar glaring at us.

"I'm sorry. We were talking—"

"No excuses! That is a yogurt trilogy, which I had to torture a man into making. So eat!"

She stood there until we picked up our spoons and started shoveling it in. Tasted like yogurt to me. Everyone else was finished and leaving the table. Charlotte Oakley came by.

"What are you two talking about? You look like you're sharing atomic secrets." She was smiling and her voice was only friendly. A beautiful nice woman. Anyway, why should she be worried? She won any contest in the room. Whenever I'd looked at her, I'd noticed at least two men staring at her each time. Who wouldn't?

"Charlotte, the most amazing thing! James Stillman was Miranda's boyfriend when they were in high school."

"Really? I loved James. He reminded me of Hugh when he was young."

That was it! I'd not been able to put a finger on why I liked Hugh Oakley so much. The instant she said it, I realized a great part of my attraction to her husband was that he seemed to have the same kind of roaring spirit and curiosity as James.

"I hadn't seen him since high school. Then I went to our class reunion and heard he was dead."

She frowned. "A bad place to hear something like that. James was the Prodigal Son always sneaking back in through the dog door. The original Bad Boy, and always a pleasure! Any time we spent time together he absolutely melted my underwear. I would have eloped with him any time. But that *girlfriend*, Kiera! She went from zero to bitch in two seconds."

"What happened to her?"

"Wait a minute, I have a picture of them."

"You do?" Hugh sounded as surprised as I did.

"Sure. The time we all went to Block Island?" Charlotte carried a small purse but had a large wallet wedged into it. She took it out and rummaged through. "Here you go."

She passed me a photo and although I took it, I couldn't look immediately.

"What's the matter?"

"It's hard—the life I never lived is right here. On this piece of paper."

"Nah. Do it, Miranda. Then you won't be haunted."

I took a deep breath and looked. James, Charlotte, and Kiera were smiling at the camera. He had short hair, which was a shock, because when we were together he wore it down to his shoulders. He looked older. There were wrinkles, and the gaunt face he'd had in high school had filled out some, but there was that same smile with the white, white teeth. Long artistic hands.

My eyes filled. "I can't stand it."

"He was great. You would have loved him."

"I *did*." I looked at Charlotte and tried to smile.

BABE RUTH'S
SMALL HEAD

IN THE MONTH that followed I didn't think much about the Oakleys. Business picked up, and I met a man who went from Promising! to Forget It! in just four dates. Do(u)g Auerbach came to town and we devoured each other for the weekend he was there. Twice I had tea with Frances Hatch. After the second time, she said there was a brain behind my face and she liked me. That made me feel very good. I said I liked her too. She responded playfully "But do you want to love, or *be* loved?" For a long time the question fluttered around my mind like birds that fly into a building but can't get out again.

Doug said that while in Germany he had watched a TV documentary about people who had sexual fetishes for amputees. The show was very calm and informative and without any attitude. They showed snippets from amputee porno films, magazines, social clubs, and even comic books.

"I'm a hip guy. You know, try not to judge others, be as open as possible. But I saw this show and my mouth dropped open. I kept wondering, do I live on the same *planet* as these people?"

Frances liked to talk about sex, so I told her about it.

"What's the matter with you, Miranda?"

"What do you mean?"

"You sound so prissy. Wouldn't you go to bed with a man without a leg or an arm if you loved him?"

"Yes, of course."

"What about a woman?"

"I can't imagine loving a woman that way."

"A child?"

"Frances, you're just trying to provoke me."

"How old is a child to you? How old would they have to be before you would sleep with them?"

"I don't know, seventeen?"

"Ha! A lot of men made love to me before I was seventeen and that was eighty years ago."

"Yes, but you've led a pretty unique life compared to most people."

"So what? Know when *I* think a person is old enough to make love? When they become interesting." She held a cane in her hand and knocked it on the floor.

"I don't think you should run for president on that platform, Frances. They might burn you at the stake."

"I know. I'm too old. My heart doesn't live here anymore. That's why memories are good: you wake up every morning and put them on like hand cream. That way, the days can't dry you out.

"Listen, Miranda, I have a favor to ask. Do you know the painter Lolly Adcock?"

Hugh Oakley's face came instantly to mind. "Funny you ask. Someone was talking about her just the other day."

"A *miserable* woman, but quite a good painter. I have a small watercolor by her I want to sell. Would you be willing to look into the best way for me to do it?"

I told her about James Stillman and me, about his dealings with the Adcock estate, and what happened to him afterwards.

"Too bad you two didn't meet when you were older; you'd probably be happily married with a house full of kids. But that happens: we keep meeting people or having experiences at the wrong time. The greatest love of my life was a man named Shumda, but I didn't know that till I was ten years smarter. When we were together, I was just a kid auditioning different men for mad love affairs. I was looking for heat, not light.

"You know how we look back and say, 'Gee, I was dumb when I was seventeen.' What if you look at it the other way—seventeen-year-old Miranda looks forward at you now. What would *she* have to say about what you've become?"

"What would seventeen-year-old me think of me now?" I laughed.

"Exactly. She'd probably be furious you *didn't* marry this James and save him."

Hugh had given me his business card at the party. I called and we made an appointment to meet. Frances gave me the Adcock painting to show him. I was surprised she was willing to trust me with something so valuable.

"You can only steal it. But if you do, then you won't be able to come back and visit. I'd rather know me than rob me."

The day before our meeting, Hugh called to say he had to go to Dublin immediately. We could cancel the meeting, or he could arrange for one of his assistants to see me. I said the assistant would be fine. If necessary, we could meet after he returned. When I put the phone down I was disappointed, but nothing more.

An hour before the appointment, I had a confrontation with the man I had been dating. He came into the shop all excited about a new video camera he'd just bought.

Within fifteen minutes he was insulting me. He said I was cold and calculating. I'd squeezed him empty like a tube of toothpaste, then dropped him in the trash. I let him go on until all he had left was splutter.

"I have an appointment now. I have to go."

"That's it? That's all you're going to say?"

"Haven't you said it all?" I stood up.

I don't know what my face said at that moment. My heart and stomach were calm. More than anything, I was glad it had come to this. Now I wouldn't have to diplomatically sashay around him anymore. I'd have guessed my expression was nothing but empty. Who knows? Whatever was there, his eyes widened and he slapped me across the face.

Staggering backward, I banged into a metal filing cabinet. The edge of it stabbed me in the small of the back. Crying out, I fell to my knees. I saw his feet coming toward me. I curled my body inward, sure he was going to beat me.

He started laughing. "Look at you! That's where you belong, on your fucking *knees*. Let me get a picture of this. I want to remember it."

I heard a whirring sound and, fearfully looking up, saw the camera up to his eye, pointing at me.

"This I gotta have. What a memory!"

It went on forever but I wasn't about to do anything to anger him further.

"Miranda, get off your knees, honey. You don't have to beg me for anything. You're the liberated woman." He dropped the camera to his side and walked out.

MY MOTHER USED to hit me. Long after I'd grown up and could talk to her about such things, I asked why. She refused to admit she ever had. I said, "Don't you remember the time I broke your purse and you slapped me?"

"Oh, well of course, *then*. Dad gave me that bag."

"I know, Mom, but you *hit* me!"

"You deserved it, dear. That's not hitting."

All grown up, on my knees, petrified he would come back and do worse to me, I wondered if I deserved this too.

I could call the police, but what might he do then? I felt helpless. So tough and clear in business, I easily held my own in most situations, but most situations didn't scare you to your marrow where a child still lives and cowers at the real monsters walking the earth.

Hugh Oakley's office was in a building on Sixty-first Street. I went in spite of what had happened. I knew if I didn't, I would have gone home and been afraid. I needed something to do. This meeting wasn't so important that if I started crying again in the middle of it, I couldn't leave fast.

When I got out of the elevator, I took a couple of deep breaths and tried to pull myself together. For the next few minutes I could be cool, crisp, and professional. Try to avoid my fear that way. But when it was over I would have to return to the world where *he* lived. What could I do about that?

The door was marked simply OAKLEY ASSOCIATES in the same letters Hugh had used to write down the book title for me at the party. As I put my hand on the brass doorknob, I heard, faintly, a violin inside the office playing something sprightly. I felt a jolt of joy. The unexpected music said there were still lovely things on earth. I went in.

The outer office was furnished with antiques and paintings, but there was no sign of a receptionist. The phone on the desk was lit with blinking lights.

The music grew much louder. I made out a flute and bass along with the violin. I know nothing about Irish music, but from the jump and flow, I had a hunch.

A few steps farther into the office, I called out a tentative hello. Nothing. More steps, another hello. The music kept going, light and gay as a dance. I thought, What the hell, and went toward it. There were several rooms. One was open and I peeked in. The place looked like a laboratory. Test tubes and Bunsen burners . . . It reminded me too much of high school chemistry class and I moved on.

At the end of the hall was another open door and that's where the music was. It abruptly stopped and a woman said loudly, "Damn!"

"That was good! Why'd you stop?"

"Because I blew the damned passage again!"

"Who cares?" Hugh said.

"I care."

Walking over, I knocked on the door. "Hello?" Slowly poking my head in, I saw Hugh, a man, and a woman sitting in straight-backed chairs with music stands in front of them. Hugh had a violin on his lap, the woman had some kind of flute, the man an acoustic bass guitar.

"Miranda, hi! Come in!"

"Am I interrupting?"

"No, we're just practicing. Miranda Romanac, this is Courtney Hill and Ronan Mariner. We work together."

"Your music is wonderful."

"Our lunch hour. Come on, sit down. We're going to run through this again and then we'll talk. We're playing 'Ferny Hill.' Do you know it?"

"I'm sorry, I don't."

"You'll love it. Let's go."

They started playing. I started crying. I didn't realize it until Courtney looked at me and her eyes widened. Then I felt tears on my cheeks and gave a gesture that said it was the music. And it was, more than anything else. Nothing could have been a more perfect antidote to what happened earlier. Irish folk music is the most schizophrenic I have ever heard. How can it be so sad and happy at the same time, even within the same note? Simple and direct, it tells you yes, the world is full of pain, but this is the way through. As long as you're in the music, the bad things stay away. They performed the tune perfectly. For those few minutes, I cried and was more content than I had been in days.

Finishing with a flourish, they looked at each other like kids who had sailed through a great adventure without a scratch.

"That was beautiful."

"It *was* good, huh? But let's get down to business. What have you brought us?" Hugh looked at me and obviously saw the tears but said nothing. I liked that.

I undid the strings and paper around the painting and held it up so all three of them could see it at once. They looked at it, then at each other.

"Is that what I think it is? A Lolly Adcock?"

"Yes."

Hugh took it from me. They huddled over it, making quiet comments, pointing here and there.

"Hugh didn't say anything about you bringing in an Adcock."

"I would have, if I'd gone to Dublin," Hugh said.

Ronan rubbed his mouth. "You know what my gut reaction is? Stay the hell away from it, Hugh. Even if it's real, after the Stillman fiasco, people are going to be gunning for anyone who authenticates an Adcock."

Hugh brought it close to his face and sniffed. "Doesn't smell fake."

"It's not funny, Hugh. You know exactly what he's saying."

"I do, Courtney, but that's our business, isn't it? We call them as we see them. If we're wrong, then we're wrong. Who knows, we may find out it's a fake when we check it out."

"I still agree with Ronan. Whatever we might get out of it, it's not worth the trouble." She looked at the painting and shook her head.

"Fair enough, but would you begin to check it for me?" He spoke quietly. The others got quickly out of their chairs and headed for the door.

We sat and listened to them walk down the hall. Far away, a door closed.

"Why were you crying?"

"I thought you were going to ask where I got the picture."

"Later. Why were you crying?"

"Does it matter?"

"Yes. When you came in, your face was somewhere else. Someplace bad."

"Excuse me?"

"You weren't expecting this." He held up his violin. "You had a different face on and you had to change it very fast. For one second I could see you brought something awful in from outside. The tears proved it."

"You're a good detective, Hugh."

"It's only because I care."

What could I say to that? We sat long moments in silence.

"Someone hit me."

"Do you need help with them?"

"I don't think so."

"Why would someone want to hit you?"

"He thinks I'm a bitch."

Hugh took two yellow hard candies from a shirt pocket and handed me one. As I unwrapped it, he opened the other and popped it in his mouth; then he picked up the violin and began to play quietly.

"I don't think I'm a bitch."

He smiled. "Who is he?"

"A man I've been dating."

He nodded, silently saying, Go on. He played the Beatles' "For No One."

I started out slowly but was full speed ahead in a few moments. I described how we'd met, the dates we'd had, things talked about, what I'd thought of him right up until the fateful slap.

"A painting licker."

"What do you mean?"

"There's a man in England who goes around *licking* the paintings he loves. Looking's not enough for him. He wants a more intimate experience with his favorite pictures, so when he's at a museum and guards aren't watching, he licks 'em. He has a postcard collection of each one he's done."

"Crazy."

"It is, but I understand it. I think that's what happened with your man: he couldn't have you and it drove him crazy. So he did the only thing he *could* do to own you for a few minutes: scared you. It always works. For today, or however long you're going to be afraid of him, he *does* own you."

"Damn it! Damn that power men have. Whenever they don't like something, they can always *hit* us. You'll never know that feeling. Always that little bit of fear in our heart."

"Not all men hit women, Miranda."

"But you *can,* and that's the difference."

A small white bullterrier ran into the room and over to Hugh.

"Easy! Miranda, this is Easy. Whenever we play, she runs and hides. The only dog I've ever known that actively dislikes music."

"That breed always scares me."

"Bullterriers? She's a cream puff. She only *looks* like a thief."

She looked more like a bleached pig, but her face was sweet and her tail was wagging so furiously that I couldn't resist reaching out to pat her. She moved over to me and leaned like a stone against my leg.

"Why do you call her Easy?"

"My daughter named her. No reason. I brought her home from the kennel; Brigit took one look and said her name was Easy. Simple as that."

"How many children do you have?"

"A daughter and a son. Brigit and Oisin. Oy-sheen."

"Oisin? Is that Irish?"

"Yes. Both kids were born in Dublin."

"By the way, why didn't you *go* to Dublin?"

"Because you were coming. When you said you'd be happy to see my assistant, I thought, Uh oh, when would I see her again? I knew I had to be here."

Once again I tried to figure out how to respond.

"You say things that throw me off, Hugh."

"People say I'm too direct. I didn't go to Dublin because I had to see you again. It's that simple."

Courtney called out from down the hall, asking him to come. He stood up, put the violin on the chair, and started out of the room. "I was going to call you the other day but you called me. I didn't want to wait any longer. Ever since we met, most of my days seem to be about you."

He left me sitting with Easy leaning against my leg. It took a while before my body started shaking, but when it did, it came on strong. So strong that it roused the dog from her doze. She looked up at me. I closed my eyes. My heart pounded inside its cage of bones. I couldn't wait for him to return.

HERE I AM, an old woman with a shaky hand and a cheap pen, writing about sex. Is there any greater irony? Most of the time I cannot even recall what I ate yesterday. How do I presume to remember and write honestly about that most evanescent act, fifty years after it happened?

I will stand up and walk to the kitchen. On the way I'll think about how to do it. There are some chocolate cookies left. I want to eat two and drink a glass of cold water. Eating is sex for old people.

This is my home, what's left of a life in its final few rooms. There are some photographs. My parents. Hugh and me. Zoe on the porch of this house. The only piece of furniture I have kept over the years is Hugh's easy chair. Despite having been re-covered two times it is shabby-looking now, but I would never give it away. On the table nearby is a photograph of Frances in her New York apartment. All of her possessions surround her, the paintings and rugs, that lush abundance of color so much a part of her being. The difference is, Frances *wanted* to remember everything. I don't. Better to keep my last surroundings simple. Avoid any fatal memory or malevolent connection from things best left to their uneasy sleep in my heart.

Certain things must be here. Most importantly the pile of sticks in the fireplace. Every one of those pieces of wood is important. Written on each is a date and a reason. I have never counted, but would guess there are twenty now. Hugh's collection was much larger, but he started his years before I did.

It was his idea: When anything truly important happens in your life, wherever you happen to be, find a stick in the immediate vicinity and write the occasion and date on it. Keep them together, protect them. There shouldn't be too many; sort through them every few years and separate the events that remain genuinely important from those that were but no longer are. You know the difference. Throw the rest out.

When you are very old, very sick, or sure there's not much time left to live, put them together and burn them. The marriage of sticks.

AN HOUR AFTER I visited his office to have the painting appraised, Hugh Oakley and I were walking through Central Park. He told me about the marriage of sticks and suggested I start my collection right then. I was so nervous about what was about to happen that without thinking, I did. It was from a copper beech tree. I knew nothing about trees then. Foliage, plants, things that grew. I was a city girl who was hurrying to a hotel to have sex with a man I knew was happily married with two children.

"What's the matter?" He stopped and turned me so we were face to face. We were holding hands. A moment ago we'd been racing to get to a hotel. I assumed he'd been there before. How many other women had he sped along like this, rushing to get them into bed?

"You look miserable."

"I'm not miserable, Hugh, I'm *unstrung*! Somebody hit me this morning, and now I'm here with you." I stared at our clasped hands and kept staring while I spoke. "I don't do things like this. It's everything together, full volume. Dangerous, right, wrong . . . Everything. I thought you'd be in Ireland. I thought your assistant was going to appraise the painting and I'd go home. Not this. This is all new territory for me."

He looked around and, seeing a park bench, pulled me to it. "Sit down. Listen to me. What you're doing is *right*. It's your heart and the adventurous part all saying *go*. Our checks and balances hold us back too much from risking anything.

"Don't let them, Miranda. Do it. If nothing else, you'll remember this later and say it was crazy but you're glad you did it."

My eyes were closed. "Can I ask a question? Will you answer honestly?"

"Anything."

I straightened my back. "Are you worth it?"

I heard him take a sharp breath to answer but he stayed silent a long moment. "I think so. I hope so."

"Do you go to hotels a lot with women?"

"No. Sometimes."

"That doesn't makes me feel special."

"I'm not going to apologize for the person you didn't know till today."

"That's facile, Hugh. This is a big thing for me."

"I'll do whatever you want, Miranda. We can stay here and talk. Go to a movie, or go somewhere and make love. It's all the same to me. I just want to be with you."

Two Rollerbladers pounded by, followed by a bunch of kids in crooked caps, carrying a big boom box.

We watched the parade pass before I spoke. "Know what I want to do? Before anything else?"

"What?"

"Go to the Gap and buy a pair of khakis." It was a test, plain and simple. I said it only to see how he would react.

His face lit up and he smiled. It was genuine. "Sure! Let's go."

"What about the hotel?"

He paused. When he spoke his voice was slow and careful. "You don't *get* it, do you? I'm not twenty, Miranda. I don't ride my cock around like a witch on a broomstick. I want to be you. If that's in bed, great. If not, then together is all the matters."

"Then why were we going to a hotel?"

"Because I *do* want to touch you. I thought you felt the same.

But I was wrong. Big deal. Let's go buy your trousers."

"Really?" The word came out scared.

He put his hand on my cheek. "Really."

WE WALKED OUT of the park as fast as we'd walked in. I would have given a month of my life to know what he was really thinking. He took my hand again and we kept squeezing back and forth as if to say, I'm here, I'm still with you. No matter how this day ended up, I knew I'd be running the replay in my brain for a long time.

I didn't need new pants. The only reason I'd even said it was because a few minutes before I'd seen an ad for the Gap on the side of a crosstown bus.

"Here we are."

I'd been thinking so hard about what was happening that I didn't realize we had arrived at the door of a Gap store.

"You get your khakis and I'll buy a cap. It'll remind me of today. You'll have your first stick and I'll have a baseball cap."

"Are you angry, Hugh? Tell the truth."

"I'm *excited*." Without another word, he pushed the door open and gestured for me to go in.

"In what way?"

"I'll tell you later." We walked in. He moved away from me and picked up a green sweatshirt.

Nothing else to do but find the damned pants. When a saleswoman came up and sweetly asked if she could help, I snarled out, "Khakis! I'm looking for khakis, okay?" As she backed off, her face was one big "Uh-oh."

I didn't care. I was in a damned Gap store, shopping, instead of having devil-may-care sex with a fascinating man. Why was I a coward with him? I'd done it before in a blink. That time outside the China Moon Restaurant in San Francisco? Or with the model in

Hamburg on the bed with the broken spring? I hopped into bed with other men and things had worked out fine. The memories were happy and guilt-free.

I looked around the store and saw Hugh trying on baseball caps in front of a mirror. A nice-looking man in his forties in a dark suit, pushing boys' hats around on his big head. Why *not* with him?

Because I could love him.

It began in his office when he said, "It's only because I care." As honest and simple as a piece of white paper with those words printed large and black on it. His candor disturbed me because I loved it. It seemed everything he said was either honest or interesting, usually both. He knew so much, and even if a subject had never mattered to me before once he began speaking I was hooked. Like the words he'd learned in Khalkha when he was in Mongolia researching Genghis Khan, or James Agee versus Graham Greene as a film reviewer, or the plumbing system Thomas Jefferson invented for Monticello . . .

His face was all animation, all angles and eyes. His chin was square, his teeth were smoker's yellow. There were deep wrinkles down either side of his mouth. When he smiled they almost disappeared. His eyelashes were long and thick. I didn't want to kiss him yet, but wouldn't say no if he tried to kiss me. When he asked me to lunch I said yes. When we walked out of his office and his colleagues stared I didn't care. When we stood on the street and Hugh said he wanted me, I said okay without hesitating.

In the store I walked up behind him and talked to his reflection in the mirror. He was wearing a green baseball cap tipped slightly to the right. "Will you come with me and see how these look?" I held up the pants. I had no idea what size they were. I had picked up the first pair I'd seen on the shelf.

"Sure. Did you know Babe Ruth had a small head for a man his size? Seven and three-eighths." His expression didn't change. I asked a passing saleswoman where the changing rooms were. When she pointed them out, I took his hand and pulled him behind me.

Another saleswoman stood outside the dressing rooms, but she didn't seem surprised when we entered together. It was very narrow inside. I whipped the curtain across, dropped the pants on the floor, and turned to him. A foot apart, I could smell him for the first time. We had never been this close. Orange-and-cinnamon cologne, tobacco, a slight sourness that was already delicious.

Reaching up, I slid his cap off and kissed him. His lips were softer than I had imagined. They gave nothing yet because it was up to me now and we both knew that was necessary. I slid my arms up his back but didn't pull him close.

He reached up and stroked the back of my head. We stared.

"Will we be friends too?" I slid a finger down one of the wrinkles alongside his mouth. It was so deep.

"It can only work that way." He took my finger and kissed it.

"I want to lick your spine."

Nothing else happened. We made out for a steaming minute or two, then left the dressing room smiling like lottery winners. Hugh insisted on buying the cap as a souvenir. He wore it the rest of the day as we walked around the city and deeper into each other's lives.

Whatever bad thoughts came to my mind—his nice wife, his children—had almost no gravity. The good thoughts, the hopes, the thrilling possibilities had the weight of mountains. I knew this was the beginning of something bad for all concerned, no matter how cleverly it could be justified. I had never been with a married man although there had been ample opportunities. I believed what goes around comes around. If I did the snug dance with someone's husband, surely the gods would find an appalling form of payback.

We stood outside a subway entrance. Our day was over. He was going back to his other life where his family waited for him and suspected nothing. We looked at each other with the increased hunger separation always brings.

"Are you going to get your dog?"

"Yup. Then I'll walk her home and think about you."

"I'm thinking about your family."

He shook his head. "That does no good."

"But I'm new to this. Sooner or later it's going to come out."

"Miranda, sooner or later we're going to *die*. I used to think a lot about sooner or later, but you know what? Sooner suddenly became later and I realized I'd wasted too much time worrying about it, rather than living it."

"A friend of mine asked if I would rather love or be loved. I'd rather love."

He nodded. "Then that's your answer. I have to go."

We kissed; he touched my throat, then moved toward the subway steps. Halfway down them, he turned and his face lit up in the greatest smile. "Where have you been? Where have you been all this time?"

I DIDN'T HEAR from him for two days. Imagine how loud that silence was. On the third, worried and resentful, I stopped at the mailbox on my way to the store. Inside were the usual bills and advertisements, but the last envelope in the bunch was the jackpot. My name and address were written in Hugh's handwriting. My heart started galloping.

There was a postcard inside.

A Walker Evans photograph of a tired room with only a bed and a side table with a water pitcher on top of it. The wallpaper had long since died and been consumed by the water stains everywhere. Over the bed, the slanting ceiling indicated the room probably sat right under a roof. Without the bed, it was a whore's room in *Tropic of*

Cancer, or one from an early Hemingway short story about living poor in Paris.

But like alchemy, the improbable whiteness of the sheets and pillow transformed it into a space of sex and infinity. A room you would go to with someone you wanted to fuck again and again. Then the two of you would fall asleep wrapped round each other. There was nothing special about the room except how carefully the bed had been made with ironed, brilliantly white sheets and cases. In those dismal surroundings, the two plumped pillows stood out like crisp clouds. The bedspread was a patchwork quilt. I could smell the staleness of the room, feel its temperature on my skin, and then the touch of whoever would take me there. Nothing was written on the postcard itself, but on a separate sheet of paper, this:

This is all I want with you now: a simple room, one light
in the middle of the ceiling hanging on a long line, the
kind you see in cheap apartments or hotel rooms no one
ever remembers staying in. At night the sad weak light
never reaches the far corners. It droops over a room full of
shadows. It doesn't care.

But for us, light doesn't matter here. The room is
clean and bright in the day. Maybe there's a good view out
the window. It is the *room* I want, a bed wide enough for
us to lie in comfortably. Faces close enough to feel each
other's breath.

Your skin is flushed. With my finger, I trace a line
from the ledge of your chin down the neck, your shoulder,
arm. It makes you smile and shiver. How can you shiver
when it's so warm in here?

I want this room. I want this room with you in it,
naked beside me. I don't know where we are. Maybe by

the sea. Or in the middle of a city where the noise through the window is as busy as we are.

The afternoon is ours. The evening and the night too. We'll be tired by then but we'll still go out and eat a huge meal. Your body will be wonderfully sore and raw. It will make you smile when we walk to the restaurant. I'll look at you and ask if anything is wrong. You'll say no and squeeze my arm. We'll need this time out in the world to remind ourselves there is something else besides us today, that room, our bodies.

In a noisy restaurant we'll talk quietly. Voices and faces smoothed by all those hours in bed. Anyone watching us will know we have been fucking. It is so obvious.

Later again in the room when nothing is needed, I want to sleep a few hours, and then wake with you pressed against my side. Maybe I'll reach for you. Maybe I will only touch your wrist and feel your sleeping, secret pulse. The rest can wait. There's time now.

Keep this picture with you. Put it on a table, a desk, wherever you are. If someone asks why you have it, say it's a place where you'd be happy. Look at it and know I am waiting. Look at it again.

I walked out of my building on legs made of wet spaghetti. Out on the street, the world was the same as yesterday but it took two or three blocks to regain my bearings and recognize I was still on planet earth. When I came to, I realized I had been walking with the letter clutched tightly in both hands behind my back. To hold the joy as long as I could, I stopped where I was, closed my eyes and said aloud, "I must remember this. I must remember it as long as I live."

Opening my eyes again, the first thing I saw was James Stillman. My heart recognized him before any other part did. And it was calm. It said, "There he is. James is across the street." He looked the way he had when I'd known him fifteen years before. He was unmistakable, even in the rush of people surrounding him.

He wore a suit and tie. I stood frozen in place. We stared at each other until he lifted an arm and waved to me, slowly, from side to side. The kind of exaggerated wave you give someone who is driving off in a car and you want to be sure they see you until the very last second.

Without thinking, I started out into traffic and was met by screeching brakes and angry horns. When I was halfway across, he began to walk away. By the time I reached the other side he was already far ahead. I began running, but somehow he stayed way in front of me. He went around a corner. When I got there and made the turn, he was twice as far as before. There was no way I could catch up. When I stopped he did too. He turned and did something that was pure James Stillman: He put his open hand against his forehead, then moved it down to his mouth and blew me a big kiss. Whenever we parted he would do that. He'd seen it in an old Arabian Nights film and thought it the coolest gesture—hand to the forehead, to the lips, big kiss. My Arabian Knight, back from the dead.

"I SAW A ghost and I'm in love with a married man."

"Welcome to the club."

"Zoe, I'm serious."

"Married men are *always* more delicious than single, Miranda. That's where the challenge is. And I've believed in ghosts all my life. But tell me about Mr. Married first because I'm the expert on that subject."

We were having lunch. She had come into town for the day. Married boyfriend Hector had ended their relationship and she was at the end of her period of mourning. For weeks I'd suggested a day in the city doing girl things together to take her mind off him and finally she said yes. Now I was doubly glad to meet so I could get her input on my new twilight zones.

"The ghost was James Stillman."

"Great! Where?"

"On the street near my apartment. He waved to me in that old way, remember?" I did the gesture and she smiled.

"A very romantic fellow, no doubt about it."

"But Zoe, I *saw* him. He looked exactly like he did in high school."

She folded her napkin a few times and put it on the table. "Remember when we used to do the Ouija board and contacted all those old spirits, or whatever they were? My mother believed when some people die, their souls get tossed into a limbo between life and death. That's why you can talk to them on a Ouija board or in a seance— they're half here and half there."

"Do you believe that?"

"Why else would you want to hang around life if it's over for you?"

"He was so *real*. Solid. No ectoplasm or Caspar the Friendly Ghost, hovering a foot above the ground in a white sheet. It was James. Completely real."

"Maybe it was. You'd have to ask an expert. Why would he come back now? Why not before?"

We didn't talk about it much beyond that. Neither of us knew what it meant, so further discussion was pointless.

"Tell me about your new man. The alive one."

I told her in great detail, and along the way we kept having more drinks to help us analyze my new situation.

"You know what just hit me? What if James came back as a sign to tell me not to do this?"

Zoe threw up her hands in exasperation. "Oh, for God's sake! If you're going to feel guilty, don't blame ghosts. I'm sure they've got better things to do than keep tabs on your sexual behaviour."

"But I haven't slept with him yet!"

"Miranda?"

Hearing my name spoken in a familiar voice, I turned and saw Doug Auerbach. He was staring at Zoe.

"Dog! What are you doing here? Why didn't you call?"

"I didn't know I was coming till yesterday. I was going to call later. I'm supposed to have lunch here with a client."

I introduced him to Zoe and he sat down. Soon it was clear he was interested only in my oldest friend. At first she smiled and laughed politely at his jokes. When his interest hit her, she transformed into a sexy fox. I had never seen her like that. It was fascinating how deftly she handled both Doug and her new role.

Naturally I was disconcerted. Part of me was jealous, possessive. How dare they! The rest remembered Doug's small place in my life, and Zoe's goodness. At the appropriate moment, I "suddenly remembered" I had another appointment—and would they mind if I left?

Out on the street again looking for a cab, I felt like Charlotte Oakley, the unwanted third. I shuddered and started walking as fast as I could.

ONE AFTERNOON WHEN his family was away for the weekend, Hugh invited me to their apartment. Easy the bullterrier followed me from room to room. I had on tennis shoes, so the only noise was the tick-tick of Easy's long toenails on the wooden floors.

This is where he lives. Where *she* lives. Each object had its own importance and memories. I kept looking at things and asking myself why the Oakleys had them or what they meant. It was a strange archaeology of the living. The man who could decipher it all for me sat in another room, reading the newspaper, but I wasn't about to ask any questions. Pictures of his children, Charlotte, the family together. On a yellow sailboat, skiing, sitting beneath a large Christmas tree. This was his home, his family, his life. Why was I here? Why put faces to his stories, or see gifts brought back from trips for these people he loved? On the piano was a crystal box full of cigarettes. I picked it up and read the name *Waterford* on the underside. A large red-and-white stone ball stood beside it. Crystal and stone. I stroked the cold ball and kept moving.

When I'd asked to see his home, Hugh had not hesitated a moment. They owned a house in East Hampton. The family usually went there on weekends in summer. The first time they went without Hugh, he called and told me the coast was clear. And it *was* a coast of sorts; they lived on the east, I lived on the west. If I had been his wife, I would have been enraged to know another woman was in my home, looking at my life, touching it.

So why *was* I here? If I was going to be with Hugh, why didn't I work to keep his two worlds separate and be satisfied with what I had? Because I was greedy. I wanted to know as much about him as I could. That included how he lived when I wasn't around. By seeing his apartment, I figured, I would be less afraid of what went on there.

I was right: walking through the rooms, I felt calmer seeing that only people lived here, no master race or gods, all impossibly better, stronger, and more heroic than I could ever hope to be.

As a girl, I read every fairy tale and folktale I could find. A story that began, "In an ancient time, when animals spoke the speech of men and even the trees talked together . . ." was my chocolate pudding. More than anything, I wished my own small world contained such magic. But growing up means learning the world has little magic, animals talk only to each other, and our years go over the tops of the mountains without many marvels ever happening.

What carried over from my childhood was the secret hope that wonders lived somewhere nearby. Dragons and pixies, Difs, Cú Chulainn, Iron Henry, and Mamadreqja, grandmother of witches . . . I wanted them to *be* and was still mesmerized by TV shows about angels, yetis, and miracles. I snatched up any copy of the *National Enquirer* that headlined sheep born with Elvis's face, or sightings of the Virgin at a souvlaki stand in Oregon. On the surface I was a briefcase and a business suit, but my heart was always looking for wings.

They were in his study waiting for me, but I wouldn't know that until many years later. The room was large and bare except for a pine table Hugh used as a desk. It was piled with papers, books, and a computer. On the wall facing the desk were four small paintings of the same woman.

"What do you think?"

I was so involved in looking at them that I hadn't heard him come in. "I don't know. I don't know if they're fascinating or they scare me."

"Scare you? Why?" There was no amusement in his voice.

"Who is she?"

He put his hands on my shoulders. "I don't know. Around the time we met, a man came into the office and asked if I wanted to buy them. He didn't know anything about them. He'd just bought a house in Mississippi and they were in the attic with a bunch of other stuff. I didn't even haggle about the price."

"Why do I feel like I know her?"

"Me too! There's something very *familiar* about her. None of them are signed or dated. I have no idea who the artist was. I spent a good deal of time researching. It makes them even more mysterious."

She was young—in her twenties—and wore her hair down, but not in any special fashion that gave you an idea of the time period.

She was attractive but not so much so that it would stop you for a second look.

In one picture she sat on a couch staring straight ahead. In another she was sitting in a garden looking slightly off to the right. The painter was excellent and had genuinely caught her spirit. So often I looked at paintings, even famous ones, and felt a kind of lifelessness in the work, as if beyond a certain invisible point the subject died and became a painting. Not so here.

"Hugh, do you realize that since we met, I got beat up, saw a ghost, made out in a Gap store, and now am looking at pictures of someone I've never seen but *know* I know."

"It's the story of Zitterbart. Do you know it?"

"No."

"*Zitterbart* means "trembling beard." It's a German fairy tale, but not from the Brothers Grimm. There was a king named Zitterbart who got his name from the fact that whenever he grew angry, his beard shook so much his subjects could feel its breeze in the farthest corners of his kingdom. He was ferocious and whacked off people's heads if they so much as sneezed the wrong way. But his weak spot was his daughter Senga.

"The princess was madly in love with a knight named Blasius. Zitterbart approved of a marriage between them, but one day Blasius went to battle and died while fighting another knight named Cornelts Brom."

"Blasius and Brom? Sounds like stomach medicine."

"Senga was shattered and swore she would kill herself at the next new moon. The king was so frightened that he had the kingdom scoured for every good-looking man and swore if any of them caught her fancy, he would permit the marriage. But no luck. All the most interesting men were brought before her, but she'd take one look and turn to the window to see if the new moon had arrived yet.

Zitterbart grew more and more desperate. He sent out a decree that *any* man who pleased his daughter would have her hand.

"Cornelts Brom heard about it. He'd also heard how beautiful Senga was, and he decided to have a look. The thing about Brom was, he was the plainest-looking man in the universe. His face was so forgettable people would break off conversations with him in the middle because they forgot he was there. They thought they were talking to themselves. That was why he was such a great warrior: he was essentially invisible.

"As a child he realized if he wanted to make his mark in the world he would have to excel at something, so he became the best fighter around. Plus when he was actually *in* a sword fight—"

"His opponents forgot he was there."

Hugh smiled. "Exactly. But Senga wasn't interested in great fighters, and besides, this man had killed her boyfriend! Brom was clever though and, with his forgettable face, had no problem sneaking into the city for a look at her.

"Every Tuesday the princess went with her lady-in-waiting to the marketplace to shop for food. Brom stood right next to her and watched her squeeze tomatoes, haggle over the price of cucumbers, and fill her basket.

"He instantly pitied her, and pity is a bad place for love to begin. He knew she really would kill herself because he had seen that same doomed expression of absolute hopelessness on men's faces in battle when all they wanted was the peace of death. A special despair that comes only when people have lost the way back to their own hearts. It was Brom's fault this had happened to Senga and he was genuinely sorry. Because he was a decent man, he swore that if it were the last thing he ever did, he would help her.

"Living outside the city were three minor devils named Nepomuk, Knud, and Gangolf. They did a good business trading wishes for parts of people's souls. If you wanted something, you went to these little shits and said, 'I want to be rich.' They'd look in their ledgers and say, 'We want your joy. Give us your ability to feel joy and we'll make you rich.' Most people were willing to do it too, not knowing that as soon as they did, they'd give up something much more valuable than riches."

When he said "little shits" I laughed out loud and rubbed my hands together in expectation. He sat down next to me.

"Brom went to the devils and said he wanted to make the princess happy again. This confused them because they were sure that, with his face, he would wish to be handsome. Then they got into a fight among themselves. Nepomuk wanted Brom's plain face because he knew that would make him vulnerable on the battlefield. Gangolf wanted his sense of humor because no fighter is ever great without the ability to laugh. Knud insisted on his fear because anyone living without fear is either a fool or dead.

"In the end, they settled for his courage. Brom didn't hesitate: 'Take my courage in exchange for the princess's happiness.' There was a large clock in the corner of their house. All three devils went over and blew on it. The clock stopped in mid tick and the deal was fixed.

"Back at the castle, the princess stopped looking for the new moon, put a hand over her heart, and started singing. She didn't know why, but she couldn't help herself.

"At the same time, Brom stood in the doorway of the devils' house, unable to move because he was afraid of everything. What he didn't realize was that the devils had given him Senga's fear, which was what had made her want to die. Life is full of surprises, but if you're convinced all of them will be bad, what's the point of going on?" Hugh jumped down from the table and, taking me in his arms, started waltzing us around the room.

"And?"

"And what?"

"And what happened to Brom?"

"I don't know. I haven't figured it out yet."

"You made all that up?"

"I did." He dipped me backward.

"What does it have to do with me?"

"When you find your way back to your own heart, amazing things happen. You see ghosts, you fall in love; anything's possible. I was trying to think up a great end to the story that would tell you all that. But I couldn't figure out what happened and . . .

"I wanted to tell a story that would convince you it's time, Miranda. Time to let go and start trusting me. Let it happen."

"I *do* trust you. I'm just scared." I pulled away and swept an arm in a wide arc to include his room, his home, his family. "But I'm also ready. Let's go to my place."

NEVER PET A
BURNING DOG

THERE USED TO be a neighborhood dog I liked. Since I didn't know his name, the second time he visited I started calling him Easy, after Hugh's bullterrier. The dog didn't seem to mind. A mixed breed, he had the color and markings of a cow—brown spot here, white there. Midsized, short haired, calm brown eyes, a real *dog* dog. He came by once or twice a week on his rounds. A gentleman, he invariably stood at the bottom of the porch steps and waited for me to invite him up. I was always happy to see him. When you are my age you have few visitors.

Usually I would be sitting in the rocking chair with a magazine or book or just my old woman's thoughts. That's one of the things I like about this house—it has a good sitting porch where whole chunks of a day can be spent daydreaming and contentedly watching this small district of the universe come and go. My house is just off Beechwood Canyon in Los Angeles. During the day most of my neighbors are away at work and their children are in school, so it is surprisingly quiet and peaceful for a street ten minutes from Hollywood Boulevard. Generally the only sounds are occasional snatches of conversation, the hiss of sprinklers or roar of a leaf blower, and the muted but constant hum and thump of traffic on the Hollywood freeway a mile away. It is a good house in which to be old. One floor, a few rooms, not much work to keep it clean. The porch has a view of a peaceful street and good-natured neighbors who wave or smile when they pass.

Whenever Easy came to visit I would give him two Oreo cookies. He knew that was the limit and even if I had the package with me, he would make no attempt to ask for more. The dog had his dignity and never begged or stared with "gimme more" eyes. I liked that. I also liked the way he sat beside me on the porch for a while after he had slowly eaten his cookies. He was my companion for a small part of his day, and we watched life's passing parade while I'd tell him what I had been thinking. Who wants to listen to you when you are old? A sympathetic dog is better than an empty chair.

Sometimes odd things happened. Once a bird flew so low that it almost hit him. Once a child fell off its bike directly in front of us. Easy looked at me to see if these things were all right—if the world was still in order. I said, "It's okay, nothing major," and he went back to watching or sleeping with his head between his paws. Dogs are here to remind us life really is a simple thing. You eat, sleep, take walks, and pee when you must. That's about all there is. They are quick to forgive trespasses and assume strangers will be kind.

After I heard that someone had poured gasoline over this dog and set it on fire, I realized I could no longer wait for you. These many years, your coming was the only thing I had left to hope for. I genuinely believed it would happen one day. Although I had no idea what would occur when we met, I've thought about it constantly. But after Easy was murdered I realized I had to finish this account as soon as possible because we might *not* meet before I die. Whether we do or not, this diary will be here to help you. To explain where you really came from. Perhaps that knowledge will save you from some of the awful experiences I have had because not knowing my own history ruined my life.

What is important about the death of a dog when so much else has happened over the years? I can only say it brought the realization it was no longer important whether I continued living or not. I'd thought that moment had come years ago, but I was wrong. Old age arrives like the first days of fall. One afternoon you look up, or smell something in the air, and know instinctively things have changed. I suppose the same thing is true about our own death. Suddenly it's near enough that we can smell it.

Despite that, I must continue to tell this story. Whether I am still alive or not when you read it, you must know what really happened and *why*.

IS IT POSSIBLE to properly describe the months right after Hugh and I first became lovers? That means describing happiness, and no words bear the weight of real joy. I can tell you about meals and weekend trips, conversations walking down a street on Block Island in August when the summer air was thick as breath because it was about to rain and the afternoon was suddenly purple everywhere.

Our hearts were always too full. But what does that mean? That each of us had our separate, impossible hopes, which we had brought along like secret extra suitcases.

His small touches on my arm, hair, hand always reminded me of a school of silvery fish that swam up, intensely curious, made contact, then fled at my slightest movement. But I was always moving *toward* Hugh, not away, and after a while when he touched me his hand would stay.

I have never felt so loved in my life. It made me suspicious at first. Like a turtle, I kept pulling my head back into my shell because I was certain a blow was imminent. But as our bond grew stronger, I left my head out and realized how much I had been missing my whole life.

The great surprise was how quickly we understood each other. Even in the best relationships I'd had, certain things were never communicated or understood. No matter how fluent you are in a language, situations arise that stump you for ways to express exactly what needs to be said. Being with Hugh gave me the words, which in turn helped me to know myself better. Trusting him, I opened up in an entirely new way.

Sexually he was marvelous because he had had so much experience. He admitted that for years women had drifted in and out of his life like incense. His wife knew about many of these affairs but they had come to a truce about them: so long as he was discreet and never brought home any part of these other relationships, Charlotte turned a blind eye. Was theirs then only a marriage of convenience? Did she have lovers too? No. She didn't believe in affairs and no, the marriage was strong and important.

If that was true, why had he allowed me to come into his apartment?

"Because I was already gone for you by then. Gone like never before. I would have done anything. I broke every one of my rules."

"Why, Hugh? Why *me* after all those other women? The way you describe some of them, they were incredible."

"There's never a satisfying answer to that. No matter what I say, it won't assure you or lessen your doubts. Love is like an autistic child when it comes to giving good explanations. Sometimes we love things in others they're not even aware of. Or they think are ridiculous. I love your purse."

"My *purse*? Why?"

"I've never seen a woman with such a Zen purse. You keep only the most necessary or beautiful things in there. It says so much about you, all of which I cherish and admire. I love the way you put your forehead against my neck when we sleep. And how you put your arm over my shoulder when we're walking down the street. Like two pals."

"You *are* my pal. My dearest pal. Whenever I write you a letter that's how I'll start it—Dearest Pal."

What did I feel about his wife? What one would expect, made all the more difficult by a quality I liked very much in Hugh: he said only good things about Charlotte, no matter the context. From his description, she was a loving, generous woman who made life better for everyone.

Married people often feel compelled to deride their spouse to a new lover. I knew it from my friends, and particularly from Zoe's accounts of ex-boyfriend Hector. It makes sense, but it's neither honest nor brave. We have affairs because we're greedy. Don't blame that greed on someone else. People are brilliant at justifying their motives. It's one of our ugliest talents. Hugh and I wanted each other and were willing to hurt others if it meant the survival of our relationship. There were other explanations and rationalizations, none of them true. We were simply greedy.

When did Charlotte find out about it? I think a couple of months on. Hugh never said, directly, "She knows," but things came up in conversation that indicated she did. Strangely, the more involved we became, the more like her *I* became in not wanting to know about his other life. In the beginning I was fascinated to know what they did together. Or what kind of woman he was married to. But one day that stopped. As best I could, I tried to shut her out of my thoughts and ignore the fact she was there.

It worked for a time, but six months on I answered the ringing phone and almost threw up when the tranquil voice on the other end said, "This is Charlotte Oakley."

"Hello."

"I think you know why I'm calling."

"Yes." I wanted a composed voice too. One that said, I'm ready for this, ready for you; nothing you say will change how I feel.

"My husband told me he was in love with you. I said I was going to call you. He made me promise not to, but some things need to be said before this goes further. I think you should know them.

"He was very frank about your relationship. I don't know you so I can only go on what he said. Hugh loves women and has had many lovers over the years."

"He told me." Was *this* the tack she was going to take? Try to humiliate me by making me feel like just another of his sweeties? Something inside lightened immediately. I pushed hair off my face that had fallen there a moment before, when I sat with it hanging down, like the guilty party.

"I'm sure he has. That's Hugh's way. Women love my husband because he is so honest. And funny and pays so much attention that you feel like he's your alter ego.

"What you *don't* know is his habit of choosing the same kind of woman again and again, Miranda. They're always pretty and very intelligent. They have something to say. They do interesting things with their lives. But when you get down to the fine print in his job description, they must also be *needy*. Hugh wants to save you from your dragons. He's a chivalrous man. I'm sure you need help and he's here to give it."

"I'm going to put the phone down."

For the first time, her voice became cross. "I'm telling you something that will save *all* of us time and pain! If you are anything like his other girlfriends, you love him because you need him and not the other way around. You'll fall into this relationship until you're helpless without him. Maybe you already are. But I warn you, once it happens and he grows bored with your weakness, he'll leave. He always has. That's just his way. He'll do it sweetly and it'll seem he's in so much pain that you'll think it's your fault, but it isn't—"

"How can you say these things about your husband?"

She laughed and the tone scared me; it was relaxed, *knowing.* Here was a subject she knew a great deal about. Talking to me, the beginner, was amusing.

"Has he given you the Kazantzákis autobiography to read yet? *Report to Greco.* He will. There's a line in there he loves: 'They were sparrows and I wanted to make them eagles.' "

I hung up. I had never done that before in my life. I wanted to dismiss her but couldn't because what she said was right: I *was* weak. I *did* need him.

For minutes afterward, I hated Hugh and myself equally. Why couldn't it just be an affair? I would have been content with that. Why couldn't we just have driven our car up to that point on the road and stopped? Whose fault was it that we had gone so far?

An hour later, I was still sitting in the same chair when he called. I told him about the talk with his wife and that I didn't want to see him again.

"Wait! Wait, Miranda! Please, you have to know something else. Did she describe our whole conversation? Did she tell you how it happened? I told her I wanted to separate."

"What?"

"I told her I was so in love with you that I wanted a separation."

I took the receiver away from my ear and looked at it aghast, as if it were he. "What are you saying, Hugh? You never told me this!"

"Yes I did, but you didn't believe it was true."

"No, not like that you didn't! I don't know what's going on. I *am* like your other girlfriends. Charlotte's right: I'm another weak little bird in your fan club. Why do you want to leave her—"

"Because I love you!"

"You'll leave a wife of twenty years and your kids and . . .

Bullshit! I don't want that responsibility. Or that guilt. I have to go."

"No, please—"

I put the phone down.

I TRIED TO go back to life before Hugh Oakley and almost succeeded. You can create as much work for yourself as necessary. The problem is the time *between* things, when thoughts and memories burst out of your brain like shrapnel.

I took trips to California, Boston, and London. In a dreary secondhand bookstall near the Hayward Gallery I found one of the most valuable books I'd ever seen, selling for five pounds. Any other time, I would have done somersaults. This time, tears came to my eyes because the only person I wanted to show the treasure to was Hugh Oakley.

He called constantly. If I *was* home, I'd force myself to let the answering machine kick in. His messages ranged from quiet to tormented. He sent letters, flowers, and tender gifts that stopped my breath. What he *didn't* do was show up at either my apartment or the store. I was grateful. The last thing I needed was to see him. He must have understood and accepted that, thank God.

I told both Zoe and Frances Hatch what had happened. They disagreed on what I should do. Zoe had had her share of married men and was even more skeptical than I about the possibility of Hugh's leaving his wife.

"Forget it! They all say that till they know they have you back in their power. Then they get wiggly again. A married man wants the excitement and newness of a lover, combined with the comfort and peace of his family. It's an impossible and *unfair* combination. How could you ever give him both when you've only been in his life a few months? Someone said the first wife breaks the man in, while the second gets all the goodies, but I don't think that's true. Just the opposite. Even if he leaves his wife, you'll be carrying ten tons of his guilt around on the back of your relationship until the day you die.

"Do you know the joke about the man who goes to get a new suit made? The tailor measures him and says come back in two weeks. The guy does and puts on the suit. It looks terrible. The left cuff comes down five inches too long, the lapels are completely uneven, the crotch hangs like harem pants. It's the worst suit in the world. The guy complains but the tailor says he's seeing it all wrong: 'What you've got to do is pull up the left sleeve and hold it there with your chin. Then ooch your right shoulder up five inches so the lapels are even, put your right hand in the pocket of the pants and pull up the crotch . . .' You get the idea.

"So the man does all this and ends up looking like the Hunchback of Notre Dame. But when he looks in the mirror again the *suit* looks wonderful. The tailor says, 'That's the new style these days.' So the jerk buys the suit and walks out of the store wearing it.

"He's staggering down the street like Quasimodo and passes two men. They turn around and watch him limp away. The first guy says, 'I feel so sorry for the handicapped.' The other says, 'Yeah, but what a fabulous *suit*!'

"It's the best metaphor I've ever heard for how we try to make relationships like this work. Or what we do to ourselves to make *anything* important work. Don't do it, Miranda. You've got so much going for you. You don't need him, no matter how good you think it is,"

"But what if this is *it,* Zoe? What if I walk away and it turns out this was the most important relationship in my life? What if the memory's too big and ends up crushing me?"

"If we're lucky and find Mr. Right, seventy or eighty percent is there from the beginning. The other twenty you have to create yourself. This is a lot more than twenty percent, Miranda. But if you have to do it, then do. Just make sure to put on a helmet and learn to recognize the sound of incoming shells when they start dropping. Because they will, in *clusters*!"

A LETTER CAME from Hugh:

> I had a dream last night and have no idea what it means. But I wanted to tell you because I think it has to do with us.
>
> I'm in Los Angeles and need a car, so I go to a used car lot and buy an Oldsmobile 88 from the 1960s. It's canary yellow and in good shape, especially the radio. But what's really extraordinary is, the engine is a large potato! Someone replaced the original with this giant spud. For some wonderful reason, it works perfectly. I'm driving around L.A. in my old new car with a potato engine and feeling great. I have the only automobile in the world whose engine you could cook and eat if you were hungry.
>
> One day I stop at a light and the engine stalls. That worries me, especially because the thing has well over a hundred thousand miles on it. So I pull into a gas station and tell the mechanic what happened. He opens the hood and isn't surprised at what he sees. He tells me to drive it into the garage. He and another guy winch the potato out of the car and throw it on the ground. It breaks in half. I'm horrified.
>
> Inside, like any normal tired out engine, it's glutted with thick black oil and gunk. I ask how much it'll cost to replace it. They say they can only put in a new, normal motor but it's not expensive—a few hundred dollars. Right before I wake up, I can't decide what to do. I keep

thinking, Why can't they put another potato in there. I don't want a regular engine. What does this mean, Miranda?

"How do I know what it means, Miranda?" Frances Hatch said. "I'm not Carl Jung!

"Your boyfriend had a dream about potatoes and you're asking *me* to interpret it? I'm just old. Being old doesn't mean you know more; it means you ate enough fiber. Most of my life, people didn't have psychiatry to rely on. If you had a bad dream, it was either something you ate last night or a vivid imagination.

"I don't believe in interpreting dreams. You should avoid it too. Don't worry about what Hugh's dream says; worry about what he says when his eyes are *open*. If he's not anxiety-ridden about his wife and kids, don't you be! Are you his conscience or his lover? I think it's great he'll throw everything over for you. That's the way romance should be!

"It's arrogant to think you know what's right. Morality is only cowardice most of the time. We don't avoid misbehaving because it's not proper; what we're really afraid of is how far down it looks to the bottom. It *is* far, and you may *get* killed when you hit. But sometimes you survive the jump, and down there the world is a million times better than where you're living now."

WHEN I CALLED to say I wanted to see him, Hugh asked what had changed my mind. I said the days were dead without him and I couldn't stand it anymore.

We met on neutral ground—a favorite restaurant—but we were out of there and back in my bed within an hour.

If I'd had any fears he would leave, they disappeared quickly. He moved into my apartment within two weeks. He brought so little with him that I worried he might be thinking of the move as a test drive: since all of his belongings were still at his place, he could always go back to them if we failed.

But one Saturday when he was at his office, the doorbell downstairs rang. A furniture store was there to deliver a big cushy chair I hadn't ordered. When they said a Hugh Oakley *had,* I clapped my hands. Hugh loved reading at night but said it could only be done in a perfect chair. Now he had bought one for his new home.

Charlotte refused to let me meet their children. She was convinced I was only a blip on the screen of her husband's Midlife Crisis. Consequently, when he came to his senses, they would reconcile and I'd be yesterday's news. Why expose their children to further confusion?

Hugh didn't care what she felt and was adamant about my spending time with them. I said no. They lived in a parallel universe I was not yet part of. There would be time in the future. Secretly I was petrified of what would happen when we did meet. I imagined two children glaring with fiery eyes that would melt me before I had a chance to say I would do anything to be their friend.

He missed his kids terribly, so I encouraged him to see them whenever he could. I knew in certain ways he missed Charlotte too. I was sure there were conversations and meetings going on between them that he never told me about. His emotions tacked back and forth like a sailboat in a gale.

What could I do to help? Be his friend. Let him know how much I loved and appreciated him. Hold my tongue when necessary; try to be considerate when the first instinct was to snap at anything I didn't understand or that threatened me. For all of my adult life, Hugh Oakley had lived in marriage, a foreign country I had never known. It was easy to imagine what the place was like, but imagining was like reading a brochure at the travel agency. You could never really know the place itself till you got there.

"HAVE YOU EVER heard of Crane's View?" Frances was smiling and her eyes were closed. She was sitting by a window in her red-carpeted living room, her face lit by the morning sun. A few minutes before, when I'd come in and kissed her cheek, it was almost hot.

We were drinking gunpowder tea and eating English muffins, her favorite breakfast.

"What's Crane's View?"

"A town on the Hudson about an hour away. I discovered it thirty years ago and bought a house there. It's a small place, but it has a spectacular view of the river. That's why I bought it."

"I didn't know you owned a house, Frances. Do you ever go there?"

"Not anymore. It makes me sad. I had two good love affairs and a nice dog in that house. Spent most of a year there once when I was angry with New York and was boycotting it. Anyway, I was thinking about it last week. Houses shouldn't be empty. They should either be lived in or sold. Would you like to have it?"

I shook my head and put down the cup. "You can't just give away a house. Are you crazy?"

She opened her eyes and slowly brought the muffin to her mouth. A blob of marmalade started a slow slide off the edge. Very carefully she caught it with her thumb and shoved it back onto the top. She looked at me coldly but didn't say anything until she had finished chewing. "Excuse me, I can do whatever I want. Don't be obnoxious and treat me like an old nitwit. If I want to give you my house, I'll give you my house. You don't have to *take* it, but that's your choice."

"But—"

"Miranda, you've said at least four times how you and Hugh would like to move. Your apartment is too small and you need some-place where you can start a new life together from scratch. I agree.

I don't know if you'd like Crane's View. It's a small town. There's not much to do there. But both of you could commute to the city. It's only an hour on the train and the ride is pretty—right alongside the river the whole way. At least go have a look. What do you have to lose?"

The next Sunday we rented a car, picked up Frances, and drove to Crane's View. It was the first time she had left her apartment in months. She was both thrilled and scared to be out in the world again. Most of the day she wouldn't let go of my arm but was so excited she didn't stop talking for a minute.

From their first meeting, Frances and Hugh liked each other very much. Her life and the people she'd known fascinated him. Her greatest pleasure was talking about her experiences to someone who cared. They also argued all the time, but Frances loved a good fight. Despite her great age, there was still a big fire in her that longed to be fed. Hugh sensed this immediately and to my dismay started an argument with her the first time they met. The look on her face was pure joy. In the middle of the battle, Frances slapped a hand down on her birdie knee and proclaimed, "If you hadn't said that, someone else would have. *That's* the difference between the clever and the great." Hugh hooted and said he was going to pray to Saint Gildas, who protected people from dog bites.

As we were leaving, she pulled me aside and said, "He's so different from your description, Miranda. So much better and so much more annoying!"

We visited her together after that. When Hugh did our shopping he invariably brought back a variety of Ding Dongs, Pinwheels, Twinkies, and other sweets for her. When I told Frances he was the one who bought her the junk food, tears came to her eyes. But the poster won her heart forever.

Seeing it the first time, I asked how the hell he'd found it. Hugh said only that he'd been lucky. His assistant Courtney later admitted

Hugh had all of his European contacts on the lookout for months before they tracked one down in Wroclaw, Poland. It was a large color poster from the Ronacher Theater in Vienna advertising a 1922 performance by The Enormous Shumda, "world renowned" ventriloquist and, of course, the great love of Frances Hatch's life. On the poster he is standing with arms crossed, looking huge, confident, and mysterious in a tuxedo and full-length cape. He's a handsome man with gleaming black hair combed straight back and a wicked little goatee. When Frances saw the picture, she touched her cheeks and exclaimed, "That goatee! He always put Florida Water on it first thing in the morning before he did anything else. You never smelled anything so good in your life."

As we drove out of New York City that day, she started talking about him again. "In a funny way, Shumda gave me Crane's View. Not directly. He was gone years before I ever came up here. But Tyndall lived here, and he was Shumda's biggest fan."

I turned around and looked at her in the backseat. She was wearing a tomato red wool cap and a fur coat that had seen better days.

"Tyndall, the oil man?"

Frances nodded. "Yes. We met him in Bucharest in the twenties. Back there he was just another fan of Shumda. We kept in touch over the years. In the early fifties he invited me for a weekend to Crane's View. I fell in love with the place and kept coming back. It was the perfect escape from New York and Lionel was always glad to have me.

"They had a murder there last year." She didn't say anything for a while and when I turned to check her, she was asleep. That was one of the few symptoms of her almost hundred years: she fell asleep faster than any person I'd ever known.

We rode in comfortable silence a long time. I looked out the window and watched the city turn into suburbs and then almost country. Hugh put his hand on my knee and said softly. "I love you. Know that?"

I looked at him and said, "No one in the world could be happier than I am right now. No one."

We didn't wake Frances until we saw the first exit sign for Crane's View. In fact, we didn't wake her at all: a mile before the turnoff, we both jumped when she called out, "Take the next right!"

I turned the rearview mirror to see her. "How'd you know when to wake up?"

She patted away a yawn. "Lionel Tyndall always had a crush on me. He was as ugly as an egg salad sandwich, but that was okay. I'm no prize in that department myself. No, my mistake was sleeping with him a few times. He didn't know what he was doing. But *I* did and that made him unreasonable. The guy didn't know the difference between his big head and his little one. Now go right, Hugh. That's it. We're almost there."

She continued talking as we drove toward the town. I didn't know what to expect, but what was there pretty much fit what I had imagined. Crane's View itself was cute and small. The stores in the town center were the basics—food, clothes, hardware, and newspapers—with a couple of specialty shops. It was a town built on hills and from those hills you often caught glimpses of the Hudson River below. Driving around that first day, I kept thinking, It's a nice place, a real 1950s small upstate town. But there was nothing special about it. I wondered why Frances said she loved it. Crane's View was everything Frances Hatch wasn't—quiet, slow moving, unsurprising.

"Stop here! This is the place for lunch. They've got the best pizza in the county."

Hugh braked hard and swerved into a parking spot in front of a dumpy-looking pizza joint. We got out of the car and Frances led the way inside. We were welcomed by the delicious smell of hot garlic. A couple of town studs leaned against the counter and gave us the slow once-over. We each ordered a slice of pizza; when they arrived, they were each as big as an LP record. Frances shook crushed hot pepper all over hers. We took soft drinks out of a refrigerator and sat down at a scarred table.

While we were eating, a handsome man in an expensive-looking double-breasted suit came in. He stopped when he saw us and his face lit up with a big wholehearted smile.

"Frances! What are you doing here?"

"Frannie!"

He came over and they embraced. "I am really happy to see you, old woman! Why didn't you call and say you were coming? We coulda had a dinner or something."

"I wanted to see the look on your face when you saw I was still alive. Frannie, these are my friends Miranda and Hugh. This is Frannie McCabe, chief of police. I've known him for twenty-five years. How are you, Chief?"

"Good! I'm a married man again. Magda and I finally did it, though I had to carry her kickin' and screamin' to the altar."

"Good for you! Magda McCabe, huh? That's a nice name. Listen, we're going to my house after lunch. Is everything all right over there?"

He crossed his arms and looked at the ceiling, exasperated. "Frances, have we had this conversation before? You *know* I keep an eye on the house for you! How many times do I have to tell you? It could use a paint job, but we've talked about that. Otherwise it's fine. You going to start living there again?"

"No, but they may. That's why we came up to see it."

McCabe pulled out a chair and sat down. "It's a nice house, but if you're going to live there, it needs work. Definitely a paint job, and the basement gets damp. I could introduce you to some people who'd do the job right and not charge too much."

Frances finished her pizza and brushed off her hands. "Frannie is the king of Crane's View. He knows everybody. If they're not in his family, they used to be in his gang. He was a juvenile delinquent when he was a kid. That's how we got to know each other: he broke into my house when he was fifteen but I happened to be there at the time." She turned toward him. "Why don't you go over there with us?"

"I would, but I have too much stuff to do. There's a zoning meeting this afternoon and I gotta be there. The company that bought the Tyndall house sold it after the murder there last year. Can't say as I blame them. Now a consortium's sniffing around. They want to tear it down and build a hotel or something. What's a dull little town like ours going to do with a hotel? Who's going to stay there, Rip Van Winkle?

"Anyway, I gotta go. If you two need anything, she has my phone number. I wish you *were* moving back, Frances. I'd rather visit you here than down at that creepy apartment in the city."

They kissed and we shook hands. Starting for the door, he was called back by the smirking counterman, who held out the pizza he'd ordered. McCabe grinned and went back for it.

"Is there much crime here? You mentioned a murder before."

His smile evaporated and he stared at me before answering. "That was a one-time thing. There were a lot of extenuating circumstances. Crane's View is a quiet town. Dull most of the time. Lotta blue-collar people here, some commuters. Everyone works hard. On the weekends they mow their lawn or watch a game. I've been a cop here a long time. The worst crime we have is, once in a while someone gets his car boosted. That's all.

"Listen, I really gotta go. Ms. Hatch, I will talk to you soon. And let me know if you folks are going to move in. I'll send some people over before you do to straighten the house up so at least it'll be livable when you first get in."

The counterman yodeled out, "Byyyyye, Chief!"

McCabe gave him the finger and smiled. "I don't get no respect." Then he was gone. I watched him get into a beautiful silver car and drive away.

"Drives a very nice car for a policeman."

Hugh had watched too, and he nodded. "Did you see the wristwatch he was wearing? That was a Da Vinci! We're talking about *serious* money for that timepiece."

Frances shrugged. "He's loaded. He doesn't need to be a cop, but does it because he likes it. Made a lot of money with his first wife. Something to do with television. He told me once but I forget."

"I like him. He's a tough guy." Hugh put up his fists and pretended to box.

"You *do*? He reminds me of one of the gangsters in *Goodfellas*. I wouldn't want to mess with him."

Frances patted my hand. "No, you wouldn't. He's like a Russell's viper if you cross him. But a great friend and one of the few people you can depend on completely. Shall we go? I'm excited to see my house."

This time Frances sat in the front seat and directed Hugh to the house. As we drove through Crane's View, I kept imagining myself there, walking down this street, shopping at that store. Letters to us would arrive at the small gray post office at the end of Main Street. After a while, we would know the names of the men on the orange garbage truck stopped at a corner. Young kids rode bicycles in woozy lines down the sidewalk. Dogs crossed the road at their own pace. Two girls had set up a lemonade stand on one side of a tree-lined street. The sun through the leaves dappled the girls and they frowned at us when we drove by.

"Hugh, look!"

A pretty teenager was walking a bullterrier that looked like Hugh's. The two were in no hurry. The dog sniffed something on the sidewalk, tail wagging slowly. The girl wore a Walkman and waited for him with arms crossed. She looked up as we passed and waved. Frances waved back.

"That's Barbara Flood. Good-looking girl, huh? Her grandfather was Tyndall's gardener. Turn right here."

"She's the first black person I've seen here."

Frances gave Hugh a shove. "Don't start with the liberal agenda. There are plenty of blacks in Crane's View. The mayor is black."

He caught my eye in the mirror and winked. "I was just making an observation."

"Yeah, well it weighed ten pounds. This is it. Stop here."

"*This* house? You're joking."

Frances's voice slashed down like a karate chop. "What's the matter with it?"

I bent forward for a better look. "Nothing's the matter. It's just big. You said it was small. This is not a small house, Frances."

It was blue, sort of. Blue with white trim. But the years had faded the paint to the color of a pair of old jeans. The white around the windows and door had yellowed and was peeling off everywhere. McCabe was right—the first thing it would need would be lots of paint. The house was square, shaped like a hatbox, with two floors and a large porch in front. The night before we drove there, Hugh and I had spent a whole dinner wondering what it would look like. Neither of our imaginings had come even close to this.

189 BROADWAY // CRANE'S VIEW, NEW YORK

"Here Hugh, you open the door. I want to take a look around." Frances handed him keys and walked toward the porch steps. Leaning forward, she kissed the wooden newel post. "Haven't seen you in a long time." Slowly climbing, she patted the banister as she went. At the top, she reached out and pressed the doorbell. It rang loudly inside.

Hugh put his arm around my shoulder. "Did you hear that? A *real* bell! *Ding dong!*"

I quietly asked, "What do you think?"

"I like it! Reminds me of a house in an Edward Hopper painting. It'll need a lot of work, though. I can see that already." He put his hands on his hips and looked appraisingly at the house.

"It's sure a lot bigger than I'd imagined. I thought it would be a kind of large bungalow."

Frances walked to the end of the porch and stopped. Her back was to us. She didn't turn around for the longest time.

"What's she doing?"

"Remembering, probably. Let's go inside. I can't wait to see what it's like." Hugh slotted the key and turned it in the lock a couple of times. Before pushing the door open, he slid his hand back and forth over the surface. "Nice door, huh? Oak."

It swung open. The first odors of our new home drifted out to say hello: dust, damp, old cloth, and something in complete contrast to empty-house bouquet. Hugh entered while I stood in the doorway, trying to figure out that one smell. Clean and sweet, it was not at all appropriate in a building that had been closed and unused for years. It was fresh, delicious. I couldn't put my finger on what it was.

"Miranda, are you coming?"

"In a second. Go ahead."

I heard Hugh walk across the floor, then a door creak open. He said a quiet "Wow" to something in there, then his feet started across the floor again. What *was* that smell? I took a few steps into the house, looked around, and closed my eyes.

When I opened them a moment later, the hallway was full of people. Full of children, rather, with a few adults standing around watching the show. Kids were running, jumping, making faces at each other, and playing. They ran back and forth from room to room, stomped up and down the staircase, ate yellow and blue cake (*that* was it—cake smell!), blew plastic horns, hit each other. Most wore pastel party hats. Seeing them, I realized what this was—a kid's birthday party.

I was not surprised. I must repeat that, because it is very important. From one second to the next, Frances Hatch's empty house was in a flash full of the happy chaos of a child's birthday party, but none of it surprised me. I simply watched and accepted it.

One little boy in a crooked party hat stood in the middle of the hall watching the party whirl around him. He wore a white button-down shirt, stiff new blue jeans, and zebra-striped sneakers. He looked like a miniature Hugh Oakley, even to the color and texture of his long hair and the broad grin on his face. A smile I knew so well now and loved. This had to be Hugh's boy.

He looked directly at me and did the most wonderful thing. Slowly closing his eyes, he shuddered all over. I knew it was from delight at the party around him. For it was his party, his birthday.

His name was Jack Oakley and he was eight years old. He was the son Hugh and I *would* have when we lived together in this house. We had already talked a lot about having children, joked about what their names would be. Jack and Ciara. Saint Ciara of Tipperary who put out fire with her prayers. And now here was our Jack Oakley standing in front of me, eight years old today, looking like his father. There was some of me in him too. The high forehead and upward curve of the eyebrows.

I didn't move, scared if I did, this gorgeous vision of our future would go away. The boy looked at me and, still smiling, threw his small hands in the air as if they were full of confetti.

"Miranda?"

Startled, I jerked my head to the left. Hugh walked toward me, smiling just like his son. Our son. I looked back to where the boy had been standing. Everything was gone—Jack, the kids, the party.

"Are you okay?"

"We have to live here, Hugh. We *have* to live in this house."

"But you haven't even looked around yet! You haven't moved from this spot. Come on, I've got to show you something." He put his arm around my shoulders and gently pushed me along. I went but looked back once, twice, just in case Jack was there again. The little boy, our little boy, come to show us how wonderful it would be for all of us here.

THE TARZAN HOTEL

I STOOD AT the bottom of the stairs and took a long deep breath. Thirty-four steps. After thirty-four steps I could stop and rest awhile. Just in time too because my arms were beginning to feel like pieces of chewed gum. I was holding a heavy cardboard box. Across the top was written "Sky Average." Don't ask what it meant because the contents of the box were Hugh's. Already that morning I'd taken "Pontus Harmon," "Tarzan Hotel," "Ugly Voila," and now "Sky Average" up to the room he would use as a study. The first time I'd seen him writing those strange phrases onto boxes in New York, I'd looked at them, at Hugh, then at the boxes again.

"Am I missing something? How do you know what's inside?"

He capped the thick marking pen he was using and slid it into his back pocket. "I'm a mood packer. Free form. Things go in a box that connect with each other, but leave enough room for surprise when I open it again and discover what's there."

"So what does 'Tarzan Hotel' mean?"

"I made it as a kid. I took a Buster Brown shoe box, cut it up, and painted it. I was seven. I made it into a hotel for some of my favorite toys."

"And you kept it all these years?"

"No." He looked at me and shrugged.

"Sooo, the Tarzan Hotel *isn't* in your Tarzan Hotel box?"

"No."

"Hugh, I think we've left the highway here. Should I put it into four-wheel drive?"

"No. Hand me that tape, willya? The Tarzan Hotel was where I kept favorite things. So inside *this* box are some of my favorite things. My pocketknife collection, fountain pens, some great books. That novel you gave me—*The Story of Harold*. Other stuff too, but I didn't write it down so I'll be surprised later."

"You're a strange fellow, but I like you."

HUGH HAD MADE packing up my apartment bearable. I had never liked moving. Who does? But his company and unbroken enthusiasm made the work tolerable and sometimes even fun. Frequently I would get manic and feel we had to have everything done/packed/finished in this or that period of time. He was much more relaxed about it and that mood calmed me down. Often he came to me holding some object—a lamp, a figure, a pair of German binoculars—and wanted to know the story behind the thing. He wasn't snooping or asking me to disclose any secrets; he wanted to know me through the things I owned. Frequently I found myself telling him in long detail the story behind them and, in doing so, relaxing and pleasantly reliving past times. When both of us were exhausted and dirty, we would take a bath together and then go out for a meal. Invariably we lingered at the table talking about what life would be like in Crane's View. And not only that. We talked endlessly about what life would be like together. One night after dinner he took a slip of paper out of his pocket and read a poem to me. I kept the paper and had it framed. I must have said the poem to myself hundreds of times over the years:

> If I get to love you, please enter without knocking,
> but think it over well:
> my straw mattress will be yours, the dusty straw,
> the rustling sighs.
>
> Into the pitcher fresh water I'll pour,
> your shoes, before you leave, I'll wipe clean,
> no one will disturb us here,
> hunched over, you could mend our clothes in peace.
>
> If the silence is great, I will talk to you,
> If you are tired, take my only chair,
> If it's warm here, loosen your collar, take off your tie,
> if you are hungry, there's a clean sheet of paper
> as your plate if there's food,
> but leave some for me—I, too, am forever hungry.
>
> If I get to love you, enter without knocking,
> but think it over well:
> it would hurt if you stayed away for long.

Hefting the box marked "Sky Average," I began climbing. I couldn't see a thing with it full in my arms, so I had to count steps as I went. I'd found that counting backward somehow made the climb easier. At step sixteen, Hugh called out from above. I kept going and had reached seven when he called again.

"Wait a minute!"

I heard his footsteps, and then the box was lifted out of my arms.

Immediately I felt dizzy and almost fell backward. Grabbing the banister, I steadied myself. Hugh was climbing with the box and didn't see what had happened. Just as well. It was the second dizzy spell I'd had that morning and it was disconcerting. We'd been working too hard.

Three days before, we'd rented a yellow Ryder truck and filled it with our belongings. When we were done, we stood on the sidewalk in front of my apartment building and looked inside. Hugh said it was unsettling to see all the possessions of two lifetimes stacked neatly in the back of a not-so-large truck. I kissed his shoulder for being diplomatic. Uptown in Charlotte's apartment he had a whole other lifetime of belongings, which undoubtedly would have filled several trucks, but he'd made no mention of that. He was taking a lot to Crane's View, but not so much when I knew what he *could* have taken.

When Charlotte heard we were moving out of the city, she flew into a flaming rage. From that day on, she did everything possible to make Hugh's life miserable. She was good at it. In their last civil conversation before the lawyers started circling the remains, she hit him with everything she had where it hurt most. What about their marriage, his responsibilities, their children? Did he realize what this would do to them? How could he? Was he so selfish? Did he care about three other people's lives?

"MIRANDA?" HE STOOD at the top of the staircase with his hands in his pockets, looking at me. "Are you okay?"

"Yes. I was thinking about you and Charlotte."

His face hardened. "Thinking what?"

"I was thinking there's no way I'll ever be able to thank you enough for coming here with me."

"You don't have to thank me; just love me."

"I'm so afraid I'll do it wrong, Hugh. Sometimes it feels like my heart is breaking loose because I want this to work so much. How do you love someone the right way?"

"Use plenty of butter." He pulled his T-shirt out of his pants and over his head. He dropped it on the floor, watching me the whole time. "And no margarine. Some people try to cheat by using margarine, but you can always taste the difference." He undid his belt and slid his jeans down.

"I thought we were supposed to be unpacking." I crossed my arms, then dropped them to my sides.

"We are, but you asked how to love someone the right way. I'm telling you."

"Use butter." I began unbuttoning my shirt.

"Right." He stood in white Jockey shorts with his hands on his hips. He wiggled a finger at me to climb the rest of the stairs to him. My shirt was open by the time I reached him. He slid his hands over my breasts. "Women will always win because they have breasts. It doesn't matter how big they are; just the fact you *have* them means you'll always win." He pulled me slowly down to the floor.

The wood on my back was cold. I arched up into him. "Men have cocks."

"Cocks are dumb." He kissed my throat. "Too obvious. Breasts are art."

I put my hand over his mouth. Slid my fingers back and forth over his tongue, then slid them out and wiped the wet across his cheek. It glistened. I kissed it. The phone rang. I put my hand between his legs and whispered, " 'We're not home right now, but leave a message. We'll get back to you as soon as we've come.' "

It rang and rang. "What would you do if I answered that?" He was smiling and flinched when I squeezed him too hard.

His face was a few inches above mine. Some of the bristles of his beard were gold, others black. I rubbed my hand across his scratchy cheek. Then I stopped my hand and left it there.

He stared at me. Something distracted him and his head snapped up. His eyes widened. His face changed into an expression I had never seen before on him: fury. Outrage. He leaped up. Before I could say anything, he was already sprinting down the hall.

"Son of a bitch!"

"Hugh!" I grabbed my pants and stood too quickly. Again came a whoosh of dizziness. It passed slowly and I went after him.

He was in our bedroom looking frantically around. "There was someone *here*! He was watching us. I looked up and saw a man standing in the doorway watching us!"

"Where did he go?"

"I thought in here. But he's not. The windows are closed. . . . I don't know. Jesus."

"Should we call the police?"

"It won't do any good if he's not here. When he saw that I saw him, he stepped back in here but now . . . nothing. What the hell . . ."

"What did he look like?"

"I don't know. A man. He was in the shadows. I don't know." He kept checking around. He opened a closet door. He went to a window and, throwing it open, stuck his head far out and looked in every direction.

We spent a long time searching the house from top to bottom. But Hugh was much more upset about it than I. Perhaps because he had actually seen the man. What disturbed me more was that it was the second time something strange had happened in Frances's house and we hadn't even moved into the place yet. While we searched, I kept thinking of the little boy and his birthday party. That little beautiful boy.

"LOOK AT THIS!"

An hour later I was in the kitchen making lunch when Hugh came in holding something large in his hand. Or rather his fingers—

he held it far out in front of him, as if it wasn't at all nice. I smelled it before recognizing it. A bone. The kind of big cow bone you give a dog to chew.

"Where'd you find *that*?"

"Under the desk in my room! But touch it—that's what's weird."

I pointed to the food on the counter. "Hugh, I'm making lunch. I don't want to touch a bone."

He jiggled it as if trying to guess the weight. "It's still warm. Warm and slimy. Like it was chewed five minutes ago."

"In your room?"

"Under my desk. I haven't seen any dog around here. But this thing is *warm*. Something has been chewing this bone in my room. Recently."

I put the knife down. "Do you think it had anything to do with the man you saw this morning?"

He looked at the floor and shrugged. "You mean maybe the dog was chewing this while his master was spying on us? I don't know. I was wondering along those same lines. It's weirder thinking he might have had a dog with him."

The phone rang again. I picked it up and was relieved to hear Frances Hatch's scratchy voice on the other end. She asked how we were doing. I told her about our morning of the intruder and the warm bone.

"That house has been empty a long time, Miranda. Who knows who's been going in and out of there over the years? McCabe says he's been watching it, but he can't be there the whole day long. I'd call and tell him. You two be careful."

She asked to speak to Hugh. I handed him the phone and went back to preparing our meal. When I was finished, I brought it to the table. Hugh continued talking to Frances while he ate. I was about to sit down when I realized I had to go to the bathroom.

That was one of the few annoying things about the house—there was no toilet on the ground floor. I trudged up the stairs again and walked down the hall. Approaching the bathroom, I stopped when I heard something inside: water running. The door was cracked. A moment's hesitation before I pushed it open and felt for the switch on the wall. The light came on and I saw a thin thread of water running out of the faucet. I went over and turned it off and looked at myself in the mirror. Something else. Something else was wrong but it didn't register for some moments. The doorknob. The old porcelain doorknob to the toilet had been warm when I touched it. I went back and put two fingers on it to be sure. Warm. How could that be if no one had touched it for hours? I took a deep breath and said a good throaty "Shit!" before I started out on my own investigation of the upstairs rooms. Although Hugh was downstairs, I still hated the idea of looking on my own but knew I must. I couldn't be afraid of this house and I would be if I got spooked now and ran for cover. As I opened the door of our bedroom, my hand paused on the doorknob for a moment to gauge the temperature. Cool. No problem. Our bedroom, Hugh's study, what would one day be the guest room and in time, the baby's room, were only full of boxes and stacked-up furniture. Nothing more. No shadow men or dogs chewing bones. In Hugh's room, I even got down on my knees and felt the floor under his desk where he said the bone had been. Nothing.

Then I did something that was strange but seemed right at the moment. I tipped my forehead till it was touching the floor. And I prayed. Or I said to someone powerful and important and in charge, "Please let everything be all right. Please let us be safe." And then I went back downstairs to finish lunch with my love.

I WATCHED AS a red + sign slowly appeared in the middle of the blotting paper. Though I already knew, sensed, had *felt* it for days, it was still a storm in my head to actually see the physical proof. I was pregnant. The druggist told me these home tests were usually 98 percent sure.

I bought it at a pharmacy near my store. I'd put it in my purse and carried it around for three days, equally excited and frightened to use it. Every time I took it out and read the instructions again, turned the box over and over in my hands and shook it next to my ear as if it might have something to say, I ended up dropping it back into the bag and saying, "Later."

After too many strange things happened—continued dizziness, fatigue, sudden nausea at the smell of coffee—I knew I had to find out what was going on inside me. At home Hugh had a book of medical symptoms. When I read those describing pregnancy—dizziness, fatigue, nausea—I closed the book and bit my lip. What would he say on hearing that it had happened so soon after we'd moved in together? Right in the middle of all the turmoil with Charlotte and his children. How would he react?

The day I decided to take the home test, we rode together into Manhattan on the train. Just past Spuyten Duyvil, I carefully curved our normal morning chitchat around to the subject of children. Hugh had been looking at a Sotheby's catalog of rare musical instruments to be auctioned.

He drummed his fingers on the cover. "I love Fellini films and my favorite parts are when there's a scene of a big family fest: a marriage or birthday party. Tables have been set up in an empty field and everyone's eating, having a wonderful time. A bad local band is playing, children are running around. The wind is always blowing and crepe paper or balloons are flying around, and leaves. . . ." Looking out the window, he blew breath against the glass and made a small patch of fog. He rubbed it away with the heel of his hand. "Sometimes you hear a train passing in the distance. A couple of sad toots.

"I want to be at those parties, with *my* five kids running around. They've eaten too much cake and are tired of sitting still. Or maybe they're my grandchildren and I've got white hair and am beginning to get sleepy because I've had too much wine. I love the Italians. All those big families and their kids. I love kids. I'd be so happy if we had some. But of course only if you want them too."

I stared at the vivid red cross on the test and realized I was humming the Beatles song "I feel fine." I had a plan. I put the test in a small Ziploc bag and slid it into my desk. Then I went to a liquor store and bought a bottle of their best champagne. My first thought was to go to Hugh's office and surprise him, but I realized I didn't want his assistants to know yet. I called instead and asked if we could have lunch. To my great dismay, he said no. He had to meet with clients all afternoon and might not be home till late. I was on the verge of telling him then, but that would have been wrong. Over the telephone? This was our greatest event and it deserved special treatment. The announcement had to wait till later.

I stood in the middle of Eighty-first Street with a bottle of champagne and the best news I'd ever had but no one to share them with. If only my parents were still alive.

To make matters worse, ten feet away across the sidewalk a well-dressed middle-aged woman suddenly started screaming, "Where is everyone *going*?" again and again in a voice that could have opened the eyes of the dead. In typical New York fashion, people steered a wide path around her, but I was mesmerized. Her fists were against her cheeks, and she looked like a mad Edvard Munch character. Naturally she ended up staring at me, her audience of one. Snapping out of my trance, I didn't know whether to flee or try to help her.

"Where are they *going*?" she pleaded, as if I knew who "they" were or where they were headed. She continued staring at me in the most beseeching way.

The only thing I could say was, "I don't know."

"But you have to know; you've been here longer than any of us!" And with that she moved off down the street in a swift stagger that was as awful to see as the look on her face.

After making sure she wasn't coming back, I returned to the phone booth and called Zoe. Halfway through tapping out her number I hung up, remembering she had flown out to Los Angeles two days before to visit Doug Auerbach.

Frances! Frances was always home, thank God. She answered after the fifth ring. When I asked if I could visit, she happily said, "Of course!" I went to a specialty market and bought tins of pâté and Russian caviar, a beautifully fresh French bread, and a box of Belgian chocolates.

When I hailed a cab the sun was shining brightly, but on the way uptown the sky darkened abruptly and thunder rolled. The rain began just before I saw the madwoman again. She was now walking briskly in a purposeful stride that said, Outta the way I'm in a hurry. So different from minutes before when she'd been standing on the sidewalk looking like aliens had landed inside her skull. Now she looked straight ahead and her arms pumped back and forth, rump rump rump.

But the moment we passed, her head jerked toward me. She raised a hand and shook a scolding finger. Shocked, I turned away. The rain swirled silvery down the window. The street shone glossy black. Cars hissed by. Umbrellas were everywhere. I wanted to look at her again but was afraid. The rest of the ride uptown I tried to keep my eyes closed. I listened to the rain and the bumpity-bump of the tires hitting ruts in the road. I thought of the baby. I thought of Hugh.

Arriving at Frances's, I paid the driver and ran across the courtyard into her section of the building. The rain soaked the paper bag full of food and I felt it coming apart in my hands. I stopped on a landing and took the things out. Cradling them in my arms, I started up the stairs. They weren't heavy, but in a moment they were much too heavy. Suddenly I was dizzy and too hot to go on. I was barely able to lower myself to a step without keeling over. I put the food down and put my head in my hands. Was this what pregnancy was going to be like? Nine months of feeling great and then abruptly feeling like you were going to keel over?

Normally the building was as loud as a train station. Kids ran shouting up and down the stairs, dogs barked, radios and TVs blasted. Today it was virtually silent but for the rain pattering outside. I sat trying to will the dizziness away so I could go up and tell Frances my joyous news.

At the same time, it was enjoyable sitting there alone on that cold step, listening to the rain outside plink on metal, splat on stone, gurgle urgently down into the drains. I had never realized before what a variety of rain sounds there were. Rain had always been rain—something to avoid or watch dreamily through a window. It made the familiar world wet and shiny and different awhile and then you forgot about it till the next time. But alone now surrounded only by rain noises, I was able to recognize more and more distinctions: rain on wood, sliding down glass, rain on rain. Yes, there was even a sound to that, but a hidden one, altogether secret.

I lifted my head and said aloud, "That's not right. No one can hear those things." But I was already hearing other things too: conversations, channels changing on a television, someone peeing hard into a toilet. What's more, I knew *exactly* what each of the sounds was. Feet crossing a floor, a cat purring, a person licking their dry lips in sleep, toenails being clipped.

I looked around to check if any doors were open nearby. No. Only the rain outside and now this relentless cascade of sounds falling over me. From behind those closed doors, from apartments twenty or thirty feet away. Noises I shouldn't have heard. Impossible from where I was sitting.

Back in some bedroom behind closed doors where two kids were supposed to be taking a nap, one little boy was whispering to his brother, both of them under the blanket on his bed. Somewhere else in the building a woman sang quietly along with the radio in her kitchen as she washed dishes. It was the Dixie Cups song "The Chapel of Love." I heard the rush of aerated water in the sink, the squeak of the sponge on glass, her quiet melancholic voice.

"I fuck you good. You know I fuck you good."

"Fuck me *hard*."

I could hear their grunting breath, the smack of kisses, hands sliding over skin. I could hear everything. But where *were* these people? How was this possible?

I stood up. I didn't want to hear. But none of it would stop. Cars ssh'd and honked outside on the street, a heating pipe clanked in the basement, pigeons chuckled on the windowsill, food fried, people argued, an old woman prayed. "Oh God, you know how scared I am, but you not helping me through this." All the sounds of a rainy day in Manhattan were too near and I couldn't stop them. I covered my ears and shook my head from side to side like a wet dog. For a moment the sounds of the world stopped. Silence again. Beautiful, empty silence returned.

But then *it* came and it was the biggest sound of all. My heart. The dull, huge boom of my beating heart filled the air and space of the world around me. I could only stand and listen, terrified. What was worse was the irregularity. Boom boom boom, then nothing for seconds. It started again, only to go and stop and go with no evenness, no rhythm or structure. It beat when it felt like it. Then it stopped. It was moody. It did what it liked. But it was my heart and it was supposed to be the steadiest machine of all.

I knew it was me because I had had arrhythmia all my life. A few years before it had grown so serious that I spent a night in the hospital being rigorously tested and monitored by a twenty-four-hour EKG.

The loudest noise I ever heard pulsed and stopped and pulsed again but with no pattern, no safe recognizable rhythm. Maybe it would beat another time. Maybe not.

"Miranda? Are you all right?"

A moment passed before my mind focused on her voice and face. Frances stood several steps above me. She wore a red robe and matching slippers, which made her intensely white skin glow in the dark of the stairwell.

"What's the matter, dear?"

Her voice brought things back. I tried to speak but couldn't. She slowly worked her way down. When she got to me she put a hand on my elbow. "I was sitting by the window and saw you come in. I got worried when you didn't ring."

She helped me up the rest of the stairs. Without that help, I don't know how I would have made it.

"IT'S ALL MY fault."

"Don't be ridiculous, Frances. Unless you made all these things happen to me." I tried to sound facetious, but the words came out sounding self-pitying.

"You don't understand; it's more complicated than that." She began walking around the room.

I had just finished telling her everything. From the day I saw the ghost of James Stillman on the street, right up to the impossible sounds I had heard out in the hall. Once I'd started, the whole story leaped out like an animal that had been trapped in a cage too long. Simply recounting all of the strange events made me feel better.

Frances was silent throughout and spoke only after a long pause. "I knew you were pregnant the day we went to Crane's View. I don't know if you remember, but when we got to my house I stood on the porch and asked to be alone while you two went in."

"I remember that. Hugh mentioned it."

"I didn't want you to see my face because I might have given it away. That's when I knew."

"How, Frances? Are you psychic?"

She shook her head. "No, but when I was a young woman in Romania I met people. Shumda introduced me and they taught me some things. That was the greatest mistake of my life: they were willing to teach me much more but I wasn't interested. Incredible. Incredibly stupid.

"Shumda was Romanian. He had been raised in the country, and to country people, real magic is no big deal. Things like that *shouldn't* be a big deal. They are to us because we're so sophisticated and skeptical that we're above all that primitive hocus-pocus.

"But there *is* another world, Miranda. Most of us refuse to accept that because it scares us. It threatens to take away our control. But that won't make it go away. Let me read you something." She walked to a table and picked up one of the many notebooks she kept around the apartment. She called them daybooks and filled them with her thoughts and quotes from things she had read and liked. She leafed through this book. "Here, listen to this: 'Maybe what comes from elsewhere will make me do crazy things; maybe that invisible world is demonic and should be excluded. What I can't see, I can't know; what I don't know, I fear; what I fear, I hate; what I hate, I want destroyed.' "

"But Frances, I do believe in those things. I always have. I've just never had any contact with them until now. Did you really know I was pregnant that day? How?"

"Your smell. And the color of your fingertips."

"What does a pregnant woman smell like?"

"Like hope."

I smiled and felt my spirit lift. "It's possible to smell hope?"

She nodded. "When you know how."

"And what about the fingertips?"

"Look at them."

I held up my left hand but saw nothing at first. Then I gasped. The tips of my fingers were changing colors—the colors of clouds on the sky. As if a strong wind was pushing fleecy clouds across the sky, clouds that were white, purple, orange-red. They moved over my fingertips in a passing rush. The colors of storms, sunsets, early morning. All of them together flying across my fingertips.

I guess I made some other noise because the moment I did, the colors disappeared and my fingers returned to their proper color. I kept staring at my hand. Eventually I looked at Frances again but with a whole new perspective.

"*That's* what I saw when we were in Crane's View. You can't because you haven't been trained. I did it to you now so you could see for yourself."

"All women have that? On their fingers? All of them when they're pregnant?"

"Yes."

"And you learned how to do that in Romania?"

"Among other things."

"What else, Frances? What else do you know?"

She sighed loudly. "Not enough. I was too young to appreciate what they were offering. Knowledge pursued me, but I was faster. When you're young you're only interested in parlor tricks, Miranda, things that can impress others or get you in the door.

"But these people, and they were from all walks of life, were willing to teach me incredible things because I was with Shumda. If only I'd had the patience and dedication! I met a Yezidje priest, people in the Sarmoun Brotherhood. . . . You can't imagine who I knew when I was there. But none of it penetrated. The young are like rubber—everything bounces off them.

"Shumda called me *bimba viziata*, his spoiled child, and I was." She sighed again and rubbed her hands up and down her sides. "You talk to shadows too much when you get old. Old memories, old regrets. I could have learned so much when I was a young woman, but I didn't and that was a great mistake. But I do know some things. I knew you were pregnant. I know that what you're going through now is a result of that pregnancy."

"And James's ghost? Or the noises I heard outside? The little boy in our house?"

"They're part of it. Believe me, it's all necessary for you now. Something enormous is about to come into your life and all of these things are part of the overture." She walked over, put her hands on my tense shoulders, and kissed the top of my head. It was the first time Frances had kissed me.

WHEN I GOT back to Crane's View, the rain was having an intermission and the sky was full of black fat thunderclouds. After getting out of the train I stood on the platform and stared at that turbulent sky, remembering my fingertips and what had happened in Frances's apartment earlier. The day had exhausted me, but I decided to walk the mile to our house. I wanted the exercise. The air smelled delicious and ripe as it always does in the country after rain.

As I walked and breathed deeply of the thick air, I kept thinking about what she had told me. More than anything else, "there is another world" kept chiming in my head like a clock striking twelve. Like it or not, that world had become part of mine. I would have to accept it and go wherever it led me. But how would it affect my relationship with Hugh? And our child?

Frances told me about a dull man she knew who suddenly, in

middle age, was able to see what people would look like when they were old. For the rest of his life he had to live with that . . . talent? Curse? What would you call it?

Another man suddenly developed a frighteningly accurate ability to read palms. That lucky fellow went mad because it reached a point where he could see nothing else but people's palms and the certain fates that awaited them.

"Need a ride? You look tired."

I looked up and saw Chief McCabe leaning on the roof of his car in front of the bakery. He held a French cruller in one hand and a small carton of milk in the other.

"No, thank you. I just got off the train and this walk is bringing me back to life. But I have a question."

He grinned and nodded. "You don't want a ride but you got a question. Okay. Shoot."

"Have you ever known anyone with special powers? People who could tell the future or read palms, that sort of thing?"

He didn't hesitate. "My grandmother. Spookiest person I ever knew. Always knew when you were lying. The family legend. No one of us ever lied to her because she always *knew*. Worst part was, if you did lie, she hit you. Lie—BANG! When I was a kid she must've got me a thousand times! Shows how smart I was, huh? Why do you ask?"

I didn't even know McCabe, but for a moment I wanted to tell him everything. Maybe after what had happened that day, I just needed a friend.

"Oh, yeah," he went on, "and Frances Hatch too. She gets tuned into weird channels too sometimes." His car radio squawked and he bent in to listen. I couldn't make out what it said.

"Gotta go. Someone's screaming up on Skidmore Street." He popped the rest of the cruller into his mouth and took the milk with him when he got into the car.

He drove off before I could tell him. It was a Japanese woman. A Mrs. Hayashi. I had never seen her before. She had taken too many pills and the hallucinations were driving her mad. Her children stood on windowsills in a high building waving happily to her down below. Bye-bye Mama. Then one by one they jumped. She watched as they dropped through space and hit the ground directly in front of her. I saw her face, the wide open mouth screaming to her sanity to help.

Outside her small house on Skidmore Street, neighbors stood worriedly at the window watching her on the floor, pulling her hair and screaming in a language none of them understood.

I saw it.

FIVE HOURS LATER Hugh came in looking pale and very drawn. He went into the living room and sat down in his new chair and let out a low groan. I got him a drink and asked if there was anything I could do. Unsmiling, he kissed my hand and said no. Sweet man that he was, he looked up with weary eyes and apologized for not being able to make lunch earlier. He'd had an awful day. An important deal for a rare Guadagnini violin fell through. He had argued with his assistants. Charlotte called and accused him of terrible things.

I sat on the floor next to him and leaned my head against his leg. I had wonderful news to tell him but didn't. After dinner. I would cook and it would be wonderful, the most delicious meal I'd ever made. After dinner, when we both felt better and the day was ours again and the moment was right for such a surprise. *Then.*

We sat in silence. It started to rain again. When he spoke, Hugh's voice was flat and toneless, as if it had been washed of all color.

"Know what I love? In the summer when you leave the windows open in the bedroom and go to sleep. There's a breeze blowing you can just feel on your face. As you're drifting off, the wind picks up, but you're too sleepy to do anything about it.

"Then in the middle of the night, a big bang wakes you up in a second. A storm's *raging* outside and all your windows are flapping back and forth. Like they're applauding. Like they're applauding the storm.

"So you get up, sleepy as hell but wired from the shock, and go around closing them. Everything's wet, the windowsills, the floor. . . . While you were sleeping this thing blew in and drenched everything.

"The best part is standing at the open window and getting wet. I put my hands on the sill and stick my head out into it. The wind's whipping, things are tremendous out there. It's three in the morning and no one's around to see it. Only you. The whole show's just for you."

I put an arm around his leg and squeezed tightly. His hand was on my head, ruffling my hair. Neither of us moved for minutes. The only things that changed were the sounds of the wind outside. Hugh's hand stopped moving. The rain gradually slowed and stopped too. Everything stopped. The silence was thick as fur. Despite all the surprises and excitement of that bizarre day, the next minutes were the most peaceful and fulfilling I ever knew.

When I finally moved to get up, because my back was beginning to hurt, because it was time to cook our dinner, because afterward I could tell Hugh about our baby, his hand slipped from my head. I saw that he was asleep.

He was dead.

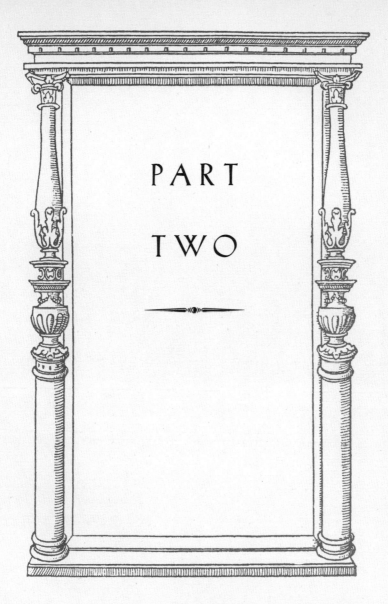

PART

TWO

SIN TAX

THREE DAYS AFTER his funeral I saw Hugh again.

Standing at the kitchen sink, I looked out the window at the small yard behind the house. I could not feel my body. I could not feel anything. Since his death, I had moved through the days in a walking stupor and felt best there.

What had surprised me was not the horror of the loss, but the gain of so many terrible things. The gain of time: if he were here now, we would be doing this together. Now there was nothing to do. If he were here now, I would be doing this *for* him. Now there was nothing to do. If he were here now I would touch him, talk to him, know he was in the next room . . . the variety was dreadful, endless.

As was the space around me. The space in our new double bed, the house, the life we had just begun together. Hugh's empty easy chair, the empty shoes lined up carefully in his closet, the table with only one place setting.

The silence grew palpably larger, the days longer, the nights indescribable. And there was a sudden, almost religious importance to objects—his coffee cup, his razor, his favorite recipe, television show, color, tree. I stared at his moving boxes with the funny names on them. Tarzan Hotel. Sometimes I reached in and touched an object. Some things were sharp. Some smooth. Always Hugh's. A silver penknife with a broken blade inscribed *Sarajevo* on the side. A cranberry baseball cap with *Earlham* across the top. A volume of poetry titled *The Unknown Rilke*. Horribly, I turned two pages into it and read this before it registered:

> *Now we awaken with memories,*
> *facing that which was; whispered sweetness*
> *which once pierced and spread through us*
> *sits silently nearby with its hair all undone*

Another box contained some of the sticks he had collected. When I saw them I immediately left the room.

I scoured my mind for things he had said, his opinions, beliefs, jokes, anything mentioned off the cuff, in passing, in earnest. Anything. I wrote it all down because I wanted every trace of Hugh Oakley for me and our son. I sat in his chair for hours and hours trying to remember everything. But it was like picking up rice grain by grain after spilling an entire bag on a white floor full of cracks. It went all over and so much of it was invisible.

Holding a glass of water in my hands, I stood at the kitchen window staring out at the yard. Before I realized it, I was smiling. I had remembered something new: Hugh saying we should plant pumpkins and sunflowers out there because they were the clowns of the flower kingdom. How could you not laugh at a pumpkin? How could sunflowers not make you smile? I drank some water and felt it cool down my throat. I put the glass against my forehead and rubbed it back and forth. The telephone rang and I closed my eyes. Who would it be this time? What on earth could I say to them? Leave me alone. Can't you all just leave me alone now? I opened my eyes again.

Standing twenty feet away across the yard were Hugh and the little boy I had seen the first time we visited the house. The phone rang again. Hugh looked exactly as he had the day he died. He was dressed in the same clothes—dark slacks, white shirt, the blue tweed sport jacket from Ireland he liked so much. The phone kept ringing.

Over that noise, I heard something tapping. I didn't recognize what until I looked down and saw my shaking hand. The water glass rat-a-tatted against the metal sink.

The little boy turned around and knelt down. The answering machine clicked on. I heard my calm voice say the old message: "We're out now, but please leave a message. . . ."

Barely able to control my shaking hands, I slid the window up and called Hugh's name. Called it, cried it, whispered—I don't know how it came out. He looked at me and gave a small breezy wave, as if I were calling him for lunch and he'd come in a minute. But he had heard me! And he was really there! But he was dead. But there he was.

I was so amazed, so riveted, that I didn't notice what the boy was doing. Didn't see him pick up the stone and throw it.

It hit me in the face. I grunted and staggered back. Hands over my eyes, warm blood already gushing over my fingers. Stepping on something, I twisted my ankle hard and fell down. I tried to put out a hand to stop the fall. But it was so slick with blood that as soon as it touched the floor, it skidded sideways. My head hit with a loud thud.

I lay on my side and tried to blink, to clear my head. Everything had slowed almost to a stop. Blood was in my eyes and I couldn't really open them. I was viciously dizzy. I lay still and heard myself pant. When I could, I wiped my face and opened my eyes. I saw the rock on the floor. That is what I had tripped over. It was brown and silvery and huge. A big rock on the kitchen floor. I remember thinking even then, even there, What's this rock doing here?

And then something else. Nearby a child was laughing.

None of it was clear to me. I tried to focus my mind on this thing and that—getting the blood out of my eyes, seeing clearly, regaining my balance. But reality was tipped on its side and I could not right it. The child's laughter remained above and inside and around my confusion. It was the only constant and it was very clear.

"WHAT HAPPENED TO you? This is a bad cut."

"I fell."

The doctor stopped bustling for the first time since entering the room. An ugly woman with a monk's haircut, she narrowed her eyes. "You fell?" She was wearing white surgical gloves and she pointed a finger at the bandage on my forehead. "That doesn't look like a fall, Ms. Romanac. Are you sure?" Her smile lasted a second. We both knew what she was saying. "It looks like you were struck with something. Something heavy and sharp." Her voice rose indignantly on the last word. Her stern face was ready to be outraged. If I didn't tell her the truth, I would feel that rage. She moved and spoke with the undiscerning sureness of a hanging judge. I was glad I didn't know her.

I started to shake my head but my neck hurt terribly, so I stopped. "My neck hurts too."

She put a hand on it and gently felt up and down with her fingers. "That's normal. It's either the trauma from the fall or you jerked it unnaturally and twisted the muscles. It'll go away in a couple of days. But this is what really concerns me." Again she pointed to my forehead. "We don't usually see this kind of cut from a fall."

I took a deep breath and let it out in an aggravated, tired-of-this whoosh. "No one *hit* me, Doctor. All right? I'm alone. The man I lived with died a few days ago."

Her expression remained unchanged. Emergency room doctors have heard every lie and story in the world. "I'm sorry. But a wound like this usually indicates abuse. I could explain the technicalities of it to you, but that's not necessary. Are you on any kind of medication?"

"No. I was given Valium but I don't take it."

She went to her desk and scribbled on a pad. "Here is a prescription for a muscle relaxant for your neck, and this one is for pain. Are you seeing anyone? A counselor or a therapist? They can be very helpful when you've lost someone close."

"Ghosts," I wanted to say. I'm not seeing a therapist but I *have* seen ghosts. One even threw a rock at me.

"Thank you for your concern, Doctor. Do I have to come back here?"

"Yes. I'll need to remove the stitches in a week."

I stood up very slowly but still my head throbbed and pain went down the back of my neck in a fiery shot. I wanted to be out of that room, away from that aggressive, offensive woman, out in the world again. All I wanted was to be out on the street.

"We also have the results of your pregnancy test and sonogram, Ms. Romanac. They were positive."

My back to her, I tried to turn my head but the pain said no. I turned completely around to face her. There was nothing to say. I already knew it and had taken the hospital test as an afterthought. The day Hugh died I knew I was pregnant but never had the chance to tell him. That was the worst. The absolute worst part.

"You could talk to our counselor about that as well."

I didn't understand what she meant. She saw the question on my face and tightened her lips.

"The child. If your partner is gone then perhaps you might want to consider terminations. . . ."

I caught the gist of what she was saying more from her tone of voice than from the actual words.

"I'm having this baby, Doctor. Can I go now?"

"Would you like to know if it's a boy or a girl?"

I started for the door. "It's a boy. I already know."

Her voice was haughty and dismissive. "No, actually it's a girl."

MY LOVER MADE the best sandwiches. He loved to cook, but sandwiches were his specialty. He made pilgrimages to special bakeries around Manhattan to buy *the* perfect California sourdough bread, Austrian dreikornbrot, Italian focaccia. He experimented with exotic ingredients and condiments like piri piri, wasabi, mango chutney. He poured thin trickles of specially prepared kurbiskernol onto bread and warmed it before he did anything else. He owned the most beautiful and ominous set of Japanese cooking knives I'd ever seen. I think he enjoyed sharpening and caring for them as much as he liked using them.

All of these things went through my mind as I opened the refrigerator door to look for something to eat an hour after returning from the hospital. One day he was dead. Four days later he was buried. Three days later I saw him standing in our backyard with a child who had never been born. One week. Exactly one week to the day ago I discovered I was pregnant and Hugh died.

On a shelf was a large slice of fontina, his favorite cheese. He would cut a piece and hold it in an open palm, telling me to look— look at this masterpiece of *kasekunst.* Some of his "cheese art" and an apple. I would be able to eat those small things without getting sick, wouldn't I? Dinner. I had not eaten for a long time. I wasn't hungry, but I had to eat regularly now. For the child. For the *girl* inside me. Girl or boy, it was Hugh's child and I would care for it with every cell in my body.

I wasn't afraid to be in the kitchen again. Opening the front door an hour before and stepping into the house, I had been, but it passed. I turned on all the lights and walked from room to room. Sometimes I said out loud, too loud, "Hello?" But that had only been to fill the space and the silence around me. When I had seen that every room was empty, I was okay. I was even able to walk into the kitchen and look out the window at the backyard again. Night had come and there was nothing to see out there.

I turned on the radio and was pleased to hear the last part of Keith Jarrett's *Köln Concert,* one of my favorite pieces of music. Set the table and eat something so you have strength. I took a canary yellow place mat out of a drawer, and a large blue plate from the cupboard.

The refrigerator was full of Hugh's things—the Lavazza coffee he liked so much, the fiery Jamaican sauce he used to make jerk chicken, sesame oil, lime pickle. I saw them and knew each could break my heart if I started thinking about them. There were the cheese and apples, and now it was time to eat. Take them out. Close the door. Remember to clean out the refrigerator sometime soon so you don't keep bumping into those things.

When the Jarrett finished, some awful grating jazz replaced it. I switched the radio off. The silence around me was suddenly huge and rising like a tidal wave, so I quickly turned on the small television across the kitchen table. Hugh loved TV and made no excuses for watching infomercials, bowling, mindless situation comedies. Oddly, he usually watched standing up, even if it meant standing there for hours. At first having him standing two feet away while watching *Friends* made me uncomfortable, but gradually I grew to like it.

Part of living with someone is growing to enjoy their eccentricities. Hugh Oakley sometimes slept in his socks. He wrote notes to himself on his index finger in green ink, was suspicious of microwave ovens, and watched television standing up.

What do you do with your love for someone when they die? Or the memories they've left? Do you pack them up in moving boxes and write strange names for them across the top? Then where do you put them and the rest of a life you were supposed to share with a person who left without warning?

Switching through the channels, I thought of Hugh's box marked "Tarzan Hotel" and how he enjoyed not knowing what was inside. He'd once said, "Never try to avoid the rain by walking close to a building. You always get hit by the big drops falling from the roof." Thoughts, pictures, memories of him flooded me.

I would have been swept away if a high tweedly whistle from the television set hadn't begun playing "Ring's End Rose," a happy Irish song about new love that was one of Hugh's favorites. Before I focused on the TV to see why it was being played, I thought, This is what it's going to be like now and maybe forever—everything will be Hugh Oakley. I'd better get used to it or it will drive sorrow and remembrance into me like a mallet driving a stake into soft earth.

•On the television screen, Hugh sat by the side of a swimming pool playing an Irish pennywhistle. In the pool, Charlotte and the now familiar little boy held hands and danced together to his music.

Hugh looked ten years older—heavier and redder in the face, less hair, the kind of slow carefulness in his movements you see in aging people. He might have been in his late fifties. His great years had passed; he was at the age where you take what you can get. But his expression blazed happiness watching the two dancers, and it came through in the way he played.

Charlotte looked gorgeous. Although she was a decade younger than Hugh, she too looked older than when I had last seen her. Her still lovely figure was accented by a simple black one-piece bathing suit that emphasized her high square shoulders and long neck. Her platinum hair was cut very short and smart. She wore minimal, chic steel-rim eyeglasses. The severe, scaled-down look suited her brilliantly. It said, Yes, I'm older, but I know exactly what to do with it: pare my beauty to its essence so that what's left shows only the best.

"Daddy, come in! You promised you'd come in."

"Daddy's happy playing for us, honey. Come on, let's you and me dance some more."

They did, and there was so much love around the three of them that I cringed. Hugh played "Foggy Dew." Hugh was on television. Hugh ten years older, balder. Hugh still alive but with Charlotte again. And their son.

They danced and splashed and sang along. Still playing, Hugh stood up and did a jig by the side of the pool. The boy jumped around and threw himself into Charlotte's arms. Her glasses flew off but with the most beautifully precise gesture she snatched them out of the air before they hit the water.

When he had finished playing, Hugh walked into the house. The boy grabbed onto the side of the pool and tried calling him back. Hugh only waved and kept going. He went through the kitchen, the living room, out to the front porch. Opening a mailbox there, he took out a handful of letters and magazines. Shuffling through, he didn't stop until he uncovered an oversized postcard.

On the front was a photograph of a picturesque port with white-washed buildings set against a green hillside and the bluest sky. He turned the card over. The handwriting was instantly recognizable. Mine.

Hugh,

I'm on Samos and it's nice. Traveling here has been good for me because the Greeks are in no hurry. It's easy to follow their lead. I saw a man drive his motorbike right into a taverna, they give you a whole lemon to squeeze over your calamari, and the air smells of hot flowers.

I often eat at a place called the Soapy Grill. They make a delicious gyro sandwich of pita bread, lamb, french fries, and tzatziki. It reminds me of the ones you used to make for us. What was that line? Even a single hair casts its shadow. In this case, it's a single sandwich.

When does it end, Hugh? When will I be able to go around a corner of my life and not run into you, your sandwiches, your ghost, my memories, what *was*?

You once said, "everything flows." But it doesn't, Hugh. Too many things stop, and no matter how hard you try, they can't be moved. Like memory. And love.

Miranda

He finished reading and clicking his tongue, shook his head. "Samos. Samos." He said the word twice, as if trying it out on his tongue. The expression on his face was clear: relief. He wasn't in the least sad I was gone.

"Darling, did the mail come?" Charlotte walked into the room followed by a young dalmatian that was growling and pulling on a pink towel she held behind her. Hugh held out my postcard. She looked at it and, raising an eyebrow, asked, "Miranda?" He handed it over with no hesitation. Tipping her head in a way that indicated her glasses were too weak, she read it quickly and handed it back.

"How long has it been since you last saw her? Eight years?"

He bent the card in half. "Nine. A long time."

"But she's been writing you ever since." It was a statement, not a question.

He lifted a hand and shrugged as if to say, What can I do?

The dog put its front paws on him and stretched languorously. Hugh grabbed its head and kissed it.

Charlotte patted the dog. "Isn't it strange? Miranda's the only one of your girlfriends who's stayed true to you. All the trouble and pain you had with her at the end, but a decade later she's still sending you postcards from her travels."

Tongue lolling out of its mouth like a long red belt, the dog started humping Hugh's leg. They laughed. Hugh said, "Perfect timing," and pushed him down.

The boy rushed into the room. "Dad! It's getting dark outside. The eclipse is starting! Come on!" He took his father's hand and, finding him immovable, rushed back out of the room.

Charlotte's mouth tightened and she gestured toward the boy. "What if you *had* stayed with her? Then we'd never have had him."

Hugh reached out and touched his wife's cheek. "But I didn't stay with her. Don't think about it, sweetheart."

"I think about it all the time. Thank God you stayed."

"You won, Char. Look at these postcards. She's pathetic."

She touched a finger to his lips. Be careful what you say.

THE TELEVISION PICTURE changed abruptly to a scene from *Amarcord,* Hugh's favorite film. Above the TV noise, a sound rose behind me that was difficult to place. But then I knew it—toenails clicking across a wooden floor.

I turned as the young dalmatian entered my kitchen. He plopped down on the floor and stared at me. His tail began to thump. The same dog that had been on television with Hugh's family a moment ago was now here with me.

"His name is Bob."

Nothing is more ineffable than a voice, yet a few remain recognizable as long as we live. Even if we lost them a lifetime ago. James Stillman stood in my doorway. But this was James the man I had never known, the face I had seen only once, in a photograph.

He was thinner, hair fashionably short, the beginning of a few concentric wrinkles framing the corners of his mouth. But his eyes were the same. Eyes I had once memorized—a rascal's eyes, the eyes of a guy who's got tricks up his sleeve or a great joke to tell. He leaned easily against the door frame, hands deep in his pockets, one leg crossed nonchalantly in front of the other. He did it all unconsciously. His mother used to call it his Cary Grant pose. I smelled his cologne. I smelled the Zizanie cologne and somehow that was the most shocking thing of all. It made it all the more real. Dreams don't smell.

The dog jumped up on him and scrabbled furiously for his attention. James picked him up. Bob went nuts. He wiggled and licked and twisted all at the same time. It was too much, and James put him down again but continued to scratch his frantic head.

"I remember your dog, Miranda. What was its name?"

"Oscar."

He grinned. "Oscar! That's right. Loudest dog I ever knew. Remember how he snored? And farted?"

"James—"

He held up a hand to stop me. "Not yet. Let me get used to you again." He crossed the kitchen and came close. My God, that too-sweet cologne. His trademark. The first man I ever knew who used cologne every day. He used to steal the beautiful silver bottles from Grieb's pharmacy. I hadn't smelled it in years but the memory was like a flashbulb going off in my face.

Hands still in his pockets, he leaned forward until we were inches apart. What I wanted to know, had to know, was, how much was he here? If I reached out and touched him would he be skin and bones, *real,* or a ghost, a shade, my imagination gone screaming?

He shook his head and closed his eyes. "Don't do it. You don't want to know."

I shivered and pulled back. "You know what I'm *thinking*?"

"No, but it's in your eyes."

I put my face in my hands and lowered it to the table. The wood was cold. My skin was hot. I no longer understood anything.

There was a deep, abiding silence.

Slowly I began to hear noises. The volume rose. Higher. Together, they were familiar. Years-ago familiar.

Rushing, the slamming of metal, everything loud, jarring. Many voices, laughter, scuffling feet, and movement. A clanging bell. *School?* The bell that rang eight times a day in my high school when class was over and you had three minutes to get to the next?

These sounds were so recognizable. I lifted my head and saw. It was all familiar, blood familiar, but because it was impossible, it still took time to understand, to *register*. I was back in school. I was back in high school!

Faces from so many years ago swirled and streamed around me. Joe del Tufo, Niklas Bahn, Ryder Pierce. A football whizzed through the air and was caught with a two-hand slap by Owen King.

"Mr. King, give me that ball."

Miss Cheryl Jeans, the algebra teacher, stood in the doorway to her classroom. Tall, thin as a pencil, she gestured for Owen to hand over the ball. She was so beautiful and good-natured that she was one of the most popular teachers in school.

"Come on, Miss Jeans. We won't do it again."

"Get it after school, Owen. Right now it's mine. Hand it over."

He gave her the ball and kept staring at her even after she turned and walked back into her room.

School. I stood in the hall of my high school surrounded by many of the same people I had seen at the reunion months before. But there they had been adults, what they would turn into years after leaving this place and going out into life. Here they were teenagers again with the bad haircuts, braces on their teeth, and unfashionable clothes that had been so cool and necessary to us fifteen years earlier.

I stood transfixed. Kids I'd known, hated, loved, dismissed, worshipped, pushed by on their way to class, the toilet, out the back door to sneak cigarettes. Tony Gioe. Brandon Brind.

And then *I* walked out of a classroom with Zoe. Eighteen-year-old Zoe Holland and Miranda Romanac passed within two feet of where I stood. Both smiled conspiratorially, as if something funny and secret had just happened and they were savoring it between them. To prove it was real, I was blasted with the smell of strong perfume. Jungle Gardenia—that cheap stuff I wore every day to high school. The two girls continued down the hall and I followed. They didn't notice. I walked parallel with them and neither noticed.

"I don't *believe* it! Miranda, you're telling the truth? You absolutely swear to God?" Zoe's eyes were alive with curiosity. Miranda's face stayed blank and emotionless, but then she couldn't hold it anymore and burst out laughing. "We did it."

Zoe brought her books to her face and stomped her feet. "Oh God! Come in here!" She pushed Miranda down the hall and into the girls' bathroom. They went to the mirrors and rested their books on adjoining sinks. "And?"

Miranda looked in the mirror and made a moue. "And *what?*"

Taking her shoulder, Zoe turned her around hard. "Don't fool around, Miranda. Tell everything."

"When he picked me up last night he said we were going on an adventure. I went, 'Uh-oh,' because you know what James means when he says that. He drove to Leslie Swid's house and parked down the block. It was dark inside the house because the Swids are out of town, right? James said we were going to break in."

Zoe looked at the heavens. "Oh my God! And you did? You broke into their house with him? You're a criminal!" She giggled.

"He promised not to do anything—we'd just go in and look. So we snuck around the back of the house. Naturally I was so scared the police were going to come that I had seven heart attacks. But James tried all the windows and found one he could open with this tool he had—this car tool thing. So he opened the window and we climbed in. It was scary, but exciting too. We went around the house just looking. When we got to her parents' bedroom, he took me and pushed me down on the bed and . . . it happened."

"Was it good? Was it great?"

"First it hurt, then it was nice. I was just basically scared, Zoe. I didn't know what I was doing."

I had never slept with James Stillman in high school. I had never slept with anyone in high school. Why was I lying to my best friend?

Something touched my shoulder. Adult James Stillman stood directly behind me.

"Come. I need to show you something."

Although I didn't want to leave, I followed him.

James hurried down the school hallway through swarms of kids and clamor. Through fifteen- and sixteen-year-old lives hurtling along toward anything that looked interesting, glowed, or blinked brightly, anything enormous or tempting or even dangerous, up to a point. Following him was like swimming in a sea of ghosts from a time of my life that was suddenly furiously *there* again.

None of the kids noticed us. Perhaps because we were adults moving through their world—which meant we were invisible. What we did was of no concern to them.

"Where are we going?"

"Outside."

We walked down the hall to the back door and out to the school parking lot. It smelled of dust and fresh asphalt. It was a hot, still day. The weather would probably change later, because everything felt too thick and heavy. Insects chirred around us. The mid-afternoon sun glinted off a hundred car windshields. James stopped to get his bearings, then started off again. I had questions, but he clearly had a destination in mind, so I held my tongue and followed silently. We wove in and out of the cars and motorcycles. Here and there I recognized one from so long ago. Mel Parker's beige VW. Al Kaplan's Pinto with all the bumper stickers on it. One read: NEVER TRUST ANYONE OVER THIRTY.

James walked to the other side of the lot and only then did I see where he was going. The old green Saab his parents gave him when he got his driver's license was parked near the exit to the street. How could I forget? He always parked his car there so we could make a quick getaway after school. I saw two people sitting inside.

James was sitting inside. Eighteen-year-old James, and a policeman. Although it was very hot, the car windows were rolled halfway up, but I could hear what they were saying. The policeman was talking. His voice was slow and genuinely sorrowful.

"There were two of you up there at the Swid house last night, James. You and a girl. So don't keep denying it because then you're insultin' my intelligence. People saw you two and wrote down your license plate number. Are you going to tell me who she is? It'll make it easier on you."

"I was there alone, really!" James's voice was respectful, eager to tell the truth.

The cop sighed. "Son, it's going to be very hard on you this time. We've let you get away with a lot of crap over the years, but not this time. You broke into a rich man's house and people saw you. You're definitely going to have to do some hard time for it. Maybe if you tell me who the girl was, I can talk to the judge—"

"Honest to God, it was just me. I don't know why they saw me with anybody."

Adult James asked me, "You don't remember this, do you?"

"No."

"Senior year. Two months before graduation. We went out one night to eat ice cream. I told you I wanted to do this—" He gestured toward the car. "—sneak into the Swids' house and look around. You were supposed to say yes, Miranda. We were supposed to go in there and end up having sex. That was to have been our first time. The night that would have changed everything. Because the next day I was *supposed* to be arrested. Arrested and sent to prison for breaking and entering."

"But we didn't do that, James! What are you saying? What is this?" My voice was shrill and frantic. It knew nothing but still it was denying everything. The sun was in my eyes. Any way I turned, it jabbed me like an accusing finger.

James shook his head, exasperated. "I'm saying everything's written, Miranda. The biggest secret of life: Fate *is* determined, no matter how much you deny or try to fight against it. But you've challenged your fate your whole life. And gotten *away* with it!

"You and Hugh were not supposed to stay together. He was fated to go back to his wife and have that little boy with her. That's what the scene on TV was for: to show you how his life was supposed to have happened. You two were supposed to have a quick, red-hot affair. You were supposed to end up writing postcards from exotic places telling him how much you missed him.

"But none of it happened. You were able to change things. You changed fate. Again. Hugh stayed past the time he was supposed to and then he died. No reconciliation with his wife, no little boy Oakley, mother Charlotte, father Hugh. None of it *happened*, Miranda."

He stopped abruptly and the racket of summer's million insects instantly filled the air. Behind it, young James and the policeman continued talking in the car.

"What about the birthday party I saw the first day we went to the house? What about that little boy?"

"Never happened because he was never born. He was supposed to be born, but he wasn't."

"But you didn't go to jail either! That was good!"

"No it wasn't. That's where I was supposed to have straightened out. The experience would have terrified and changed me forever. I had always been dancing around the flames, being bad, taking chances. But going to jail would have thrown me into the middle of the fire. It would have been hell. When I got out, I was supposed to get a job I liked and meet a woman who was right for me. And then I was supposed to have died an old man." He chuckled, but it was a black, bitter sound. He pointed to one side of his nose. "See this mole? The little one? When I was old it went cancerous but I didn't take care of it and it killed me." The same chuckle, even more venomous. "Not a hero's death, but nicer than driving a car into a pylon when I was barely thirty, chasing after a mean bitch with Russian poetry tattooed on her wrist."

A loud bell clanged inside the school. Within seconds, doors slammed open and hundreds of kids flooded out. Almost instantaneously the parking lot was filled. Cars started, horns honked goodbye, kids shouted and talked, hurrying toward the street and freedom. The necessary part of their day was over, and after hours in class, all were eager to get to the good part.

James and I watched them leave. It didn't take long. I remembered that from the old days. You were out of the school building and somewhere else as fast as you could move.

Minutes later a few stragglers still stood around the back door chatting with my old chemistry teacher, Mr. Rolfe. A bunch played basketball at the other end of the lot. Several cars remained, including the green Saab. The policeman and young James continued talking. It was supposed to be the first day of the rest of his life.

But it never happened. Because of me.

FEVER GLASS

MCCABE AND I looked at each other, waiting to see who would go first. The nurse at the reception desk had given us directions to the room, but once we'd stepped out of the elevator, we stood still, each hoping the other would make the next move.

"Go ahead."

"That's okay. You first."

"What was the room number again?"

"Ten sixty-three."

Unlike other hospitals or rest homes I'd visited, this one smelled altogether different. It was unnerving. None of the blunt, spiritless odor usually so prevalent in those places—disinfectant, medicine, and sickness mixed together so that it reeked of nothing good, nothing that gave comfort. Unable to stop myself, I raised my head and sniffed the air like a hound trying to recognize a scent.

McCabe saw me and spoke without hesitation. "Turkey. Smells

like a turkey dinner in here. I noticed it first thing when we came in. Come on, let's find Frances." He started down the hall looking left and right for room 1063.

I HAD AWOKEN in bed in the Crane's View house fully dressed, a quilt over me, head on a pillow, arms at my sides. Normally it took time for my mind to clear, but not *that* morning. Instantly I remembered what had happened the night before with Hugh and his family on the kitchen television, and then going with James to visit our old high school.

All my life people joked that I looked dead while sleeping because of the position in which I lay. Once settled and asleep, I usually never moved. This morning I lay wondering how I had managed even to reach the bed. Then the telephone rang. Picking it up, I didn't recognize McCabe's voice until he identified himself and said Frances Hatch was in the hospital. She had called him from there and asked that both of us come to see her as soon as possible.

His voice was edgy and irritated. "What I don't understand is why she's not in Manhattan. She's up in a place near Bronxville called Fever Glass or something. Strange name like that, but I've got it all written down. She gave me directions. Can you be ready in an hour? I'd like to get going."

THE BUILDING WAS one of those expensive, ludicrous copies of a Tudor mansion only rock stars and other momentary millionaires buy or build these days. First we passed through high, scrupulously trimmed hedges that hid the grounds from the street. Then, at the top of a long curving driveway, Fieberglas Sanatorium sat on a small rise amid acres of beautifully tended land that must have cost a fortune to maintain. Looking around, you got the feeling it could have been a golf course, an expensive research facility, or a cemetery. Or maybe all three in one.

McCabe pulled into one of the many empty parking spaces in front of the main building and turned off the motor. He had been playing a Kool & the Gang CD and the abrupt silence was unsettling. It emphasized, Here we are and now we have to do something.

He looked in the rearview mirror and ran his hands through his hair. "Pip-pip. Tut-tut. This place is all English wannabe. They *wish* they were *Brideshead Revisited*. Wouldn't wanna be sick here. I'm sure they're big believers in high colonics."

I looked out the window. "You're sure she's here? It doesn't look like a very Frances place."

"True, but this is it."

We got out and walked across immaculate white gravel to the front door. McCabe opened it and motioned for me to enter. Inside, I was surprised to see large numbers of people milling about the entrance hall. Some were in robes and slippers, others were fully dressed. We went to the reception desk and asked for Frances. Checking a computer, the nurse apathetically tapped a few keys. I glanced at McCabe. He was a handsome man, no doubt about it. I wasn't crazy for the gelled hair, but in his double-breasted suit, white shirt, and black silk tie he looked very dashing.

"I'm sorry, but she's not allowed visitors right now."

McCabe took out his police badge and held it up for the woman to see. When he spoke, his voice was low and kind but there was no mistaking the authority it carried. "Just tell us the room number. And the name of her doctor."

The woman twitched uncomfortably in her chair. But there wasn't much she could do. "Ten sixty-three. Dr. Zabalino."

"Zabalino. That's great. Thanks very much." He took my arm and neither of us spoke until we'd reached the elevator across the hall. He pressed the orange button and stared at his feet.

"What if she really *is* too sick for visitors?"

The doors slid opened. The car was empty. We stepped in and they shut quickly. I pressed three.

"Miranda, how long have you known Frances?" He stood too close to me but I didn't mind because it wasn't male-female or sexy in any way. McCabe was in close on all accounts; he touched, he poked, he patted people on the shoulder. Most of the time I don't think he even knew he did it. He also spoke in a tone of voice that said he knew you intimately; you could tell him anything and it would be okay. He made contact in all ways, and even if you had done something wrong his touch or voice held you in place. It was nice.

"Not that long. A few months. Why?"

"I've known her twenty-five years. She's the world's most independent person. But when she does ask for something, do it and don't let anything stop you. She calls up and says she wants to see us here? We *run,* Miranda."

Several doors were open as we walked down the hall. In one room a very old man lay in bed with his eyes closed. Seated next to him on a wooden chair was a small girl. She wore a large red watch on her wrist and stared at it, eyebrows raised. She spoke to the old man and I realized she was counting seconds for him. Although his eyes remained closed, he was smiling.

Two doors down I was startled to see a small black dog sitting alone in the middle of a perfectly made bed. There appeared to be no one else in the room. I couldn't resist touching McCabe's sleeve and pointing. When he saw it he did a double take and stopped.

"What the hell?"

The dog saw us and yawned. McCabe stepped to the door and peered at the small shield giving the patient's name. "Frederick Duffek. Is a Duffek a breed of dog?" He took a step to the right so he stood in the center of the doorway. "Frederick? Where's your master?"

"Yes?" A gigantic middle-aged man appeared from behind the door a foot from McCabe. His bald head shone like it was oiled and he wore pajamas the color of old ivory. McCabe wasn't fazed. "Hey! I saw your dog there on the bed and was wondering—"

The man put a hand on McCabe's chest, pushed him back out into the hall, and shut the door in his face. Frannie looked at me, delighted. "What a fucking nutty place, huh? That guy looked like Divine. Maybe the dog's part of his therapy."

"Maybe we should find ten sixty-three."

But there was one more snapshot before we reached Frances's room, and that one stayed in my mind. All the other doors on the hall were closed except the one next to 1063. It was wide open.

Inside was a young woman. On first sight, her back was to us. She wore a baggy black sweat suit and her legs were spread wide. She looked like an inverted *Y*. On the floor in front of her was a very large blue-gray stone shaped like a rough egg. It would have been a strange sight anywhere. In that quiet, forbidding place, it was outrageous.

She panted hard three times—hoosh hoosh hoosh—bent down, and like a seasoned weightlifter hoisted the stone up to her stomach. Then she blew out the same three short pants and lowered it to the floor. Pause, then three pants and up again. McCabe hissed, "Jesus!"

The stone was almost to the floor. Letting it thud down, she spun around. She was remarkably beautiful.

"Dr. Zabalino?" She had a marvelous smile. When she saw us, it fell noticeably. "Oh, hello. I thought you were my doctor."

McCabe stepped into the room and looked quickly behind the door to check if anyone else was there. "Why are you lifting a rock? In your hospital room? Is that good for you?"

"It's part of my meditation."

"*Meditation?* Who's your guru, Arnold Schwarzenegger? Ooh!" He smiled lewdly and reached into a pocket. "My telephone's ringing. I love vibrating phones. I could let it ring all day." He took out a small gray one. It sprang open in his hand. "Hello? Well, hi, Frances. Where are we? Not far. We could be there in, oh, eight seconds. Yeah, we're here. Next door to you, with the woman who picks up the rock? Uh-huh. No problem." He closed the phone and looked at me. "Frances says she'd like to talk to you first. I'll wait outside."

The woman put her hands on her hips and frowned. "Excuse me, but who *are* you two?"

Walking toward her, McCabe spoke quickly, as if he didn't want her to get a word in edgewise. "We're visiting your next door neighbor, Frances Hatch. Would you mind if I tried that before we go?" Bending down, he put his arms around the stone and made to jerk it up. His eyes widened and he spluttered. "How heavy is this thing?"

"Seventy kilos."

"A hundred and fifty pounds! You can lift it up and down like that? How do you do it?"

I caught his eye and gestured I was going. The woman asked me to close the door. Outside, I walked the few steps to Frances's room. As I reached for the knob, someone nearby went, "Psst!" and I looked up.

Hugh and Charlotte's little boy stood in a doorway across the hall. He wore the same striped swimsuit he'd had on when I saw him on television in the kitchen. His feet were bare. Worse, there was a small puddle of glistening water beneath each foot. As if he had just stepped dripping wet out of a swimming pool.

Instinctively, I looked at his hands to see if he held another rock.

"I'm not gonna go away." His voice was a child's, and held the terrible note of unending threat only a child's voice can. Do you remember that? Do you remember how frightening and all-encompassing it was to be threatened by a classmate you hated because you feared them all the way into the marrow of your bones? You knew you could never defeat them, never, because they were stronger or prettier (or stronger *and* prettier), or smarter or bigger or horribly, monstrously mean. And because you were young and knew nothing of life, you knew this person your own age—seven, eight, nine—would always be nearby and a permanent menace until the day you died.

That is what I felt and the feeling was not small. A paralyzing dread came over me because this boy did not exist but was there nevertheless, ten feet away, looking at me with loathing in his eyes.

He began to sing. "In Dublin's fair city / Where the girls are so pretty—" His voice was sweet, mischievous.

I took a step toward him. "I don't know what you *want* from me! What can I do? What do you want me to do? I don't understand." Unintentionally I reached out toward him. Arm extended, palm up, a beggar's hand: Please help.

His face was blank. He gave me a long look, then stepped out of the doorway and walked away. His feet left wet prints on the linoleum all the way down the hall. He began to sing again. "—I first laid eyes on Sweet Molly Malone."

"Please stop."

Nothing.

"Tell me what I can do!"

He never turned. Reaching the door, he pushed it open and was gone.

WHEN I ENTERED the room, an imposing woman stood above Frances, taking her pulse. She had a big sweep of lustrous black hair spun up and around her head like a cone of soft ice cream. Thick eyebrows, large eyes, small features, white skin. She wore a black Chanel suit that contrasted vividly with numbers of gold rings on her fingers and bracelets on her wrists. If I saw her on the street I'd have thought, Money, showoff, businesswoman, or wife with an attitude. Attractive without being special, her black eyes announced she knew exactly what she was doing. When she spoke the timbre and authority of her voice reinforced that.

"Can I help you?"

"Doctor, this is my friend Miranda Romanac. Miranda, Doctor Zabalino."

The doctor turned one of the bracelets on her arm. "The boy is telling the truth: he *won't* leave. You must make him go away."

Appalled that she knew what had happened outside, I barked back, "How do you know about that? Who are you?"

Frances feebly propped herself up on her elbows. "Don't be afraid, Miranda. I called you here because I'm sick. Very sick. The doctor says I might die, so I have to tell you some things. It's essential you know them.

"The first is, if anything happens to me, Zabalino can help you. If you need advice, or a place to stay, you can always come here and you'll be safe. From anything.

"But now you have to go back and live in the house. Stay there until you've found who you are. After that it's your decision whether to stay or leave."

"What am I supposed to do there? Help me, Frances. Give me some direction!"

"I can't because I don't know. But the house is the key, Miranda. The answers are all there."

"Is that why you gave it to us?"

She shook her head. "No, but it's the place where Hugh died and that's its importance. The same thing happened to me in Vienna with Shumda fifty years ago. I had to stay until I discovered who I was.

"Tell Frannie I can't see him today. But tell him his wife is very ill and must have a thorough examination. She can still be saved but *must* be checked immediately."

The door opened and McCabe strode in like the mayor of the place. "Hiya, Frances. What's going on, girls? Am I supposed to stay next door with Rock Woman?"

I heard something. I couldn't recognize *what* but instinctively knew it was bad. The way your head snaps back from a revolting smell before the brain registers.

The noise got louder.

"What is that?"

They all looked at me. The women traded glances.

McCabe shrugged. "What's *what*?"

"Don't you *hear* it? That breathing sound? Loud breathing?"

He rubbed the side of his chin and smiled. "Nope."

Frances and the doctor were not smiling. They looked as upset as I felt. "Miranda, you have to go. Right now, get *out* of here! Take Frannie. Go back to Crane's View. Go to the house."

McCabe was facing me, his back to the two women. "What's goin' on?" He looked happily baffled, as if a prank was being played on him.

Behind him, Frances called his name. He turned. Nothing passed between them—no look, touch, word, or gesture. But he suddenly spun back to face me and his expression was four-alarm fire. "We gotta get out of here! Miranda, come on. Come *on!*" He took my arm and tried to push me toward the door.

I hesitated now, certainly frightened, but also determined to find out something. "What is it, Frances? What is that breathing sound?"

Zabalino spoke in a warning rush. "It's *you*. It's part of your self waiting outside. You must go now and find answers. It won't hurt you, or us, if you leave now."

"But Frances said if I was in trouble I could come here—"

"Later. Not now. Until you find out certain things and then decide what to do, none of us are safe while you're here. It's waiting. It can't touch you while you're inside. It's as close as it can get and wants you to know that. Fieberglas is a haven, but not for you yet.

"Frances never should have asked you here. First you need to know who you are. Until then, it—" Zabalino pointed outside, where a frightening and unknown part of myself was breathing loud and close against the walls of this dubious place.

Fear made my feet feel like they weighed two hundred pounds. Strangely, a line from childhood shoved its way to the front of my mind and kept shouting itself over and over. It was the Big Bad Wolf's threat to the Three Little Pigs as he stood hungry and full of murderous confidence outside each of their houses, knowing he was about to eat the inhabitant: "I'll huff and I'll puff and I'll blow your house down."

"Miranda, come *on*." McCabe took my arm. I shook him off.

"Frances, did I cause Hugh's death?"

"No, definitely not."

"But you have to help me! I don't know what's happening!"

Outside the noise got louder. The breathing faster, somehow thicker.

"Go back to Crane's View, Miranda. The answers are there. If not, then I don't know anything. It's the only thing I can tell you that might help." She was about to say more but Zabalino touched her arm to stop. Frances Hatch licked her thin lips and stared at me with pity. And apprehension.

WHEN I WAS a girl I contracted meningitis. One summer day I came in from playing with Zoe Holland to tell my mother I had a headache and my neck hurt. She was watching television, and without taking her eyes from the set, she told me to go lie down. When her program was over she would come in and take my temperature. I went to my room and quickly fell asleep. When my mother came in she could not rouse me. The most interesting part of the experience was that although I had slipped into a coma, all the while I was completely aware of what was going on around me. I simply could not react to it. When mother panicked because she could not wake me up, I heard everything. I just couldn't open my eyes or mouth to say, I'm here, Mom, you don't have to scream.

I was aware of the ambulance men coming in and working on me, of being carried out of the house and the sounds we made while leaving, of the ride in the ambulance to the hospital, everything. It was not like a dream so much as like being behind glass or some kind of thin curtain, half an inch away from the regular goings-on of life. Two days later I woke from the coma when I felt the urge to go to the bathroom.

Riding back to Crane's View with McCabe, I thought about those days and what it had been like to be conscious but in a coma at the same time. There but not there—cognizant but completely cut off. Now much the same thing was happening. Since witnessing the phantom boy's birthday party, I had been watching my life take place from the *other side* of something. Something impenetrable and mysterious. My life was *over there,* not where I was. Or it was life as I had once known it. And there was nothing I could do to get back to it. What would going back to the house in Crane's View do to help? But what alternative did I have?

THE ACCIDENT MUST have happened only minutes before we came around the bend. Smoke was still rising in a sinuous cloud from beneath the crumpled silver hood. A sharp thick smell of hot oil and scorched metal filled the air. The song "Sally Go Round the Roses" blared from inside the car. No one else was around. The song bored through the strange silence surrounding us on that narrow road a few miles outside of Crane's View.

McCabe cursed and slewed hard to the right a hundred feet

behind the wreck. We bumped onto the unpaved shoulder of the road and stopped amid a loud whirl of flying stones and dirt. Without saying anything, he jumped out and ran across the road to where the BMW was rammed so hard into the telephone pole that its front end was two feet off the ground. Some kind of grim liquid dripped steadily out the bottom of the car. I assumed it was water until I saw the dark color. I looked up the length of the telephone pole. Strangely enough, birds were perched on the black wires, looking busily around and chirping at each other. The wires jiggled a bit under their slight weight.

McCabe ran to the passenger's side and bent down to look in the window. I was right behind him, my hands pressed tightly against my sides.

He spoke calmly to whoever was inside. It was almost beautiful, how sweet and warm his voice was. "Here we are. We're here to help. Anybody hurt? Anybody—" He stopped and stepped abruptly back. "Bad one. Bad one." Before he turned to me, I saw inside the car for the first time.

Hugh Oakley was impaled on the exposed steering column. His head was turned in the other direction so I couldn't see his face, thank God. Charlotte Oakley had not been wearing a seat belt and had gone full force into the windshield. The safety glass had stopped her, but her head had hit with such impact that there was an enormous crystal spiderweb on the glass. What was left of her beautiful face looked like a piece of dropped fruit. A section of the black steering wheel lay in her lap, evilly twisted, looking like some odd tool. The child, their boy, was in the backseat, dead too. He lay on his back, both arms above his head, one eye open, one closed. He wore a T-shirt with a picture of Wile E. Coyote holding a stick of dynamite in one paw. The boy's head was bent at a fatal angle. But most important, he was older than when I had seen him only an hour before in the hall at Fieberglas. He had *aged*.

Staring into that car full of bodies, I knew what this was.

What would have happened if Hugh had lived, eventually left me, and gone back to Charlotte? This.

They would have had the boy and been happy for some years. Maybe eleven or twelve, maybe thirteen. Then one day they would go for a ride in the country in their elegant new silver car. And it would end like this: a face like a burst plum, Wile E. Coyote, the wrong beauty of a cracked glass spiderweb.

When McCabe walked back to his car to get a cell phone and call in the accident, my "coma" still surrounded me, protecting me. In any other situation, seeing Hugh Oakley like that would have driven me mad. Now I just stayed by him and listened to the eerie, beautiful song coming from the radio. I didn't even feel bad, because I knew this was not true; this was *not* how it happened. He had died with his hand on my head, quietly, just the two of us, at the end of a summer evening rainstorm. That way was better, wasn't it? Quietly, in love, with the second half of his life to look forward to, living with someone who loved him more than she ever thought possible? I would have given him everything. I would have pulled down planets to make our life work. I looked at him. I had to ask a question he could never answer because he was dead. Dead everywhere. Dead here, dead in my life.

"Which life would have been better for you? Which one would have kept you whole?"

Unconcerned, the birds above us hopped on and off the wires, chatty and busy with the rest of the day.

THE SLAP OF NOW

I RETURNED TO Crane's View with a member of the town's volunteer fire department. McCabe remained at the scene of the accident. After the fire truck and ambulances had arrived and the personnel had done everything they could, he'd arranged for me to go home with a friend of his.

We rode in silence until the man asked if I knew the victims. I hesitated before saying no. He tugged on his earlobe and said it was a terrible thing, terrible. Not only because of the accident, but because the Salvatos were fine people. He had known Al for years and even voted for him when he ran for mayor a few years before.

Baffled, I asked whom he was talking about. He threw a thumb over his shoulder. "The Salvatos: Al, Christine, little Bob. Hell of a nice family. All dead in one crash like that. Heartbreaker.

"Being on the fire department, we gotta be at most of the pile-ups. 'Specially the bad ones. But these are the hardest. You come onto an accident scene, which is bad enough, but then you look in the car for the first time and you *know* the people? Jesus, there they are, dead. I'm tellin' you, sometimes it makes me think about maybe quitting."

I turned 180 degrees in my seat and gaped out the rear window; then I turned back. "But did you look *inside* the car? Did you actually see your friends in there?" It was a demand, not a question, because I had seen it too, *them*—Hugh, Charlotte, the whole horror.

"Sure I saw it! Lady, waddya think I'm talkin' about here? I pulled Al off a steering column that was about two feet deep up his chest! Damned *right* I saw. I was six inches away from his face."

I watched him silently until it was clear he wasn't going to say anything else. I swiveled in the seat again to look out the back window. We were almost to Crane's View.

When we drove through the center of town I remembered how excited Hugh and I had been the day we moved in. We wanted to do everything at once—unpack the truck, go into town and check out the stores, take a long walk to get a feel for what Crane's View was really like. Because it was a nice day, we chose the walk and ended up by the river watching boats pass. Hugh said, "Nothing could be better than this." He took my hand and squeezed it. Then he walked away. I asked where he was going but he didn't answer. I watched as he wandered around, his eyes on the ground. Eventually he leaned over and picked up a small brown stick about the size and width of a cigar. Holding it up, he waved it back and forth for me to see.

"I've been waiting for just the right moment to look for this. Now's the moment. Here with you, the water, the day . . . The perfect time to find my first Miranda stick."

He came over and handed it to me. I rubbed my thumb over its surface and then impulsively kissed the stick. "I hope there will be a lot more."

He took it back and slid it into his jeans pocket. "This is one of the big ones for me. I've got to take care of it."

I GOT OUT of the car wondering where Hugh's stick was. I waited until the car had gone around the corner before I turned to look at our house. I felt nothing—no dread or anxiety, not even the slightest shred of curiosity. Judging by the events of the last two days, there was no other option but to go back inside and face whatever was waiting for me.

Staring at the place I had so recently and happily thought would be our house, our *home,* for the rest of our lives, I remembered something Hugh had done that disturbed me.

One night in my New York apartment, he called to me from the bedroom. When I got there, he stopped me with an arm across the door.

"Do exactly what I tell you, okay? Look quickly and tell me what you see on the table next to the bed. Don't think about it. Just look and say."

Puzzled, I complied. Something dark and odd-shaped was exactly where my bedside lamp usually sat. I squinted once to see better but it didn't help. I had no idea what it was. My wondering went on until he dropped his arm, walked to the bed, leaned over, and switched the lamp on. It *was* my lamp, only he had laid it on its side in such a way that it was impossible to recognize from a distance.

"Isn't that strange? Just the smallest twist of the dial away from normal—one click—and everything we know for certain vanishes. Same damned thing happened to me this morning. There's a vase in the office we've had for years, a nice Lalique piece. But someone knocked it over or whatever. When I saw it like that today, on its side, it was unrecognizable. I couldn't tell *what* the thing was. I stood in the hall glued to the spot, wondering, What-the-hell-is-that? Then Courtney walked up, righted it, and there it was again—the vase."

I wasn't very wowed and he must have seen that in my expression. He put both hands on my face and squeezed my cheeks. "Don't you see? Nothing is ever finished. It's all evolving; everything has a hundred new angles we've never seen. We get jaded, but then something jarring like this happens and we're bewildered by it, sometimes even pissed off, or delighted. That's what I keep trying to be—delighted by what I don't know."

It was a sweet and very Hugh insight, but it didn't do much for me. I kissed him, straightened the lamp, and went back to cooking our dinner.

That night I was awakened from a deep sleep by a touch—across my face, between my legs, up and down my side. My tingling body and foggy mind were rising in happy concert and I was moaning. When it happened, either the sound or the cause froze me and I threw my arm out to the side as hard as I could. It smacked Hugh on the forehead a great resounding *wap!* Crying out in surprise, he fell back holding his head. A moment later we were laughing and touching and then ended up doing what he had intended in the first place.

Afterwards, Hugh went back to sleep but I was marooned awake. In the silent boredom of three in the morning, I reran the events of the day, remembering what had happened earlier with the crooked bedside lamp and what he said about it. Waking to his touch was the same thing. Unlike him, I had not been delighted by what I didn't know. On the contrary: unexpectedly caressed by my lover in the middle of the night, I had come awake swinging. Unable to stop the line of thought, I scrolled through other memories, realizing I could apply this dismal insight all over the way I had lived. I lay there feeling as stiff and inflexible as an old woman's neck.

ON THE SIDEWALK in front of our house, I remembered this. What would Hugh have said? What would he have done if he'd been in my shoes the last few days? I didn't know anything about what was going on in my life anymore. He was dead and that same crooked lamp sat by our bed upstairs. Such a nice house too—square and solid like a dependable aunt. With a porch that was perfect for a hammock and small talk, iced tea in the summer, a battered bicycle leaning against the wall. A porch for children to play on. If I closed my eyes I could hear kids chasing each other across the wooden floor. Be careful! Slow down! How many children would we have had? How many bikes would have been leaning against the wall, sleds?

I took a step toward the house, hesitated, then took another. Finally I took big fast strides. A car horn honked nearby. I jerked my head but raced up the stair. At the top I avoided looking in the windows. What if there had been something inside, something new that would deter me from going in again?

Jamming my hand into my back pocket, I pulled out the New York Mets key ring Clayton Blanchard had given me when I worked for him. Just thinking his name calmed me some. If there was still Clayton, then there was still New York and old books, some kind of order that existed, hot coffee and cold soda, a place where you could step and not fall off the edge of the suddenly flat earth. Love was in that place, sanity too. I needed to get back there both for myself and our child. Memories and this baby were Hugh's legacy to me. Neither could function in the strange reality I had been shoved into.

I put the key in the lock and turned. Or tried. Because the key would not turn. *Could* not turn. I tried again with no success. I twisted the doorknob. It would not turn but it was warm. As if someone had been holding it just before I touched it. I shook it, pushed in and out, tried the key again, tried turning the knob. Nothing.

Leaving the key in the lock, I stepped over to one of the windows and looked in. Nothing. Inside, the house was dark. I could just make out the shadowy shapes of our furniture in the living room: Hugh's new chair, the couch. Without warning I felt a sheer need to be inside the house, no matter what waited in there. I went back to the door and tried everything again, this time with the fury and strength of impatience—the lock, the knob, push, shake. Nothing.

"Temper, temper! What are you doing, trying to kill the door?"

Both hands on the knob, I looked over my shoulder. McCabe stood on the sidewalk with his arms crossed. He slipped a hand into a pocket and took out a pack of cigarettes.

"What are *you* doing here? I thought you had to stay . . . back there."

"I did what was necessary. You tell what you saw; they fill out their forms. . . . Only so much you can do. I was worried about you, so I thought I'd come by and see if you were all right before I went down to the station."

"Thanks for your concern! Listen, did you know the people in that accident?"

"The Salvatos? Sure. She and the kid were sweet, but Al's no loss to mankind."

"Salvato? That was the name? They're from Crane's View?"

"Yeah. Al owned a couple of stores downtown. Green Light Al Salvato. We grew up together. Why?"

"I . . . don't know. When I looked in the wreck, I thought I knew the people."

McCabe took a deep breath and let it out quickly, his cheeks puffed out. "That's a tough moment for anyone. Especially if it's your first time. I never get used to it. I guess you were confused."

I knew full well it *was* Hugh and his family in the silver car. There was no doubt about it.

"I saw you fiddling with the key. Is there a problem?"

Gesturing toward the door, I gave a defeated laugh. "I can't get into my house. Something's wrong with the lock. The key won't turn and neither will the doorknob."

"Can I try?" Flicking his half-smoked cigarette away, he climbed the stairs to the porch, took the key, and tried it himself. Once. Nothing. It was a small gesture but I liked him for it. He didn't try to be a *man* about it by fooling with the key for five minutes until the lock submitted and he had shown me up. He tried once, failed, handed back the key.

"You got two choices, then. We call a locksmith for, like, fifty bucks even though I know a guy who'll give you a discount. Or you can pretend you don't see this. . . ." He brought something out of his pocket and showed it to me. A lock pick—I recognized it from a hundred TV shows. "You want to give it a shot?"

"I'm happy to save fifty dollars."

"Well, let's see."

He slipped the awl-like thing into the lock and wiggled it around a couple of times. He stopped, made one more small movement with his hand, and there was an audible click. He turned the knob and the door opened.

"Cha-cha-cha." Standing back, he made a sweeping gesture toward the door. "Open sez me."

I started in but stopped. "Look, I'm sure you've got a million other things to do. But would you mind coming in with me just for a few minutes? I'd feel so much better if I had company in there awhile."

He looked at his beautiful watch. "Sure, I got time. We'll give the place a once-over." Without waiting he walked in. A moment's hesitation and then I followed.

"Uh-oh, did you leave something on the stove?"

"No."

"We better look in your kitchen first." He went right toward it. For a second that confused me until I remembered McCabe had often been in the house when Frances lived here.

As if reading my mind, he said, "This house used to be full of weird smells. You never knew what would hit you when you came in. Sometimes ambrosia, sometimes Perth Amboy. Frances ever make you pecan pie? Sometimes great, other times absolute dog food. You'd be cleaning your teeth for three days. She was the damndest cook. Great soups, terrible meat. Never let her cook you meat! Once for my birthday—" He shoved the kitchen door but nothing happened.

"You lock this?"

"No."

We stared at each other.

"Interesting." He pushed again, but nothing happened. Under his breath he began whistling the Beach Boys song "Help Me, Rhonda." He slid his hands into his pockets and immediately took them out again. He gave the bottom of the door a small kick that sounded way too loud in the silent house. He whistled some more. "This is interesting. Maybe it explains why you couldn't get in from outside." Taking a magenta credit card out of his pocket, he slipped it in the crack between the door and the frame and slid it upward. There came a small metallic *tink* on the other side.

"There you go! I remember there's a hook and eye on this one because I put it in for Frances years ago." He pushed the door open.

First came the smell, then the smoke. Not much of it but enough to stiffen the neck and make you scared. Brave McCabe walked straight into the room. Seconds later there was a metallic scraping, a crash, and he fell down right in front of me.

"What the *fuck*—"

Pieces of metal covered the kitchen floor; glass too. Some were whole, others broken or in jagged fragments. Many were blackened, others actually smoking. The largest was immediately recognizable— a silver trunk lid from an automobile with the BMW insignia emblazoned on it. There were more silver pieces among the others—the silver of Hugh's wrecked car.

McCabe stood up, hands bleeding. Dazed, he looked at me. "What is this shit?"

I knew what it was. I knew too well. I never should have brought him into the house. Whoever was in here, whoever was *in charge,* wanted me alone in the house. Without knowing it, I had broken the rules. Now poor McCabe and I would pay for my mistake.

I turned and walked quickly out of the room to the front door. Of course it was locked. I grabbed the doorknob and tried turning it, but nothing moved, not an inch. It felt welded shut. I knew it was useless to try finding another way out of the house.

I went back to the kitchen. McCabe stood at the sink washing his hands. He did it slowly and precisely. Despite what was happening, he appeared in no hurry. I couldn't think of anything to say because whatever came out would sound absurd.

With his back to me, he murmured, "It's here again, isn't it? That's what this is all about." He took a red dish towel off a hook by the window. Drying his hands, he waited for my answer.

"I don't even know what *it* is. Strange things have been going on ever since Hugh and I moved in."

"Is that why Frances wanted us to come see her? Tell me the truth, Miranda."

"Yes. But how do you know about it? What is it?"

"Frances called it the Surinam Toad. That comes from some line by Coleridge—the poet? She made me memorize it. 'My thoughts bustle along like a Surinam toad, with little toads sprouting out of back, sides, and belly, vegetating while it crawls.'

"When I was young it tried to kill me, but Frances saved my life. It happened here in the house." He sat down at the table. He slowly looked at the debris around the room and pursed his lips. "Here we go again. I thought all that was over a long time ago. The fuckin' toad is back."

I went to a drawer and took out a box of Band-Aids. I handed them over and sat down across from him. "Can you tell me about it?"

"I *have* to tell you about it now. Remember when you asked me if I knew anyone who had powers? Frances has powers. She—"

There was a loud scraping sound. I jerked in my seat and looked across the room. The trunk lid was moving. It dragged slowly across the floor toward us. The other pieces began moving too. The room was filled with the racket of this terrible slow scraping sound everywhere, the long high screech of sharp metal edges digging a path. A deep white line appeared behind the trunk lid as it gouged a wavy path across the wooden kitchen floor.

I reached across the table, and slid my hand across his cuts. Blood was still oozing from them; it spread onto my fingers. Standing, I walked to the closest piece of metal and wiped the blood across it. The movement, the sound, everything stopped instantly. The silence was immense.

McCabe stuck his hands under his armpits, as if trying to hide them. "What'd you do? Why did it stop?"

I couldn't answer. I wasn't sure. Instinctively I had known how to stop the pieces from moving, but *how* I knew was unclear. My mind worked furiously to put it in focus.

A house! It was like a house I'd lived in all my life. It had a certain number of rooms I knew by heart, every angle, the view from each window. But suddenly this house contained twice as many rooms, all filled with unfamiliar things. But it was my house. It had always been my house—I just hadn't known about these extra rooms and what they contained.

McCabe glared at me, hands still hidden. "Huh? You know things too, don't you, Miranda? How did you know what to do?"

"Blood stops it. I . . . I just know blood stops things."

"Yeah, great. But what now? What the hell happens now?" Without waiting for an answer, he left the room. I stood and listened while he did exactly what I had done—went to the front door and tried to open it. I heard his steps, the door rattling, curses when it wouldn't open.

His steps crossed the floor again but instead of returning to the kitchen, they began climbing the stairs. He was talking but I couldn't make out his words. I looked at the debris around the kitchen and part of my mind thought it was funny. Miranda's junkyard. Come into my kitchen and find a bumper for your BMW. Then I'll make you lunch. Part of you stops being scared when the sane world of a moment ago goes mad.

If Hugh had been in the backyard the other day, he might still be around. I had nothing to lose. "Hugh? Are you here?"

Nothing.

"Hugh? Can you hear me?"

The kitchen door swung open. But it was McCabe.

"Come with me. Hurry up."

I followed him out of the kitchen and trailed behind as he started back up the stairs.

"You like dolls?"

His question was so absurd and out of place that I stopped climbing. "What?"

"Do you like dolls? I asked if you like 'em." His voice was urgent, as if everything depended on my answer.

"*Dolls?* No. Why?"

Narrowing his eyes, he stared at me as if he didn't believe it. "Really? Well then, that's bad news. 'Cause they're in the same room as before. So I guess the same *goddamned* thing's happening again! Only Frances isn't around to get us out this time."

"What are you talking about, McCabe?"

"You'll see."

Then the realization hit me. "I *did*. I used to love dolls when I was a girl. I collected them."

When we reached the first floor he walked down the hall to Hugh's and my bedroom and threw open the door. "*Somebody* likes dolls."

Before moving to Crane's View, we had bought a new bed. There should have been only two things in that room—the new bed and a small leather couch I had owned for years. Nothing else.

Instead, our bedroom was full of dolls. On the new bed, the couch, most of the floor. They were stuck on the walls, across the entire ceiling, the windowsill. They blocked most of the light from coming in the window. Hundreds, maybe even a thousand dolls. Large ones, small; flat faces, fat faces, round; with breasts, without; wearing jeans, dirndls, evening gowns, clown costumes . . .

All of them had the same face—mine.

"Leave me alone in here, Frannie."

"What? Are you crazy?"

"That's what they want. They want me alone in here."

He glared but didn't speak.

"The same thing happened in here with Frances, right? In *this* room. The same thing. Were there dolls?"

His eyes dropped. "No. People. People she said she knew from a long time ago."

I was about to respond when the first voice spoke. A child's, it was quickly joined by another and then another until we were surrounded by a deafening cacophony of voices saying different things at once. We stood in the doorway listening until I began to make out what some of them were saying.

"Why do we always have to go to Aunt Mimi's house? She smells."

"But you *promised* I could have a dog."

"Dad, are stars cold or hot?"

On and on. Some voices were clear and understandable. Others were lost in the surrounding swirl of tones, whines, whispers. But I understood enough. All of them, all of these words and sentences, were my own, spoken in the various voices I had owned growing up. The first one I disentangled was the line about the stars. I knew it immediately because my father, an astronomer, had loved it and repeated it to others throughout my childhood.

My Aunt Mimi *did* smell. I hated visiting her.

My parents finally relented and gave me a dog, which was stolen three weeks later. I was nine at the time.

If I had remained in that bedroom long enough, I assume all the words of my lifetime would have been repeated. Instead of life passing in front of my eyes, my words were entering my ears. Some of them tweaked memories, most were nothing but the verbal spew of twelve thousand days on earth. I once read that a person speaks something like a billion words in the course of a life. Here were mine, all at once.

"Go out. Wait downstairs."

"Miranda—"

"Do it, Frannie. Just go."

He hesitated, then put his hand on the doorknob. "I'll be outside in the hall. Just outside if you need me."

"Yes. All right."

The moment he closed the door behind him, the room fell silent.

"Miranda, would you do me a big favor?"

There had been so much noise, so many loud and clashing voices seconds ago that this one with its simple question rising so suddenly out of the new silence was especially disturbing. Because it was a *man's* voice and very familiar.

"Sure. You want a backrub?"

"No. I'd like you to go with me to the drugstore."

"Right now? Dog, I've got to be at the airport in a few hours and you know how much I still have to do."

"It's important, Miranda. It's really important to me."

My back was to the door. Turning around, I saw an entirely different room behind me: a hotel room in Santa Monica, California. Doug Auerbach sat on the bed in there. A game show was yapping on the television. Doug was watching me as I came out of the bathroom wrapped in a white towel.

It was the day we went to the drugstore because he'd dreamed about doing that together. The day I flew back to New York and saw the woman in the wheelchair by the side of the freeway.

I stood in the corner watching a part of my life happen. Again. Only this time there were two me's in the room—the one living the moment and the one who watched.

"What's wrong with this picture?" James Stillman said as he walked out of the bathroom. Dog Auerbach and Miranda continued talking. They did not react to him. "Where's Waldo?" James smirked, and that look, that one precise facial expression I remembered so well down the years was as frightening in that moment as anything else.

"Why am I here, James? What am I supposed to do?"

"Stop whining and asking questions. You're here because someone *wants* you here, Miranda. Figure it out! Stop playing the poor little puppy. You waste so much time crying *why me.*"

His voice was cold and mean. I stared at him and he stared right back. I began to move around the motel room, looking carefully at everything, hoping for a clue, listening to the two talk. Light from the window lit the half-filled water glass on the night table. An orange candy bar wrapper lay twisted on the floor. A book. A green sock on the bed.

"Can I touch things?"

James smirked again. "Do whatever you want. They don't know we're here."

I reached out and touched Doug's arm. He didn't react. I shook him, or rather I shook but he didn't move. He continued talking. I picked up an ashtray and threw it across the room. It banged loudly against a wall but neither of them acknowledged the sound.

I walked to the window and looked out. The afternoon sun was a used-up yellow-orange. Out on the sidewalk a bum wearing a brightly colored serape and a black beret pushed a supermarket cart filled with junk. Two kids on skateboards whizzed by. He shouted at them.

The first surprise was that I could hear every word the bum said, although the window was closed. Next was the realization, like a hard, unexpected slap in the face, that I suddenly knew everything about this man. His name was Piotr "Poodle" Voukis. Sixty-seven years old, he was a Bulgarian émigré from Babyak who had worked as a janitor at UCLA for twenty years until he was fired for drinking. He'd had two sons. One was killed in Vietnam.

On and on, my mind flooding with every detail of this man's life. I knew his most intimate secrets and fears, the names of his lovers and enemies, the color of the model motorboat he had built and sailed in Echo Park with his sons when they were young and life was as good as it would ever get for him. Then I saw the room at UCLA hospital where he spent desolate months sitting by his wife's bed as abdominal cancer dissolved her insides until there was nothing left but a dark and fetid pudding.

Everything about him, I knew everything in his now dim and addled brain.

Aghast, I turned away. The second I did, my mind emptied and I was myself again. *Only* myself.

For a moment.

James said something and without thinking I looked at him. At once I saw the rushing view through the windshield of his car as it sped toward his death in Philadelphia. I saw the tattooed words on his last lover Kiera's wrist. I experienced his feelings for Miranda

Romanac—nostalgia, resentment, old love ... all wrapped tightly around each other like leaves on a cabbage.

As with the bum on the street, the moment I looked at James Stillman I became him.

This time I screamed and staggered. Because of a fear that was not my own: James was absolutely petrified of me. Having become him, I knew why he was afraid and what had to be done. I am not a brave person and have never pretended to be, so what I did next was the bravest act of my life. I have regretted it ever since.

Looking around, I saw what I needed, but was so unbalanced that I scanned the room twice more before it registered. A mirror. A small oval mirror above the desk.

I looked into it.

A MAN IN a black suit and floor-length silk cape stood alone in the middle of the stage of a giant theater. He was tall and handsome, immensely alluring in a frightening way. Everything about him was black—his clothes, patent leather shoes, gleaming hair like licorice. Even the intense whiteness of his skin accentuated the darkness. Just looking at him, I knew here was a man capable of real magic.

Staring directly at me, he said my name in a thundering voice. How could he know my name when I had never seen him before this night? With one languid hand, he beckoned for me to join him on stage. I looked at my mother and father, who were sitting on either side of me. Both smiled their permission and enthusiasm. Father even put his hand against my back to move me more quickly. The audience began to applaud. I was terribly embarrassed to be the center of attention, but loved it at the same time. I sidled out of our row and walked down the wide aisle to a short staircase on the side of the stage.

At the top of the stairs an easel supported a large poster announcing the name of the performer:

THE ENORMOUS SHUMDA
SHUMDA DER ENORM
BAUCHREDNER EXTRAORDINAIRE

As I climbed the stairs the audience clapped harder. Worrying I would trip and fall in front of everyone, I walked carefully to center stage, where the man in black stood.

He put up a hand to stop the applause and it died instantly. There was a stop while all of us waited for what he would do next. Nothing. He simply stood there with his hands behind his back. It went on too long. Unmoving, he stared into the audience. We waited restlessly but it went on and on.

Just as people began to whisper their dismay, shifting impatiently in their seats, a dalmatian wandered out onto the stage. It darted back and forth sniffing the floor excitedly and came to us only after it had jittered around like that awhile. Some in the audience laughed or scoffed out loud.

Shumda did nothing to stop the titter. He continued his silence and staring. We stood in front of hundreds of people but the only thing that had happened since I'd stepped onto the stage was the arrival of the dog. When it felt like the whole theater would explode with tension and exasperation, the dog leaped in the air and did a perfect back flip. On landing, it bellowed out in a beautifully deep man's voice, "Be quiet! Have you no manners? What's the matter with you people?"

Deadpan, Shumda looked at the dog, then at me. He gave me the smallest possible wink. He looked back at the audience, same deadpan, and slipped his hands into his trouser pockets.

After the dog spoke, gasps and shocked yelps of laughter burst from the audience.

The dog then sat down and adjusted itself until it was comfortable. It continued in the same pleasingly virile voice that was not at all like the ventriloquist's, "Since you seem displeased with Shumda, I will now take over the show. Master, if you please?"

Shumda bowed deeply first to the audience, then to the dog. It dipped its head as if acknowledging the bow. Then the man in black turned and left the stage.

When he was gone and there was no possible way the ventriloquist could be within fifty feet of the animal, the dog spoke again.

"And now for my next trick, I would ask the young lady—"

Pandemonium. How could the dog speak if the ventriloquist was now off the stage?

The animal waited patiently until the audience quieted. "I would ask the young lady to step to the front of the stage and hold her arms out from her sides."

I did it. Four feet from the edge, I stopped and slowly lifted my arms. Because I was standing so far forward, I couldn't see the dog when it spoke again. I looked out over the sea of attentive faces and knew they were looking at me, me, me. I had never been so happy in my life.

"What is your favorite bird?"

"A penguin!" I shouted.

The audience roared and applauded. Their laughter continued until the dog spoke again.

"A formidable bird, certainly; one with great character. But what we need now is a championship flyer. One with wings like an angel, able to cross continents without stopping."

I licked my lips and thought. "A duck?"

Another gale of laughter.

"A duck is a brilliant choice. So, my dear, close your eyes now and think of flying. It's daybreak; the sky is the color of peaches and plums. See yourself rising off the earth to join your fellow pintails on the journey south for the winter."

I closed my eyes and, before I knew it, felt nothing beneath my feet. Looking down, I saw that nothing *was* beneath my feet: I was a foot, then two, five, ten feet above the stage and rising. I was a child and was flying.

As I rose, I began to float out over the audience. Looking down, I saw people with their heads bent back, all of them staring at me in wonder. Mouths open or hands over their mouths, hands to their cheeks, arms pointing up, children bouncing in their seats; a woman's hat fell off. . . . All because of me.

Where were my parents? I could not find them in the dark mass of heads below.

I continued to float out until I'd reached the middle of the theater. Once there, I rose even higher. How did the birds do this? How heavy humans were! Gently I rose again. My hands were spread in front of me but not far out—more like I was playing a piano. I wiggled my fingers.

My body stopped as I floated seventy feet above the crowd in the center of the theater. No wires attached to my back, no tricks, nothing but the genuine magic of a talking dog.

Time stopped and there was complete silence in the theater.

"What are you doing? Are you mad?" Below, Shumda marched quickly out onstage, looking up at me and then at the now cowering dalmatian.

"But, Master—"

"How many times have I told you? Dogs cannot do these things! You don't know what you're doing!"

Tentative laughter from the audience.

"Bring her down! Immediately!"

But I didn't want to come down. I wanted to stay weightless for the rest of time while people below looked up and wished they could be me. Staring forever, rapt, at me the angel, the fairy—*I could fly!*

"Bring her down!"

I dropped.

Falling, I saw only faces. Horror, surprise, wonder frozen on their faces as they saw me drop straight at them. The faces grew larger. How fast does a child fall? How long does it take till impact? All I remember is fast and slow. And before I was scared, before I could even think to scream, I hit.

And died.

PAINTING HEAVEN

"DARLING, ARE YOU all right?"

The words poured slowly into my mind like thick, glutinous sauce. Brown gravy.

With great difficulty I opened my eyes and squinted hard at the first thing I saw. It was awful. Jarring and fragmented, the colors were a bad, gaudy, incomprehensible mix adding up to nothing but mess. If they had been brass instruments, their squawks and squeals would have made me cover my ears and run away.

But as my head cleared, I remembered with a terrible sinking feeling that what was in front of me was mine—I had painted it. I had *been* painting it for months and months, but nothing I did made it better. Nothing.

Maybe that's why I had been having the blackouts with increasing regularity. Lying on my back longer and longer each day painting the fresco on the ceiling of the church. The church I had connived Tyndall into buying. The fresco that, when finished, was supposed to have convinced the others I was a real painter. Not just everyone's mistress. Not just the great pair of tits who the famous ones let stay because I was always available. The Arts Fucker, as De Kooning called me to my face. But when I was done, they would see. See that I was far, far better than any of them had ever imagined. My fresco would prove it.

It had begun as such a wonderful idea. And the only reason for continuing to see Lionel Tyndall. Let him screw me to his heart's content. Make him crazy for me; make myself into his drug. Then when he was hooked, use him. Use his money and connections to get what I really wanted—the respect of the likes of de Kooning and Eleanor Ward, Lee Krasner and Pollock. Yes, even that bastard.

One of the few interesting things Tyndall ever said was about them, the great ones: They had no empty space around them. He was right. My dream was to bring them here and show them what I had accomplished. How good the heaven was I had painted on the ceiling of Lionel Tyndall's church. The church he bought me out of the deepness of his lust and his pockets.

In a sketchbook, I had written a line from Matisse that became my essential rule: "I tend towards what I feel: toward a kind of ecstasy. And then I find tranquillity." Since beginning the church project, I had done everything I could to follow my instincts, to "tend towards" what I felt. But sadly what I felt was nowhere near what I had painted. Worse, I could no longer imagine even getting close. No empty spaces around them? There was nothing *but* empty space around—and in—what I had created.

What's worse, going through life trying to find your passion but never finding it, or *knowing* what you want but no matter how hard you try, never being able to accomplish it? I had wanted to be a painter for fifteen years and had done everything I could to achieve it. But it hadn't happened, and, horribly, it was beginning to look like it never would.

"Darling? Are you all right?"

Tyndall's voice sniveled up from below and made me shudder. He didn't care if I was all right; he wanted me to come down so we could go outside and make love in his car or under a tree or in the water or somewhere. That was our unspoken deal. He bought the abandoned church outside East Hampton and gave me everything I needed to paint it. In return, I was expected to climb down and play with him whenever he called.

But the blackouts I'd been having? Those dangerous spells once or twice a month where everything simply fell away and I came to with no memory of them happening?

"Why don't you come down and we'll have some lunch. You've been up there since seven this morning."

I stared at the ceiling and thought about his hands, his breath on my neck, the thin musky smell of his body when he got excited.

I turned on my side to look down at him. As I did, there was a loud sharp crack from below. Alarmed, I tried turning completely over. But all at once there was a second crack, a high *wheee-yow* of scaffold metal bending, and everything collapsed.

I dropped.

The last thing I saw, before a metal bar snapped off the scaffolding and flew through my throat, was one of the faces I had painted on the ceiling.

SCREAMING. THERE WAS screaming all around and not just human. Metal—the scream and grind of metal against metal for seconds, then gone. Nothing breaking or snapping this time, only meeting. Meeting for earsplitting seconds in a fast hot sparking touch and gone. We flew. The car rocketed forward. I opened my eyes again onto bright sunlight after the tunnel's blackness. We twisted, rose, turned. A fresh gust of screaming from the children in our car. We went up up up, almost stopped, then fell into the intricate loop and swing of the roller-coaster track.

I looked at James. His hair was flattened against his head. Staring straight ahead, he wore a crazy adrenaline smile. As we sped along I kept watching him, trying to find in his face what had been palpable all day but not clear until now. The moment he turned and looked at me, I knew: I no longer loved him.

It was my eighteenth birthday. James had suggested we go to Playland to celebrate. It had been a wonderful day. We were leaving for different universities in two weeks and had never been closer. But now I knew we would not go beyond those two weeks. No matter what we'd said about writing and calling and Christmas vacation isn't so far away . . . I no longer loved him.

As the roller coaster curved and fled down the track toward the now visible end of the ride, I let out a sob so strange and violent that it sounded like a bark.

"DO YOU KNOW what I love about you?"

We sat on a bench eating cotton candy and watching people pass by. I pretended to be busy working a piece of the sweet pink gunk off my fingers and into my mouth. I didn't want to know what James loved about me, not now, not anymore.

"I feel famous in your arms."

"What?"

"I don't know. I just feel famous when I'm in your arms. When you're holding me. Like I mean something. Like I'm important."

"That's a really nice thing to say, James." I couldn't look at him.

But he took the cotton candy out of my hand and turned my face to his. "It's true. You don't know how much I'm going to miss you next year."

"Me too."

He nodded, assuming we were thinking the same sad thoughts, and that made me feel even worse. I felt my throat thicken and knew I was about to start crying. So I squeezed my eyes closed as tightly as I could.

INSTANT SILENCE. IT was huge after the roar of the amusement park ride. When I looked, thirty-year-old James sat in the bay window across the Crane's View bedroom watching me. All of the dolls were gone. It was once again the room I had shared too briefly with Hugh Oakley.

"Welcome back. What'd you learn on your tour?"

"All those women were me. The little girl flying, the painter, me with you at Playland. . . . All lived different lives but they were the same . . . person inside. And the only thing they thought about was themselves. They were all total egotists. Were there others? Have I lived other lives, James?"

"Hundreds. They would have shown you more of them but you're smart—you saw it with the three most recent."

"And all of the people in them were connected." I touched my ten fingertips together. "Shumda was Frances's boyfriend. The little girl went to his show. And the woman painting the fresco was Lolly Adcock, wasn't she?"

James nodded and said sarcastically, "Who tragically fell to her death just before the world recognized her talent. She died in 1962. Miranda Romanac was born in '62. The little girl died in 1924. Lolly was born the same year."

"You were involved in that scandal about the fake Adcock paintings. And Frances owned a real one."

He pointed at me. "So did Hugh, but didn't know it. Those four pictures of the same woman he had? Lolly painted them when she was studying at the Art Students League."

"They're paintings of the little girl who fell at the theater, aren't they? What she would have looked like if she'd lived and grown up. Lolly thought she was imagining them. That's why I felt so strangely about those pictures. Like I knew the woman in them even though I'd never seen her before."

James winced and drew a short harsh breath. "How do you know that?"

"*How?* For God's sake, James, what do you think I just went through? What do you think all this is all about? Don't play games. I thought you were here to help me."

"No, you're here to help me. Miranda. You're here to get me the fuck out! I'm not here for you—I'm here for *me*. Let me go free, please! I've done everything I can. I've shown you what I know. You knew about those paintings; you knew who the subject was. I didn't. Don't you see? I'm done. I've given you everything I've got. So let me go now. *Free me!*"

"Why is all this happening to me now? Why suddenly now?"

He shook his head. "I don't know."

"Where is Hugh now?"

"I don't know."

"Who am I?"

Leaping up, he started toward me, furious. "I don't know! I'm here because I was supposed to tell you what I knew. What I know is, you're reincarnated. Everything in all of the lives you have lived is interconnected. Everything. And each time you've lived you cared only for yourself. The girl in the theater was a bratty, selfish kid. Lolly Adcock used people like toilet paper. You . . . Look what you did to me, even after you knew you didn't care anymore. And Doug Auerbach. The guy with the video camera who came into your store and hit you. You broke up Hugh's marriage because you were selfish and you wanted him. . . . Always *you first,* no matter what."

"Why did they make you come for me? Who are *they*?"

"Miranda? You all right in there?" McCabe's voice through the door made both of us turn. James gestured toward it.

"Your friend's waiting."

"Who are they, James? Just tell me that."

Lifting his chin, he slowly twisted his head to one side, like a confused dog.

"Miranda, open up!"

"I'm okay, Frannie. I'm coming."

James's voice was a high plea. "Please—*let me go.*"

Without looking, I opened my left hand. Lying on my palm was a small silvery-white stick. Written on it in perfect brown calligraphic letters was *James Stillman.*

It began to smoke. It flared into rich flame. Although it burned brightly in the center of my hand, I felt no heat or pain. It was hypnotic. I couldn't take my eyes away. The flame danced and grew and spread up my arm. I felt nothing.

Someone said my name but I only half heard the man's voice. James? McCabe? I looked up. No one was there—James was gone.

Then pain came like a roaring explosion. My arm was agony. I screamed and shook it, but the flame only ate the wind thus created and blossomed upward. My skin went red, orange, molten, and shiny as oil.

But from somewhere inside, from *someone* I was but had never known, I knew how to stop it. Sweep the fire away like a live cigarette ash. With my free hand I brushed it and the flame that devoured my arm slid slickly down and dropped onto the floor like some kind of jelly.

The door behind me banged open and McCabe was there, pulling me by the collar out of the room. I could barely move. My arm did not hurt anymore. I wanted to watch as the flame spread across the floor, caught on the throw rug and jumped to the bedspread.

"Come on! Come on!" McCabe jerked me and I stumbled backward into him. The bedroom smoked and burned, flames rising high off the blazing bed, licking, blackening the ceiling.

As Frannie pulled I knew what had just happened to me but could not frame it clearly in my mind. When James asked me to free him and without warning I felt the stick in my hand, I was the other person. The one who had conjured stick and flame from nowhere. The one who had lived all the lives and understood why. The one capable of hearing impossible noises in Frances Hatch's building. The one I would soon know too well and fear.

She knew how to free James Stillman and keep pain away from a burning hand. But the moment I heard my name called and looked up, I was Miranda Romanac again and *she* was only mortal.

Out in the hall, McCabe slammed the door shut behind us and looked worriedly around. "Should we try to put it out or just get the hell out of here?"

"We can't get out, Frannie. The house won't let us. It's haunted. By my ghosts now. I brought them in when I came."

He remained silent. The fire crackled two feet away.

"It's the same thing that happened to Frances when I was a kid."

"The same thing?"

"No, but it's the same, believe me. You're right, we can't get out of here now. *You* gotta figure a way to do it."

"What did Frances do?"

"She went to the attic. Did something up there. I never knew what."

I looked toward the ceiling. "There is no attic."

McCabe looked up. "Sure there is, I been there a hundred times."

"It's gone. There's no more attic, Frannie. The house changes."

He opened his mouth to answer but a muffled thumping explosion behind the bedroom door stopped him. "What the fuck are we gonna do, Miranda? We gotta go somewhere!"

"The basement. It's in the basement."

"*What* is?"

"I don't know, Frannie. I'd tell you if I did. But it's in the basement." I saw my arm. The one on fire moments before. There wasn't a mark on it.

"Wait a minute. Just wait a second." McCabe sprinted down the hall and around a corner. Everything stunk of smoke. It poured from beneath the door into the hall, oozing along the floor.

I had been in the basement only a few times. There were two large rooms. Hugh said when we had some money we would do something interesting with the space. Hugh. Hugh. Hugh . . . There was a light in each room down there and one at the top of the stairs. I tried to picture it all and what could possibly be down there that was so important.

Frannie jogged back down the hall looking baffled. "You're right, there's nothing there anymore. Used to be a door in the ceiling with a latch you'd pull and a folding ladder would come down. But it's all gone. There *is* no fuckin' attic!"

"Forget it. Let's go."

"The house is going to burn down and we're gonna be in the goddamned basement!"

I led the way. Down the front stairs, a left turn, and just before the kitchen, the white basement door. McCabe reached for the knob. I stopped him. "Let me go first."

The dank odor of damp earth and stone. A place where the air never changed, a breeze never blew through. Clicking on the light at the top of the stairs did little good. No more than a sixty-watt bulb, it illuminated only a few steps down and then the rest fell away into a brown darkness. I took firm hold of the rickety banister and started down.

"I hope to God someone's called the fire department by now. They're having a busy day."

"Be quiet, Frannie." The only sound then was the muted clunk of our feet going down wooden stairs. At the bottom, the basement floor was bumpy and felt like hard-packed earth. It was about ten feet from the stairs to the first room. The door was half-closed but the light from inside sent a weak ray out across a patch of floor. I walked over and pushed the door open.

Days before, I had helped Hugh carry things into this room. It had been almost empty but for a couple of broken lawn chairs and an archery target with only one leg. We stacked our empty boxes and suitcases against moldy walls and discussed whether we should even try to clean the room a little. Years of neglect had left it looking like a typical moldy basement room where you store unimportant things and promptly forget them forever.

But the room I entered now was luminous, transformed. Painted a happy pink orange, the once-shabby walls were covered with pictures of Disney creatures, giant George Booth bullterriers, Tin Tin and Milou, characters from *The Wizard of Oz*. On the spotless parquet floor sat a pile of stuffed animals and other cartoon characters: Olive Oyl, Minnie Mouse, Daisy Duck.

In the center of the room was the most extraordinary cradle I had ever seen. Made out of dark mahogany, it must have been hundreds of years old; it looked medieval. Particularly because of the intricate carving that covered every square inch of its surface. Angels and animals, clouds and suns, planets, stars, the Milky Way, simple German words carved with the most devoted precision: Liebe, Kind, Gott, Himmel, unsterblich. . . . Love, child, God, immortal. How long had it taken the artist to create it? The work of a lifetime, it said everything about love any hand could express. It *was* love, carved out of wood.

Overwhelmed, I crossed the floor thinking about nothing else but this exceptional object.

"Miranda, be careful!"

His voice and the sight of what was in the cradle arrived simultaneously.

"Oh my God!" The child living in my body, Hugh's child, lay in that cradle. I recognized her the moment I saw her. I touched my belly and began to tremble uncontrollably. None of this was possible, but I knew without question that this was our baby, our daughter. Even my jaw was shaking when I managed to say quietly, "Hi, sweetheart."

She lay on her back in a pajama the same happy color as the room. She played with her fingers and smiled, frowned, smiled, all concentration. She looked like Hugh. She looked like me. She was the most beautiful baby in the world. She was ours.

But she would not look at me even when I moved to the cradle to stare. Having controlled my shaking, I reached down to touch her. As my hand moved toward her, she began to fade. No other way to explain it. The closer I got, the paler she grew, then white, transparent.

When it first happened, I snatched my hand back. She returned. Everything about her became visible again. The cradle, her bedding, the room—all remained as it was, but not our baby. I could not touch her. It was not permitted.

Out loud but only to myself I said, "But I have to touch her. I need to touch my baby!"

"You can't." I looked at McCabe. His face was twisted in fury. "Don't you understand? It's a setup, Miranda! Just figure out what you're supposed to do. We're standing below a burning house. That's the only real thing here."

I could not accept that. I reached for my baby again, but the same thing happened. She faded. She never looked at me. My hand stopped. "She doesn't see me. Why doesn't she see me?"

"Because she's not *here*, goddammit! The room's a trick. The baby's a trick. It's all illusion. Let's get out of here! Let's look in the other room and then get the hell out."

"I can't. I have to stay here."

"Not possible." He stepped around me and picking up the cradle threw it against the far wall. It bounced off, hit the floor, and rolled over face down. One piece broke off and skidded back almost to my foot.

Horrified, I rushed to the cradle and turned it over. It was empty. Aghast, I put my hands in, but there was no child, no blanket or bedding, nothing but the empty smoothness of the wood. I was so confused I didn't even think about McCabe or what he had just done. The baby was gone. Where was my baby?

"Can we go now? They're waiting." The voice behind me was different. I turned and saw . . . Shumda. The Enormous Shumda, Ventriloquist Extraordinaire, Frances Hatch's lover, the man who killed the little girl who was once me. McCabe was nowhere to be seen and I knew why.

"It was you all along, wasn't it? Upstairs, with the fire and the talking dolls? The whole thing *was* a trick; McCabe never came back to the house after he dropped me off."

He bowed. "Correct. I'm good at voices. But we really do have to get going."

"Where? Where's my baby? Where did she go?"

"That's for you to decide. Let's go!"

"I'm not going with you."

"Oh, but you *must*. Clarity awaits, Miranda!" He said it with the exaggerated voice of a bad actor making a thunderous exit.

I didn't move. His expression slid from big smile to not happy.

"It was my baby, wasn't it?"

"Yes. Come along now and you can see her in the next room. She's there."

"I don't believe you."

"You can believe him." Hugh appeared in the door holding the baby in his arms. She was chuckling and hitting his nose with a tiny open hand. "Miranda, you have to do this. There's no other way."

I stretched out both hands to him. Hugh. With our baby.

He smiled. "It's all right, Miranda. Shumda's telling the truth— go with him and it'll help you understand everything." Before he turned and left, his eyes fell on the cradle. They moved to the piece of wood that had broken off. It lay near my foot. He looked at me and I knew he was saying something important.

"All right."

The three of them left. I picked up the wood and slipped it into my pocket. I walked out of the room and across the cellar. The only sound was my shuffling footsteps. The air smelled heavily of dirt and damp. My face was very hot. I could smell my own sweat.

The door to the other room was closed. I grabbed the knob and tried to pull the door open. It was very difficult to move and scraped loudly across the uneven floor. When it was half-open I stopped to take a slow deep breath. I wasn't ready for this but it had to be done. My heart did a few strange misbeats in my chest. I pulled again, hard, and the door came fully open.

What I expected was another room the same size as the last. That's all. No real idea of what would be in there, but definitely not what was there.

A ramp—a wide gray concrete ramp leading upward to lights. Brilliant lights against a black night sky illuminated something I couldn't see yet but which appeared to be . . . a stadium? A playing field? Giant banks of lights at fixed intervals shone down on what I could only guess was a field. I walked through the basement door and onto the ramp.

Stopping there, I looked left and right. It *was* a stadium. Walkways went off to either side and connected to other ramps. I had been to football games in college and later to Yankee Stadium with a boyfriend who was crazy for baseball. This was a very big stadium. I had walked through a door in the basement of my house in Crane's View into the bowels of a colossal sports stadium.

There were no other people around, which made things even more ominous and disturbing. Thirty feet away I saw a brightly lit concession stand, but no one was there—no salespeople or customers.

"Hello?"

Nothing.

What was I supposed to do? I walked farther up the ramp to see what this was about. Hugh said I should do this. Shumda said I could see our baby if I entered this place.

My heart kept misfiring in my chest. I put a hand over it. Okay, it's okay. After a few steps I stopped, and looked over my shoulder to see if the basement door was still behind me. It was. I could go back. I hesitated. But nothing was there; everything was in front of me. I walked up the ramp, into the stadium.

MY FOOTSTEPS ECHOED around me until I was almost at the top of the ramp. Then the noise inside the stadium rose up like a wave. You know it because you've heard it before: at a baseball game or rock concert when you return to your seat after buying a hot dog or going to the bathroom. That big noise is there but it's in the background for the moment. Your own steps are louder till you reach the top of the ramp and walk in. Next twenty thousand people and their life-sounds envelop you in a second. Talk, movement, laughter, shuffling, whistles—all together in one mighty hullabaloo.

The stadium was packed with people. I stood at the entrance and paused to soak up the picture. Thousands of people. Every seat appeared filled. In that first glimpse I did not look at anyone carefully because I was taking in the whole picture. I was surprised to see nothing laid out down on the field, no football goalposts at either end of a marked field, ten-yard line, end zone. No baseball diamond with home plate and perfect white lines marking the base paths. The field was a manicured lawn with nothing but the greenest grass glowing even greener beneath the blazing arc lights. I heard snatches of conversation and laughter, feet scraping across the stone floors, clapping. Someone far away hooted. More. So much more. The human rumble of tens of thousands of people in an enclosed place.

Hugh stood out on the field holding our baby. There was no one else out there but the two of them. They looked so small in all of that green space. He was staring at me but made no gesture for me to join him. I gave a little wave. He made the baby's arm wave back. What was I supposed to do? Why were we all here? Who were these people? What was this stadium?

As these thoughts tumbled around in my head, the noise dwindled, decreased slowly, wound down to almost nothing. It was almost quiet. That's when I looked around to see how others were responding to the new eerie quiet. And something else. Cologne. The scent of an exquisite and very familiar men's cologne made me search for its source. Diptyque. I even remembered the name.

Looking to the left, I was shocked twice. Because everyone was watching me. And because I saw my old friend Clayton Blanchard, the man who had introduced me to both bookselling and Frances Hatch. It was *his* cologne I had smelled. Sitting no more than three feet away, he was dressed beautifully, as usual—perfectly pressed dark suit, multicolored silk ascot, white shirt. I mouthed his name and a silent question: Clayton? Here? He smiled.

Next to him sat a boy I didn't recognize at first. But all at once I did. Like a swimmer struggling up from deep water, my memory rose to the surface, slowly but when it broke through I knew him. Ludger Pooth. That was his ridiculous name. His family lived next door to mine on Mariahilferstrasse in Vienna in 1922. He and his friend Kuno Sandholzer once lured me to the attic of our building and made me pull down my underpants. They thought they were making me do something terrible, but I didn't mind. Just so long as they paid attention to me. Ludger wore a brown tweed golf cap that he kept tugging on. I remembered the gesture very well.

Next to him was another person I didn't initially recognize, but his name too quickly came to me: Viktor Petluchen, the first man Lolly Adcock ever slept with. Scanning the hundreds, the thousands of faces watching at me, I soon recognized everyone I saw. Names. More and more of their names came to me and with them the stories that went with the names.

In my past lives I had known every one of these people. I began to remember those lives, these faces. How we met and parted, what they had meant to me. All of them were in this stadium.

How many people do we meet in a lifetime? How many have an impact on us, and vice versa? Imagine being surrounded at one moment by every person you have ever known—some for an instant, some your whole life. All of them are watching you because the only thing that links them together *is* you. You are their thread.

Now imagine there is reincarnation. Imagine all the people of *all* your lives, together. . . .

It grew even quieter. There was noise, a quick cough, a shoe scraping across the floor, hurried whispers. We were all waiting for what came next. I could not stop looking around because each new face brought back another memory.

These people wore the clothes of their time, so there was an incredible array of dress and looks. Men were decked out in worker's overalls, in rough linen, rags, and double-breasted suits from Hunts-man of Savile Row. Thick mustaches or shaved heads, fur hats, as-trakhans, baseball caps, sandals, wooden clogs, spats, leather boots up to the knees. They carried guns at their sides, briefcases. Women wore high powdered wigs, bonnets, dirndls, floor-length robes, a pink Chanel suit, a T-shirt advertising the rap group Black-Eyed Peas. People's names I had said hundreds of times sometimes hun-dreds of years before came back like forgotten facts: Viktor Petluchen, Henry Allison, Jasna and Flenda Sukalo. Elzbieta Dud-zinska. My friend Dessie Kimbrough, the English ambassador's daughter, who fell from the Reichsbrucke and drowned in the Dan-ube on New Year's Day, 1918. 1949, 1971, 1827, 1799 . . . Each of my lives, all of my years, all the living and the dead people I had ever known, together in that stadium. The thousands and thousands.

When I could bear it, I turned back to the field, feeling their eyes on me, waiting to see what I would do next. Down on the grass Hugh stood next to a young woman I did *not* know. The baby was no longer in his arms. Watching this new woman, I tried to remember her face, but nothing came.

"It's your daughter when she grows up." Hugh's son with Char-lotte, my nemesis, walked up the aisle toward me.

I glared at him, not trusting one word. He sensed it and his expression hardened. "It's true. I don't care if you believe me. Go see for yourself."

I made a wide circle around him and walked down the stairs. There was a small open gate at the bottom. I went through it and onto the field. Hugh and the young woman watched me, smiling. She looked at Hugh and he nodded eagerly. She touched his forearm and came toward me. I stopped and caught my breath.

She was tall and plain-looking and had big hands, my hands. Her smile was lopsided and heartbreaking. She had her father's brown eyes and eyebrows that turned up at the ends.

"Mama?"

As I was about to say "Yes, yes, yes, it's me, I *am* your mother," the world behind us erupted. For an instant our eyes met and I'm sure we both wore the same terrified expression. It was the crowd. The tens of thousands of people gathered together were suddenly screaming their collective fury, their hatred and resentment of me.

Because somewhere in the course of their lives I had selfishly used every one of them. Used them in small or large, forgotten or impossible-to-conceive-of ways to get whatever it was I wanted at the moment. I had loved them and tricked them or hated them and forgotten them, had ignored them, paid them court, stolen their hearts or said no when they offered them. I had gone into their lives blind; I had gone in knowing everything. I took their love, I took their hopes, I took their time, and I paid them no respect.

Some of them had asked for something back, some for a lot back. Each time I gave only what I wanted or had a surplus of and wouldn't miss. They gave what they cherished or what kept them alive, what made them tick or gave them faith. What they got from me in return was nothing, wrapped in a fine empty box with tinsel and glitter on it. Most people steal because they believe what they steal should belong to them anyway. To me it wasn't theft, it was barter: I'll trade you what I don't need for whatever it is about you I want. That's fair.

They shook their fists; some faces were purple or dead pale. One woman was so furious she wept. One man, driven mad, was throwing something at me. Nothing. He held nothing in his hand but was trying to throw something anyway. He did it over and over. Their hatred was crushing, resentment as thick as stone, hot as flame.

And all of it was my fault.

In the midst of this frenzy, Hugh's son walked out onto the field and stopped a few feet from me. Another casualty. A child my self-ishness had stopped from being born. He brought two closed fists

218 / Jonathan Carroll

up to the sides of his mouth. Then his index fingers came slowly out and pointed down. Like teeth. Like fangs.

"You're a vampire."

And I heard the word above the roar because I had already realized that was what this was all about.

I spun around to see if Hugh and the girl had heard, but they were gone. I stood looking at acres of perfect green grass, wishing with all my might they would reappear so I could say something, anything, to them to explain. But there was no explanation. There was only that black word and it was the truth. Vampires take the one thing that keeps a person alive. Sometimes it is blood, sometimes hope, love, ambition, or faith. I took them all.

Behind my back the noise stopped. Not even the sound of the wind. When I turned, only the boy was still there. The stands were completely empty. He stood in the same spot, his hands at his sides.

I took a step toward him but this time *he* pulled back, afraid I would touch him.

I tried to speak but my throat was thick and dry. "What's your name?"

"Declan." He said it beautifully, melodiously, as if it were the easiest word in the world to say. "It's the name of a saint."

I smiled, remembering Hugh and his saints.

"I'm going to go now, Declan. I understand why they wanted me to come here, but I don't need to see any more. I understand everything. Is that all right? Can I leave?"

"I guess. I don't know."

I walked back across the field, through the gate, up the steps past the empty seats. At the top I almost turned around for a last look, but I knew that might kill me and there were things I had to do before I died.

THE HISTORY
OF SHADOWS

OUR HOUSE WAS not on fire when I reached the top of the cellar stairs. No surprise. But what did startle me was how I perceived the house and the objects inside as I walked through it on the way to the front door.

Before Hugh and I ever became intimate and I was wrestling with whether or not I should let myself fall for him, I said, "I don't want to fall in love with you. It would be too big a memory."

Now as I walked through our home, *everything* was too big a memory. From the antique brass letter opener on the side table to the four paintings of young Lolly Adcock on the living room wall, it felt like I was walking through a museum of myself. Almost everything held brilliant, crushing memories of the time when I didn't know the truth about myself, when I was only a woman in love with a man and a vision of life with him I thought sound and possible.

I stopped and picked up things because the impulse was irresistible. A pair of scissors we'd used to open boxes, a postcard from the electric company saying we were now registered customers. Artifacts in my museum, objects and ephemera from a stone age when I guilelessly believed in a just God, believed that people had only one life to live, and evil was a word most suited to the Bible, history books, or silly movies. Charming and quaint as a hand-carved cradle, our house and what it contained was the beautiful dream you had last night that, on waking, you ache not to forget, but inevitably do within minutes.

As I was passing the living room, something nudged my mind and I went in to find a book Hugh had once shown me. *Favorite Irish Names for Children.* I looked up the boy's name.

Heaven gave Saint Declan a small black bell, which he used to find a ship for himself and his followers. Later, that bell overtook the ship and showed Declan where to establish his monastery off the Waterford coast. Declan Oakley. The kind of beautiful name a child hates when they're young because it's strange and foreign-sounding, especially in America. But he would love it when he grew older. Declan. I said it aloud.

"Actually, the formal name is Deaglan. Emphasis on the second syllable." Shumda stood outside on the porch. The window was closed but I heard him perfectly. I hadn't paid close attention to what he looked like the first time I saw him in the cellar. He appeared to be about thirty-five and similar to the portrait on the old poster Hugh had found for Frances. But if he was thirty-five in the 1920s, he would be well over a hundred today. The man on the porch did not look a century old.

"Come outside. It's a nice night."

"Why are *you* here? Where's James?"

"You set him free, Miranda. Remember? Now he's just a puff of smoke. Good closure! Besides, he's not one of *us*. Not one of the chosen few. He's only dead. Dead people are not high on our food chain."

"But why did you come?"

"Because they told me to escort you through the next stage of your . . . pilgrimage. It's more involved, but that's enough of an explanation for now. You know those stories about after-death experiences? How dead loved ones come to greet you and take you toward the Light? Beautiful, and not a word of it is true. But in your case it is, sort of. Although you're not dead. And neither am I." He threw up both hands in quick denial. "That's the beauty part. Oh, I think you're going to like this. It just takes getting used to. Are you going to come outside? Should I come in? Or I'll huff and I'll puff and I'll blow your house down." He ballooned his cheeks and closed his eyes.

"Go away."

He stretched both arms out to the sides hands closed. He opened them slowly and in each was a small black bell. Saint Declan's bell. Fingers extended, he gave each a shake. Their tinkle was light and crystalline. "I can go. But what if you have questions?"

"I don't want you to answer my questions."

Pouting, he jingled the bells again. "Brave girl. Dumb girl." He put the bells on the windowsill, crossed the porch, and went down the stairs to the street. I hurried to the window to make sure he was gone.

Then I picked up the telephone and made two calls. I needed a taxi and I needed to make sure Frances Hatch was still at the Fieberglas Sanitorium.

"I GOTTA TELL you, lady, this ride's gonna cost you money. It's about a half hour, forty-five minutes from here."

"I understand that. Could we go now?"

"You betcha."

We had been under way a few minutes before the cab driver spoke again. "You ever heard about bed mites?"

"Excuse me?"

"Bed mites. Ever heard of them?" We traded looks in the rear-view mirror. "Neither did I till the other day. Was watchin' this documentary on TV about allergies. Ever notice how people think they're intellectual because they watch the Discovery Channel? Not me; I just like finding out about the weird way the world works.

"Anyhow, there was this show on about human allergies. They got a new theory that things called bed mites cause a lot of them. They're these microscopic bugs that live in our beds and pillows, the sheets. . . . They're not dangerous or anything, but they leave *droppings,* if you know what I mean. And it's the droppings human beings are allergic to. Strange, huh?"

Taken aback, I couldn't stop myself from rudely blurting, "Did you make that up?"

"Nah, really, I saw it on this show! They suggested all these ways of protecting yourself if you're allergic. Wrap your mattress and pillows in plastic, get an air cleaner to catch any droppings that might be floating in the air . . . No, it's really true."

Again we looked at each other in the mirror, and he nodded enthusiastically.

"That's horrible!"

"Not for the bed mites."

I laughed. Then I couldn't stop thinking about them, despite all the chaos surrounding my life at that moment. I envisioned a beautiful woman getting into a freshly made bed and falling asleep. And then, like a scene in a David Lynch film, the camera goes in close on her pillow. Closer and closer until we see thousands and thousands of tiny white insects scurrying around, living their lives despite a huge human head in their midst.

I knew from high school biology class the world is infested with horrid microscopic creatures living happily off and in and on human beings but, thank God, we never know the difference. Yet sooner or later some of their droppings or their germs or their simple existences *do* touch us. If we're lucky all we do is sneeze. If we're not, they kill us. The metaphor, especially at that moment in my life, was clear and forbidding.

All the conscious lies and forgotten promises we breed, the cruel gestures, small and large. The lack of gratitude and unwillingness to share, the kindness not repaid, the slight returned. The selfishness, the chosen ignorance, the pointless theft, the fuck-you-I-come-first attitude that taints so much of life. All of them are bed mites *we* create. Growing up, we're taught to accept them as a given. Age-old. Been around forever. They're part of life. But they *aren't* because in most cases when we stop and think, we're instantly aware of how to avoid producing more of these revolting bugs and their shit.

As far as other people's behavior is concerned, we learn how to "wrap our mattresses in plastic"—we learn how to protect ourselves. But more important is filtering our own words and conduct so that our "droppings" don't enter others and make them sick.

What I had learned in one hideous moment at the stadium was that life is not usually ruined by any one crowning blow, KO punch, or single act of savagery. It *is* ruined by the thousands of "bed mites" our cruelty, indifference, and insensitivity breed in the beds of those we love or know.

"Do you have any music?"

He looked down at the seat next to him. "I do, but I don't think you'd go for it. I got Voodoo Glow Skulls and Rocket from the Crypt."

"Could you turn on the radio?"

"Sure."

Thoughtfully, he searched through the channels till he came to classical music. Berlioz's "Roman Carnival" was on, and for a while it calmed my heart. The night landscape did too as it slipped by outside in intermittent patches of glitter and dark. Towns at rest, people going home. A man leaving a liquor store. A boy on a bicycle rode furiously in front us on the road, turning again and again to see where we were, trying to keep ahead, red reflectors on the pedals. The lights in one house came on like an eye opening. A van pulled into a driveway, its exhaust smoke gray over night black.

"That's funny."

"What is?"

"The drive-in movie over there. They usually stop running it at the end of summer. Who wants to go to the drive-in this time of year? It's too cold."

I looked where he was pointing and what I saw meant nothing for a moment. On the giant screen, people bustled around inside a busy store. Then Hugh Oakley entered the picture. Standing in front of a full-length mirror, he tried on a baseball cap. It was the day we almost slept together for the first time, when we went to the Gap store in New York instead and made out in the dressing room. I come up behind him with a pair of trousers in my hand and say something. He nods and follows me to the back of the store.

At a drive-in theater in Somewhere, New York, a scene from a day in my life was showing on a screen forty feet high.

"Look at that, willya? No cars in there! Who are they showing the movie to?"

The parking lot was empty.

"Could you turn the music up, please?"

THE PARKING LOT of Fieberglas Sanatorium was not empty. We arrived around nine at night, but there were still many cars parked. We pulled up to the brightly lit front door. I looked at the building and was surprised at the stillness in my heart.

"Are you visiting someone in there?"

"Yes. An old friend."

The driver ducked his head so he could see the building better through the windshield. "Must have money to be staying in a place like this."

I looked at the back of his head. The hair had recently been cut—it was all precise angles against perfectly white skin. From behind, he looked like a soldier or a little boy. "What's your name?"

"My name? Erik. Erik Peterson. Why?"

"Could you wait here while I go in, Erik? I'll pay you for your time."

"You know, I was planning on waiting for you anyway. Didn't think you'd want to stay around *here* very long, especially this time of night. You'll be going back to Crane's View?"

He turned and smiled at me. A neighborly smile, nothing behind it but a kind and considerate man.

"Yes. Thank you. But I might be a while."

"No problem." He held up a Watchman miniature television. "The last episode of *Neverwhere* is on in ten minutes. Gotta see that."

I got out of the taxi and started toward the door. Behind me he called out, "What's *your* name?"

"Miranda."

"I'll be right here, Miranda. You take your time." I took a few steps and he said, "When we drive back home, I'll tell you about hyacinth macaws."

"Are they related to bed mites?"

"No, they're birds. Another documentary I saw *after* the bed mites." He looked down. The dancing gray-blue flicker of the television screen reflected off his face. I was so glad he was there.

Opening the heavy front door this time, I was immediately struck by how quiet and empty the place was. My leather heels on the stone floors were a a riot of noise. A middle-aged nurse sat at the reception desk reading. No one else was around. I walked over and waited for her attention but she didn't look up. Reading a page of her book upside down, I saw it was poetry. The first line of one poem read: "Bend your back to it, sir: for it will snow all night."

She continued to ignore me.

"Hello? Excuse me?"

"Yes?"

"I would like to see Frances Hatch."

"What room is she in?"

"I don't remember."

The woman sighed mightily and consulted her computer. She said the room number and immediately went back to her book.

"That's a nice line."

She looked up. "What?"

" 'Bend your back to it, sir: for it will snow all night.' It's a nice line. It pretty much says it all."

She looked at me, her book, me. She snapped it shut and grew a suspicious look. I walked away.

The elevator arrived with a *ping* and the doors opened on Frances's doctor. "You're back."

"Yes. I have to talk to Frances. But first I have a question: Could you tell me, what exactly is this place? Who is it for?"

"It's a hospice. Of sorts."

"People come here to die? Frances is going to die?"

"Yes. She's very weak."

"But why here? She loves her apartment so much. Why would she come here?"

"Do you mind if I go up with you? Just up to her floor? Then I'll leave you alone."

"All right." I stepped into the elevator. She pressed the button.

When the door closed, she turned to me and asked in a low voice, "Do you know about your lives?"

"Yes."

"Would you tell me how you learned?"

I briefly described returning to the house in Crane's View, the fire, the stadium, and the word Declan had used there that explained everything. I said nothing about Hugh's and my baby. While I spoke, she crossed her arms and lowered her head almost to her chest. When I finished we were standing near Frances's door.

The doctor slowly shook her head. "Extraordinary. It's always different."

"This is *common*?"

"Miranda, everyone here has experienced the same thing as you. It simply manifests itself differently every time. All of your lives have led you here. Now you must make a great decision. You can stay here as long as you like and you'll be safe. That's one of our purposes—to protect you while you decide. The other function is to care for those who have made the decision and choose to end their lives here.

"Hospices for people like you have existed for as long as recorded history. A hotel in the Pyrenees, a youth hostel in Mali, a hospital in Montevideo. There is an inscription over one of the tombs in the Valley of the Kings in Egypt—"

"What decision are you talking about?"

"Frances will tell you, but I think you already know. All of those people in the stadium hated you because you took something essential from the life of every one of them. People use the word *vampire* because it is something so foreign, so impossible to imagine really existing that we shiver at the thought and then laugh it off as idiotic fantasy. Dracula? Sucking blood and sleeping in a coffin? Silly. But if you look up the definition it says 'one who preys on others.' Everyone does that, but we have nice rational explanations for it. Until you look more closely.

"I think you must talk to Frances now. She'll answer the questions you have." She turned to leave. I touched her arm.

"Wait! But who are you?"

"Someone like you. I was in the same situation as you are but made my decision a long time ago." She touched my hand. "At least you'll have clarity now. I learned how important that is, no matter where it leaves you in the end." She walked soundlessly down the hall and out the door at the other end. The same door Hugh's son had used earlier. Today. All this had happened in one day.

I knocked softly on Frances's door and pushed it open. The first thing that hit me was the perfume. An aroma like the most wonderful flower shop. I hesitated in pushing the door further. The flood of colors and shapes drowned the eyes. For a second I couldn't even find the bed. When I did I had to smile because Frances was sitting up straight reading a magazine, looking totally oblivious to the paradise surrounding her.

Then I heard music. It was classical, lilting and summery, something I had never heard before. It reminded me of Saint-Saëns's "Aquarium." Before speaking, I let my eyes and ears calm down.

Still flicking through her magazine and without lifting her eyes, Frances said, "Close the door, girl. I don't want people seeing me in this nightgown."

"The room is so beautiful, Frances. You always know how to do up a place."

"Thank you. Come in and sit down. There's a chair in here somewhere. Just shift some flowers."

"Who sent them to you?"

"The Shits. But we have other things to talk about. I assume that's why you're here in the middle of the night?"

"Yes. But could you turn off the music while we talk?"

She stared at me blankly, as if I had said something complicated in a foreign language. "The *music*! No, I can't do that. It's piped in. There's no control."

"What if you don't want to hear it?"

She started to say something but stopped. "You grow used to it. Forget the music, Miranda. Tell me what happened to you. And give the details—they're very important."

I told her everything, including seeing Hugh and our child. It didn't take long. It was disturbing to finish as quickly as I did. In the end, each of us has only one story to tell. It takes a lifetime to live that story but sometimes less than an hour to tell it.

The only time Frances showed real emotion was when I told her about Shumda. She grilled me on what he looked like, what he said, how he acted. Normally very pale, her face grew redder as I talked. Eventually she put a hand over her mouth and kept it there until I finished describing the last thing he said to me before walking off the porch. She stared at the window and seemed to be putting both her thoughts and her emotions together.

"Your name in Vienna was Elisabeth Lanz. Your death was the most celebrated scandal of the day because so many people were in the theater when you fell. Shumda was a great star then. People came from all over Europe to see him. The chief of police was in the audience that night and personally arrested him.

"The *Landesgericht*. Shumda used to like to say that word to me when I visited him in his cell. He spoke perfect *Hochdeutsch,* of course. He was a superb ventriloquist because he loved languages. He spoke four. He could be happy just saying words in different languages because they were so delicious to him. Some people love the taste of chocolate; Shumda loved the taste of words. *Landesgericht, crépuscule, piombo, zvinka.* I can still see him: lying in bed after we'd made love, rolling difficult words off his tongue and smiling. He liked to talk as much as he liked to screw.

"He had led a charmed life, so he never truly believed they would punish him for your death. But it was a political year in Vienna and politicians love a scapegoat. Here was this showman, a ventriloquist

230 / Jonathan Carroll

from Romania, who had killed one of the city's young flowers in front of hundreds of people. The case against him was clear. There was no question they would have executed him if I hadn't saved him."

"How did you do that?"

"I traded my life for his."

"How did you . . . What do you mean?"

"Look at your hand, Miranda."

I looked but saw nothing.

"No, turn it over. Look at your palm."

It had no lines. Every one had vanished. My palm was smooth as paper. Smooth as skin anywhere else on your body, but not the hand. Not where your past and future are supposed to be mapped out by fate and will.

Disbelieving, I could not raise my eyes when Frances spoke again.

"Miranda!"

"What is this? Why—"

"Listen to me: There *were* lines on your hand when you entered that stadium. They disappeared when you realized what you are."

"A vampire? When I realized I had lived all these lives? That's when the lines disappeared?" I needed to repeat what she had said so I could fix it somewhere in my reeling mind. Despite the effort to remain sane, my voice teetered on the brink of something very bad. I could barely control myself.

It felt like the big bang theory was being played out all over again—in my brain. Everything I knew was speeding outward toward the farthest reaches of space. Maybe in a few billion years the fragments would have slowed and cooled enough again to allow some life again, but right now they were only flying *out*.

Frances held up her own right hand, palm out. Covering it were lines and ridges, highways crossing and separating, a lifetime of lines on skin, a detailed albeit chaotic map of the many days of Frances Hatch.

"What are you saying, Frances?"

She slowly raised her left palm. It was blank. I looked quickly at my left but it was as blank as my right.

She brought the hands together and folded them in her lap. "Palmists disagree about what the individual lines on a hand mean, but most concede those on the left indicate what you're born with and the ones on the right are what you've done with them. Left hand," she raised her blank one. "Right hand."

"Why are both of mine blank?"

"Because now that you have discovered who you really are, you *have* no fate anymore. Everything from this point on is up to you." She licked her lips. "You're different now."

"From what I learned today, I've been different all my life. All my *lives!*" I said the last word like a hissing snake.

"But now you know the truth about who you are. That changes everything. Now you can do something about it, Miranda. Everything is up to you from this point."

I looked at my smooth palms again, not sure of what to say or ask. "Tell me about you and Shumda."

"I haven't seen him for seventy years. Not since the day I saved him. That's part of how this works—if you sacrifice yourself for another person, you will never see them again. In most cases, because they never want to see *you* again. They don't like to be reminded of what you did for them. But if they're young, they never know it happened, because they don't understand.

"In other respects it's tolerable. *You* simply become a normal human being and live a normal life. You get flu, pay taxes, have kids if you want. . . . And sooner or later you die. For good. Welcome to the 'mortal coil.' No more VIP lounge for you. Watch out for cholesterol.

"I was extraordinarily lucky, Miranda. I gave my immortality to Shumda, but then went on to live a gorgeous life. Now it's over. I have no complaints." Her eyes betrayed her. As soon as she finished speaking, they shifted to the flowers as if the beautiful clusters knew a secret she didn't want told.

"But Frances, I died! I fell in the theater. I fell off the scaffold in the church—"

"And you came back. Again and again. Normal people don't. They live once and die. *We* live and die and come back. No one else does that, only us. But that's why people believe in reincarnation—because some of us *do* return, just not the ones they think. *Unsterblich*."

"What?"

"Immortal. The German word for it. Shumda loved that word. He said you had to wrap your tongue around it like a kiss."

"That word was on the cradle. It was carved on our baby's cradle."

"I'm not surprised. Everything we experience links up sooner or later. Our separate lives, the smallest details . . . nothing is left out. You met Hugh because of a discussion about your James and Lolly Adcock's paintings. You met me because of her work too. Remember those connect-the-dots coloring books you had as a child? That's us. Everything connects."

"Why now, Frances? Why am I learning this now?"

"Because of love, dear; because you're finally in love and have the opportunity to be selfless. It happens only once in a lifetime, any lifetime. There are big loves and small ones, but only one selfless love. In your case, I assume it's for your child. I would have thought it was for Hugh, but it wasn't, because you had this revelation *after* he died."

Without any warning I felt violently ill. I was going to throw up.

I slapped a hand over my mouth to try and stop it. I did, but only just.

So much had occurred since I'd learned I was pregnant that there had been no time to reflect on what it meant. But I knew what Frances said was true. The child inside me meant everything. The daughter from the man I had planned to spend the rest of my life with. The baby I had wanted all my life but avoided thinking about because the possibility of long love and children had faded as I grew older. It was a joy I tried not to think about. Getting older means you have fewer beginnings. Children are the beginning of everything again, no matter how old you are or how fixed in your ways.

The day I learned I was pregnant I had another, altogether different revelation. Riding home on the train to Crane's View, I considered the best way to tell Hugh. Somewhere in the middle of that planning, I was embraced by the thought: I will never be alone again. With this child in my life, I *would* never be alone again. It was the most warming, intimate, reassuring sensation I have ever known.

While Frances spoke, I unconsciously put both hands on my stomach, but whether for reassurance or protection I didn't know. In a whisper I said, "What's so bad about being normal?"

"Nothing. But it is entirely different from what you've known."

"Different how?"

She thought it over. Once her right hand flew up off the bed as if reaching for something in the air. Only after it had floated back to her lap and she thought some more did she speak. "Being human is a deeper, richer, much *sadder* experience than you know. Somewhere inside all of their souls, their genes, inside their cells, human beings understand this is all there is. But most of the time they can't figure out what *this* is. Your spirit is comfortable because it knows that when this dance is finished there'll be another for you. And another."

"What exactly would I be giving up?"

"Your immortality. You would give it to your child. You give it to the person you love as much as yourself. I gave mine to Shumda. They were going to kill him. I couldn't let that happen because I realized I loved him more than my own life."

"How do you give it up—is there some special way?"

She shook her head. "No. It's always different, but instinctively you'll know what to do when the time comes. It's not anything you have to think about."

"What did you do, Frances?"

She closed her eyes. "I set a dog on fire."

"Why?"

"I can't tell you. But it was necessary. When I realized that was what I had to do, I also understood it would cause the change. And it worked. As soon as I had done it, a lawyer appeared and said he could save Shumda. Herr Doktor Pongratz. I'll never forget that name. He said he had read about the case in the Viennese newspapers and had found a little-known law in the Austrian judicial system that would exonerate Shumda. And it did."

"But couldn't someone else have found that law too?"

Frances straightened up and smoothed the sheets around her. "No, because no such law existed until Pongratz found it."

"Can you give your immortality away to anyone, or does it have to be the one you love?"

"To anyone. Once you realize who you are and what you have, it's your decision what to do with it. You can give it to whoever you choose."

We sat silently amid her flowers and the piped in music. I had so many questions to ask.

"Can I have the baby even being who I am? Without giving up the immortality?"

"Yes! Of course you can, Miranda. But you'll destroy it. You'll love it and care for it and do everything in your power to give it a wonderful life. But eventually you'll destroy it because you are what you are. Your ego takes precedence over everything else. And as you've already discovered, it's not always obvious. You can't fight the instinct, no matter how hard you try. It's like pushing against the ocean.

"Whatever you give your daughter you'll end up taking back, times two. Often you won't even know you're doing it, but *she* will. As with everyone else in your life, you'll ruin things that are fundamental to her well-being. You'll ruin her dreams, sabotage her feelings of self-importance. *You'll suck her dry.* When she's your age, she'll tell cynical, embittered stories about her mother the bitch. She'll finish by saying she loves you of course, but the less she sees you, the better.

"As an adult, she'll believe the articles in women's magazines and think she's missing everything. She'll wear too much jewelry and her voice will get louder over the years as she realizes fewer and fewer people listen to what she says.

"Look around you. Watch how people function and interact with one another. You'll see this is going on everywhere all the time. People devour each other in the name of love, or family or country. But that's an excuse; they're just hungry and want to be fed. Read their faces, the newspapers, read what it says on their T-shirts! 'I think you're mistaking me for someone who gives a shit.' 'My parents went to London but all they brought me back was this lousy T-shirt.' 'So many women, so little time.' 'Whoever dies with the most toys, wins.' They're supposed to be funny, witty, and postmodern, Miranda. But the truth is they're only stating a fact: Me. I come first. Get out of my way."

"So vampires are everywhere?"

"Everywhere. They just don't have fangs or sleep in coffins."

"What will happen if I give the baby my immortality? Will she live a happy life?"

"There's no guarantee. She *will* be a vampire. But you'll be giving her an enormous chance because, if nothing else, she would have
all those lives. In a way, that's happiness. Very few of our kind have
been willing to make that sacrifice. Even when we find the love of
our life, we refuse to give them our immortality."

I told her about the cab ride from Crane's View and seeing my
life on screen at the drive-in theater.

"You're doing that to yourself. It's the immortal part of you with
the unbelievable powers. The part that was able to free James Stillman. The part that was outside this building staring in the last time
you were here. It knows you must decide now and it's afraid you'll
make the wrong choice."

"But why show me *that* scene? Hugh's dead. I can't do anything
about that."

"I don't know. But those kinds of bizarre things will continue
until you choose. Your magical side can be very persuasive, believe
me."

"Frances, that music is driving me crazy. Can you call down to
the front desk and ask them to turn it off?"

She held up a finger for me to be quiet. The pastel-colored,
ethereal music filled the room. Saint-Saëns, Berlioz, Delius—it could
have been composed by any of them. It perfectly complemented the
brilliant mass and whirl of the flowers.

I watched her face. It remained expressionless most of the time,
but now and then she flinched slightly or gave a faint smile.

"It reminds me of things I've forgotten and what I'm going to
lose when I die. 'Only in hell is memory exact.' I suppose this is how
my trip to hell begins. We forget so much over a lifetime. So many
brilliant moments and stories. How could we forget, Miranda? Why
do we let them go without a struggle? They make us, deepen us; they
define who we are. But we live these moments and forget them. We

mislay them like a set of keys. How is it possible to be so sloppy with our own life?

"Before you came in, for the first time in fifty years I remembered an October afternoon I spent in Vienna with Shumda. It was right after we'd arrived there, and he hadn't started performing yet. We took a tram to the last stop in Grinzing, then walked up through the vineyards to the Wienerwald and Cobenzl. There's a magnificent view from there down over the whole city.

"On the way home, we stopped at a *Heurigen* and had a lunch of fried chicken and new white wine. Shumda loved to talk. Almost nothing could stop him once he got going. But in the middle of our meal, right in the middle of taking a bite of chicken, he saw something behind me and absolutely froze. I'd never seen anything like it. I spun around to see what it was, but there was nothing there but two nondescript men sitting at a table drinking wine. Shumda wiped his hands carefully on a handkerchief, then reached into his backpack and took out the book he had been reading the whole summer. It was Freud's *Beyond the Pleasure Principle,* which had just been published.

"He asked how he looked. I said 'Fine, what's the matter with you?' He bit his lip and it was plain he was extremely nervous about something. Shumda was never nervous. He was the most self-confident person I've ever known. He took the book, stood up, and walked across the courtyard to the two men. As he approached, a chow chow came out from under the table and stared at him. Obviously it was protecting the men, and for a moment I thought it was going to bite him. But it was on a leash, and one of them reined it in close.

Shumda looked at the dog and then the men. He held up the book, but instead of speaking, he made the dog talk for him. *It* said, 'Dr. Freud, you have written a masterpiece. I'm in your debt.' Freud, who wasn't famous for his sense of humor, was bewildered. He kind of harrumphed a bit, said thank you, looked suspiciously at his dog, and finally asked Shumda if he was a performer. Shumda said yes very meekly and invited him to his show when it opened at the Ronacher Theater. Freud tried to smile and be gracious but he really didn't know what to do.

"We left the *Heurigen* before they did. As we were walking out, Freud and I made eye contact. Passing their table I leaned over the great *doktor,* whom I didn't know from the man in the moon, and said, 'You really should come to his show. He's a genius.' I often wondered if he was there the night you fell."

"You said you forgot things, Frances. Sounds like you remember very well."

"I'm remembering everything now. The music has been doing that to me. It brings back Freud's smell when I bent over to talk to him. The yellowness of the chestnuts on the ground in the courtyard of that *Heurigen*. They fell from the trees in spiky shells. You peeled them open and inside was a shiny brown chestnut. People collected them and fed them to the animals at the Schönbrunn zoo."

"Do you like remembering these things? You sound so sad."

"Well, it is sad watching your house burn down. When there's nothing you can do about it, you have to stand and watch. You remember the things inside you're losing. It's hard, but it reminds me of how rich my life was. God, I had a good one."

"But I'm looking at your face, Frances. You're not remembering only good things, are you?"

She wouldn't answer.

Is it better to remember all we've lost? Especially when we know it's gone forever? And what about the bad memories? The bad times, bad people, bad choices, bad plans—should we be reminded of them?

I didn't think so, especially not in Frances's case. In her retelling, even her good memories, the Freud stories and their like, trailed an aroma of melancholy and loss that stank. Even in a room filled with the most exotic flowers.

"I'll go now. I'm going back to Crane's View."

She closed her eyes and nodded. She knew I had no other choice. "If you leave here tonight, you can't come back until after you've decided. You won't be protected."

"I don't want to be protected." I bent over and kissed the old woman high on her forehead. She smelled of talcum powder. "Thank you for everything, Frances. Even after all that's happened, I still love you very much."

"And I love you. The one thing I always regretted was not having a child. A daughter. Now, having known you, I know what it would have been like and I regret it even more."

I touched her cheek and left. I walked into the hall and closed the door behind me.

After two steps I started shaking so much I couldn't move. I wasn't ready yet. I had thought I was but I was wrong. Five more minutes with Frances. A few more questions. I just needed five more minutes with my friend. Then I would be all right and able to go on to whatever was next. She would understand that. She would know how to stop my shakes and push the demons back.

I returned to her door and opened it. The music was playing. Frances sat with her face in her hands weeping so hard her whole body shook violently.

"Oh Jesus, Frances!"

She looked up. Her face was crimson. Her cheeks were shiny from tears. She waved a hand at me to leave. I did not know how to help, how to save my friend from a fate so hopeless and decided. But I could fetch the doctor. Maybe the doctor had something that could calm her down and at least let her rest.

Dr. Zabalino was downstairs in the lobby talking to the receptionist. The sight of me racing toward her must have said everything. I started explaining what happened but she was hurrying for the elevator before I was three sentences in. I started after her but she stopped and slammed a hand against my chest.

"No! If you want to stay here and be protected, don't move till I get back. But you cannot come with me! Think of Frances. Something you said obviously upset her. She's very weak and this is bad for her. I don't want her seeing you again now." She took her hand away but kept both hands wide open at her sides, as if ready to shove me again if I tried accompanying her. She walked to the elevator, entered, turned around and faced me. As the doors slid closed, she said, "Don't go anywhere. Stay here and you'll be safe."

The light above the door illuminated the floor numbers. When it stopped at Frances's, I turned and walked to the receptionist. She wasn't ignoring me or reading poetry this time. Her eyes were bright and alert, like those of a small animal that's just realized a much bigger one is very close.

"What happens now?"

"What do you mean?"

I slapped my hands down on the desk loud enough to make her cringe. "Don't give me shit! *What happens now?*"

"Usually the doctors can fix things. Dr. Zabalino is very good. She'll know how to help your friend. But it'll be harder to help you because you haven't chosen yet. That's the worst. Making up your mind, because there are so many reasons for and against it. That's why you should stay here until you've decided. Fieberglas is the safest place for you. Outside it's very, very dangerous. There are things out there—"

"Tell the doctor I left."

"You *can't!*"

"I don't want to be here. I've got to—Just tell her I left."

"But—"

The clatter of my heels against the stone floor rang out again in that quiet place as I walked to the door. Through a window, I saw Erik Peterson in his taxicab, the light from the portable TV flickering on his face. I pushed open the heavy front door. The air outside was cold and smelled of pine and stone. I felt no desire to return to the "safety" of the building.

"Erik? Let's go home."

He looked up. "You finished?"

"Yes. Do you mind if I sit next to you?"

"Not at all. Hop in." He reached across the passenger's seat and threw open the door. The overhead light came on a weak yellow. I walked around the front of the car and got in but didn't close the door. I needed a moment just sitting before my life could continue.

"How'd it go in there, Miranda? How's your friend?"

"Sick. Is this your family?" On the dashboard was a small metal frame with three oval photographs inside. A boy, a girl, a wife. The girl wore a cheerleader's sweater and flirted with the camera. The pretty woman looked straight at it, expressionless. The boy—

"Yes. That's my wife Nina, our daughter Nelly, and Isaac."

"He looks like you."

"Isaac died of meningitis two years ago. One night he didn't feel well and went to bed. The next morning he was gone." He gestured for me to close the door. I hesitated so as to have another, closer look at Isaac in the dim light. Erik started the car. The strong smell of exhaust fumes filled the air.

"I'm so sorry. What was he like?"

"Interesting you ask. Most people when they hear about it just say they're sorry. They're embarrassed to ask questions. Or they feel uncomfortable.

"What was he *like*? He was a pistol. You couldn't keep the kid down. He woke up at five every morning and went full tilt till you threw him into bed at night and shut his eyes for him. I guess he was hyperactive, but my wife said he was just too interested to sit down. We miss him."

I pulled the door closed and we drove away from Fieberglas. The gravel crunching beneath the car tires sounded very loud. As we drove onto the street I looked down at my hands in my lap and saw they were both clenched into fists. I was fearful something might stop or hold us back, but that was egotism or paranoia. Nothing stopped us; nothing met us but the night in front of the headlights.

"Once when Isaac was a little boy, I mean really little, I walked into the bathroom and saw him standing next to the toilet barefoot. The seat was up and he was dangling a foot over the bowl. I asked what he was doing, because with that kid, it coulda been anything. He said he'd bet himself he couldn't put his foot in the toilet. For some crazy reason he was frightened of doing that. So there he was standing, daring himself to do the thing that scared him most."

"Why was he afraid to do that? Had it been flushed?"

"Oh, sure." Peterson took a hand off the steering wheel and gave an airy wave. "But you know how it is when you're a kid: you got different monsters than the ones you got as an adult."

I slid forward to get as close as possible to the photograph. The boy did look like his father, but even in the picture there was a wildness in his eyes that said he *was* a pistol.

We returned to Crane's View the way we had come. Passing the drive-in theater, I worried that something would again be playing on the giant screen, but it was blank. Erik continued talking about his son. I asked questions to keep the conversation going. I didn't want to think about what to do because I knew my whole life would depend on that decision once we got home.

"Do you mind if I smoke?" he asked.

"No. God, cigarettes! I'd love one too."

He pulled a pack of Marlboros from beneath his sun visor and handed them to me. "I think I got two left in there. Have a look."

I slid them out.

He pushed in the cigarette lighter on the dashboard. "All the things we're not supposed to do anymore, huh? You know what I say? Cigarettes are gooood!"

The lighter popped out and he handed it to me. I lit up for the first time in years and took a deep drag. The smoke was harsh and raw in my throat but delicious. We sat in a nice silence, smoking and watching things pass by.

"There's a 7-eleven up here a-ways. Would you mind if I made a quick stop and bought more smokes and some other things? I told the wife I'd bring them home and she'll be real mad if I don't."

"Please, of course stop."

He sighed. "That's one of the bad things that's happened since Isaac died. Nina gets real upset about small things. Before, she was as calm as summer, but now if even the slightest thing goes wrong, she has trouble with it. I can't blame her. I guess we miss people in our own ways.

"Me, I think about all the things I'll never be able to do with the boy. Take him to see the Knicks, watch him graduate from school. Sometimes when I'm alone in the house, I go up to his room and sit on the bed. I talk to him too, you know? Tell him what's been going on in the family, and how much I miss him. I know it's stupid, but I keep thinking he's near me in that room. Nina cleaned it out completely after he died, so it's only a small empty place now, but I can't help thinking he's around there sometimes and maybe can hear me."

"What do you miss most, Erik? What do you miss most about him?" A question I had asked myself again and again since Hugh's death.

"The hugs. That kid was a hugger. He'd grab hold of you tight as a vise and squeeze. Not many people really hug you." He smiled sadly. It looked like his whole life these days was in that smile. "There aren't that many people in life who really love you either."

I felt my throat swell and I had to look away.

"I'm sorry, Miranda. I'm just talking. There's the place. I'll be out in a minute."

We slowed and pulled into a large parking lot. The store was brilliantly lit. It glowed, and the vivid colors of the products on the shelves radiated out into the night. I watched Erik walk in. He stopped to speak with the man behind the counter and in a moment both were laughing. I looked around the lot. There was only one other vehicle parked there, an old pickup truck that looked like it had traveled to World War Three and back. I twisted the rearview mirror to have a look at myself and was surprised to see my head was still on my shoulders and I didn't have big Xs over my eyes like some cartoon character that's just been knocked out.

I saw something out of the corner of my eye. Far across the parking lot, a kid on a bicycle came weaving slowly into view. My first thought was, What's he doing out so late, but as he got closer my mind froze. It was Erik Peterson's son Isaac.

He was dressed in an orange-and-blue windbreaker and faded jeans. Riding in loopy circles around the lot, he got closer and closer to the car. I knew who he was, but since I could not believe it, I looked again at the picture on the dashboard. It was him. Inside the store, Erik had disappeared back among the shelves. Outside, twenty feet away, his dead son rode a bicycle.

I opened the door and swiveled to get out. The boy stopped abruptly and put his feet down to keep from tipping. Looking at me, he shook his head. Don't move. I stayed where I was and he slowly rolled over.

"That's my Dad in there." His voice was high and sweet. He lisped.

"Yes."

"He's nice, huh?"

"He's . . . He loves you very much."

"I know. He talks to me all the time. But I can't talk back. It's not allowed."

"Can I tell him you're here?"

"No. He couldn't see me anyway. Only you. Remember you saw me before? When you were driving the other way, I was racing you. I kept up with you pretty long. I mean, I'm pretty fast for my age."

He was so sure of himself, this ten-year-old big talker out for a spin on his bike at night, checking to see if anyone was watching. It wrung my heart.

"You know Declan?" he asked.

"Yes."

A green Porsche growled in off the street and stopped a few feet away. A woman wearing a man's fedora got out. Looking straight ahead, she walked into the store.

"Women are the stones you use to build a house, men are the sticks you use to start the fire and keep the house warm."

Distracted by the jarring noise of the car, I wasn't sure I'd heard what he said. "Excuse me?"

"That's what Declan's father said."

I stiffened. "You've seen him?"

"Sure. He and Declan are together all the time. He said that today when Declan asked the difference between men and women. They were talking about why Declan never got to be born.

"See you!"

Erik came out of the store carrying a brown bag and glancing over his shoulder. Pushing the bike backward, the boy came within two feet of his father. He looked at the man as he walked past. He reached out a hand and pretended to slap his arm.

Erik stopped. For a moment I was sure he knew who was there. Isaac watched him with calm eyes. Erik moved to the left, stopped, moved to the right. He was dancing! He turned in a circle. "Do you hear it, Miranda? From inside the store? Martha and the Vandellas.

'Dancing in the Streets.' " He continued swaying back and forth as he approached the car. "One of my favorite songs. Isaac loved it too. I hear it all the time now. Funny. More than ever before, I think." He opened the back door and laid the grocery bag on the seat. "You ready to go?"

The boy nodded at me, so I said yes. His father got in and started the motor. "I got everything. Some more cigarettes too if you want one."

"Erik, if you could, what would you say to Isaac if he was here right now?"

Without hesitation he said, "I'd say I'm living, but I'm not alive without you."

ONE OF HUGH'S favorite quotes was from St. Augustine: "Whisper in my heart, tell me you are there." I suppose it has to do with God and his unwillingness to show his face to man. But in light of what had happened, I took it to mean something entirely different. I was sure "Women are the stones you use to build a house, men are the sticks . . ." was meant for me, not Declan. I was sure Hugh was whispering in *my* heart, suggesting what to do. I had already come to the same conclusion by then but his words only strengthened my resolve.

When we arrived in Crane's View and Erik dropped me off, I entered the house no longer frightened or upset. There is a calmness that comes with surrender. A peace that actually revitalizes when you know there is no other way. I knew what to do now, and no matter what happened to me afterwards, the child would be safe. That was all that mattered—the child would be safe. I would give it what I had, willingly!

The house was spotless, no sign of anything that happened there earlier. I walked into the kitchen and remembered it had all begun after I'd made myself dinner—how many hours, days, lifetimes ago? When I turned on the television and saw Charlotte, Declan, and Hugh by the swimming pool.

So what? It had to begin somewhere and that's where it did. Move on. Other things to think about now. Hunger shook a scolding finger at me and I knew I would have to eat before doing it. Opening the refrigerator door, I was greeted by an incredible array of the most extraordinary and exotic food—Iranian caviar, a box of pastries from a place called Demel in Vienna, plover eggs, Tunisian capers, olives from Mt. Athos, fresh Scottish salmon, Bombay lemon pickle, more. I had bought none of it, much less tasted most of the food on those shelves, but it didn't surprise me. The time for surprises was over. I sniffed and sampled a great deal before choosing a fresh baguette, prosciutto cut thin as tissue paper, and the most delicate mozzarella I had ever tasted. The sandwich was delicious and I ate it quickly.

There was a bottle of Lambrusco too, one of Hugh's favorite wines. I opened it and poured some into a small glass that had once held creamed chipped beef. Odd as it may sound, I wanted to toast something. That's what you're supposed to do at the end of the banquet, aren't you? Toast the host, the lucky couple, the birthday girl or the glorious country. But what could I toast on this, the last night of some preposterous part of my existence? My past lives? Here's to all the good and bad times I had but forgot and learned nothing from. Here's to all the people I knew and hurt—sorry folks, I can't remember any of you. Or how about, Here's to me—however many of us there have been.

Hugh taught me an Irish toast:

> *May those who love us love us.*
> *And those that don't love us,*
> *May God turn their hearts.*

And if he doesn't turn their hearts
May he turn their ankles
So we'll know them by their limping.

One toast came to me that was appropriate. I lifted my glass and said to the empty room, "Here's to you and the lives you lead. I hope you find your way home faster than I did." I drank slowly and emptied the glass.

On the floor in Hugh's workroom was a cardboard box filled with tools and chemicals he used to restore things. I went through it, pulling out the many different bottles, reading the labels, choosing the ones that contained alcohol or any kind of flammable substance. Our house was made of wood. It would go up quickly. I went around the ground floor pouring the strong-smelling chemicals over everything. Hugh's new chair, a couch, boxes of books, the wooden floors.

I kept spilling and watching the liquids stain new fabric, pool on the wooden floor, eat into a turquoise plastic Sky King ashtray I had given Hugh as a present. When all of the bottles and cans were empty, I stood in the front hall smelling the incredible stink of all those deadly chemicals splashed over everything in the world that had mattered to me.

I went to a window and looked out onto the porch. A car drove by outside. A white car. It reminded me of a white horse. Heroes rode white horses, heroic knights. That reminded me of Hugh's unfinished story about the plain-looking knight who fell so in love with the princess that he was willing to sacrifice everything for her. How he went to the devils and traded them his courage for her happiness. I remembered the last line of his incomplete story. "Life is full of surprises, but if you're convinced all of them will be bad, what's the point of going on?" I wanted no more surprises. I didn't trust them, any more than I believed I would be able to change anything for the better if I continued living. I would give up my immortality to the child and then I would finish it.

Still staring out the window, I felt ebullient and relieved. The world was mine because I no longer wanted to be in it. I could do this tonight or tomorrow or next week. It didn't matter when because the decision had been made and was final. No, it had to be tonight. I did not want tomorrow. I went looking for matches.

What was the name of that famous children's book? *Goodnight Moon.* Good night Hugh. Good night Frances Hatch, good night Crane's View, good night life. My thoughts chanted these lines as I searched for matches. Good night Erik Peterson and Isaac. Good night beautiful books and long dinners with someone you love. Good night this and this and this and this as I wandered through the house. The list got longer and longer as I slid open drawers and cupboards looking for something to burn up the world in which these things existed.

Just as I began to grow frustrated, I remembered seeing a pack of matches in Hugh's box of chemicals. A half-empty pack with green writing announcing Charlie's Pizza. The place where we'd had lunch with Frances the first day we visited Crane's View. The first time I saw Declan. The first time we met Frannie McCabe. First time. First time and now the last time. I would never see Declan or Frannie again. Never see this this that. A spotted dog or a marmalade cat. Goodnight life.

I found the matches and stood up, wondering only where to do it. The living room. Sit on the couch, start the fire there and finish. The walk from Hugh's room to the living room seemed five miles long. It felt like I was walking underwater. Not bad or disturbing, only slow-motion and incredibly detailed. I saw everything around me with extreme clarity. Was it because this was the last time I would see these things? Good night hall with the beautiful wood floors.

Hugh got down on his knees right there and, sliding his hand back and forth over that floor, looked up at me with the happiest smile. "This is all ours now," he said, his voice full of wonder. Good night staircase. Stopping, I looked up and remembered the day we had made love at the top. I wished I could smell Hugh in that final air. Would I see him where I was going? How wonderful to smell him one last time. I looked up the stairs and remembered him on top of me, his weight, the softness of his lips on my throat, his thumbs holding down my hands. He'd had keys in his jeans pocket that day. When he moved on me they cut into my hip. I asked him to take them out. He tossed them across the floor. They rang out as they hit and slid. Good night keys.

In the living room I stared into the empty fireplace a moment and then put my hand in my pocket. It was there. It was time, so I took it out. Because of all the mad things happening when I picked it up in the basement at Hugh's silent urging, I hadn't looked carefully at the piece of wood I now held in my hand. I had more or less forgotten about it until I was standing in the lobby of Fieberglas talking to the nurse about Frances. Then the only way I can describe what happened is that the wood *came to me* the way a good idea or real fear comes. All at once, as if through every pore in your body. Yes, it had been in my pocket the whole time, but suddenly I became aware of its presence again. Or maybe I just remembered it and, in doing so, grasped its real importance and what to do with it. A small piece of wood about seven inches long. Dark on three sides, light on the other. The side where it had broken off the baby's crib when McCabe/Shumda threw it against the wall.

There was a fragment of a figure carved on it, but the way the wood had snapped off made it impossible to decipher what it was. The back half of a running animal. A deer perhaps, or a mythological creature that fit the rest of the extravagant, fantastical world that had been carved on that wonderful old cradle. Our child's cradle, our baby girl. I thought of her, the only sight of her I would ever have. Then I thought of Declan and what his father had said. And I knew what I had to do, and it was right, but if I were to somehow survive what was about to happen, I would regret doing it forever. I looked at the wood in my hand and because I felt I had no other choice I said, "I'm sorry." I had two pieces of wood to burn. Two pieces for my marriage of sticks: The one in my hand from the cradle, and the one from Central Park I had picked up the day we knew it was going to happen. Two sticks were enough for a marriage. More would have been better. I would have loved to have a huge bundle of them for a world-sized bonfire when I was eighty years old and at the satisfied end of a marvelous life. But I had only these two and they would have to be enough. They were important though—as important as anything. One symbolized Hugh, this one our child. Where in the house was the Hugh stick? I thought but then realized it didn't matter because soon it would be gone too.

Without knowing why, I knew when I lit it, this wood would ignite as if it were made of pure gasoline. Breaking off a match from the pack, I put it to the striking pad and flicked my hand. A flame snapped open, flaring and hissing a second before taming down to the size of a fingernail. Lit match in one hand, the wood in the other. Good night life.

I looked up one last time. At the window were faces. Many many many of them. Some were pressed to the glass, distorting their features—bent noses, comical lips. Others hovered in the background, waiting their turn to get close as they could to the window, to this room, to me. And I knew all of the faces *were* me, all the me's from past lives who had come to watch this happen. To watch the end of their line, last stop, everybody out.

"Good-bye." Calmly I put the match to the wood and the world exploded.

I heard the blast and saw a blinding flash of light. Then utter silence. I don't know how long it lasted. I was somewhere else until I was back in the living room, sitting by myself on the couch, holding both empty hands in the air in total surprise. It took time to realize where I was and of course I did not believe it. Everything was so still. My eyes readjusted to the normal light in the room and the colors, the things around me, everything was exactly as it had been.

I dropped my hands to the couch and felt its rough wool beneath my palms. Turning my head slowly from side to side, I took in the view. Nothing had changed. Frances's house, our possessions, home again. Even the smell was the same.

No, there was something else. Hugh. Hugh's cologne was in the air. Then I felt hands on my shoulders and knew instantly that they were his. Hugh was here.

The hands lifted. He came around the back of the couch and stood in front of me. "It's all right, Miranda. You're all right."

I stared at him and could only repeat what he had said, because it was true. "I'm all right." We looked at each other and I had nothing to say. I understood nothing but I was all right.

"You're not allowed to kill yourself. When you burned the wood, you could only give them back what was theirs. Now you have the rest of your life. That belongs to you."

I looked at him. I nodded. All right. Anything was all right.

"Thank you, Miranda. You did an incredible thing."

I looked at him and I was empty as death, empty as an old heart that's just biding its time.

Somehow, from some place I didn't know I had, I was able to whisper, "What now?"

"Now you live, my sweetheart." He smiled and it was the saddest smile I had ever seen.

"All right."

He reached into his jacket pocket and took out something. He offered it to me. Another piece of wood. A small long silvery piece that looked like driftwood. Wood that had been floating in some unimaginable sea for a thousand years. I turned it over in my hand, examining it carefully. Shapeless, silvery, soft, old. Yes, it must have been driftwood.

When I looked up again Hugh was gone.

THERE WAS A nice song on the radio years ago. They played it too much but I didn't mind because it kept me company and I'm always grateful for that. I often found myself humming it without realizing. The title was "How Do I Live Without You?"

I have come to realize this is an essential lesson: In order to survive, you must learn to live without everything. Optimism dies first, then love, and finally hope. But still you must continue. If you were to ask me why, I would say that even without those fundamental things, the great things, the hot-blood-in-the-veins things, there is still enough in a day, in a life, to be precious, important, sometimes even fulfilling. How do I live without you? I put you in the museum of my heart where I often go, absorbing as much as I can bear before closing time.

What more can I tell you that you need to know beyond what I already have? I had a life. I never married, had no children, met two good men I might have loved, but after what I had experienced, it was impossible. I was proud of myself though, because I honestly tried with real hope and an open heart to fall in love again. No good.

I went back to selling books and I did well. Sometimes I was even able to lose myself in what I was doing, and that was when I was happiest. All the time I thought of Frances Hatch and how she had done it—lived a full and interesting life after she had cut the thread. So many times I wished I could have spoken with her, but she died three days after we last met.

Zoe married Doug Auerbach and they were happy for a long time. When he died ten years ago, I moved out to California to live with her. We became quintessential L.A. old ladies. We ate only free-range chicken and took too many vitamins. We spent too much time in malls, went to aerobics classes for seniors, wore thicker and thicker eyeglasses as the visual world became foggier and surrounded by increasingly soft edges. We made a life and watched the sun set over it.

I always woke earlier than she and made the coffee. But she was punctual, and by nine every morning she joined me in the backyard to read the newspaper and talk about what needed doing that day. We had a garden, there were a few friends, and we reminisced unendingly. Of course I never told her any of my real story.

For my birthday one year she bought me a pocket telephone. On the package was a note she had written that said, "Now you'll really be a California gal!" When I opened the box and saw what it was, I asked who on earth would ever call me? Zoe said sexily, "You never know!" And I loved her for her optimism and I loved her for the lie. I knew she had given it to me because she was worried. I had been having fainting spells, *swoons* she liked to call them, and they were getting worse. My doctor, an Irishman named Keane, joked that I had the blood pressure of an iguana. Sometimes I pretended I wasn't feeling well just so I could visit him.

But death winds the clock and one morning Zoe didn't show up for coffee. She was a robust woman and I don't think she was ever sick the whole time we lived together. When I went into her room at ten-thirty that morning and saw her lying peacefully on her side in bed, I knew. Her children, neither of whom had even the slightest trace of her goodwill and energy, came to the funeral but left on the first plane out.

STORIES WRITTEN
IN THE SNOW

THE DOORBELL rang. The old woman looked up quickly from the notebook and frowned. She did not want to be interrupted, especially not now when she was so very close to finishing. What an amazing notion—soon she would be done.

No one ever rang her doorbell anyway, that was a given. Once in a great while someone wearing a brown United Parcel Service uniform brought her a package from Lands' End or another of the mail-order companies that supplied her with sturdy practical clothes made out of warm materials like Polartec or goose down. She needed all the warmth she could get because her body felt cold almost constantly now, despite the fact that she was living in the desert heat of Los Angeles. Sometimes at night she even wore a pair of electric blue Polartec gloves while watching television. If someone had seen her they would have thought she was crazy, but she was only cold. More than wisdom, irony, grace, or peace, old age had brought cold, and she was never really able to escape it.

Pausing a moment, she remembered she had ordered nothing, so whoever was at her door now could only be mistaken or a nuisance. Would you like to subscribe to this magazine? Would you like to believe in my God? Would you happen to have a dollar for a guy down on his luck?

The bell rang again—so loud and annoying—*ding-dong ding-dong*! There was no way to avoid it. Grimacing, she put down Hugh's fountain pen and reached for the cane leaning against her desk.

She was fat now. Recently she had even begun calling herself that, although she'd known it for a long time. She was an old woman who had grown much too fat. She liked to sit. After Zoe died she had stopped going to exercise class. She liked cookies. Hugh once said, "Eating is sex for old people." Now it was true for her.

Her knees were weak. And her hips and God knows what else. It was an effort getting up or sitting down. When you were as old as she was, everything was an effort, and when you weighed twenty-five pounds too much you did a lot more with a groan than ever before. The year she died, Zoe had given Miranda the cane for Christmas. It was a very nice one too—made of oak and slightly crooked, so that it had a kind of jaunty character. It reminded her of something an Irishman would use. Ireland. Hugh always said he was going to take her to Ireland—

The doorbell rang again. Damn! She was sure she was almost finished writing her story, but now this interruption would disturb her train of thought. She didn't know if she'd be able to get back into it later. Writing demanded her full attention. More and more, her memory played hide-and-seek with her. She felt compelled to get everything down on paper as soon as she could before something inevitable and dreadful like a stroke or Alzheimer's disease roared into her brain and like a vacuum cleaner sucked it empty.

Leaning hard on the cane with one hand and pushing down on the desk with the other, she raised herself out of the chair. After a few small, unsteady, dangerous steps, she moved slowly across the shadowy room.

The room never got full sunlight. She liked it that way. She kept two lamps burning in there almost all the time. At night when she was exhausted and going to bed she would walk out and leave them on on purpose. She liked thinking her workroom was always lit. As if some kind of bright spirit was in there guarding the important things like the diary and her thoughts. Yes, she felt she left her most important thoughts in that room because it was where she did all of her diary writing. How silly. The silly thoughts of a silly old woman.

That's what she was thinking as she gradually made her way across the house to the front door. Who could it be? Why did they have to come calling now? What time was it anyway? She stopped walking and looked at her watch. It was an enormous thing, the watch with the largest face in the store—bought so that she could read the time without having to put on her glasses.

"Wow!" It was five in the afternoon. She had been writing for hours. That was good news because it meant she was inspired, anxious to know how she would end her account. That end was so near now. She felt she could reach out and touch it. When she was done, Alzheimer's or heart attack or whatever horror could take over and she wouldn't care. Really, she wouldn't care.

She peeked through the window in the front door but saw no one. If this was a prank by a neighborhood kid—ring the bell and run—she would be annoyed. But better that, because then she could go right back to work. Or maybe she would make one quick detour into the kitchen to see—the bell rang again. How could it? She had just looked and no one was there. A short circuit? Whoever heard of a doorbell short-circuiting?

Maybe someone was trying to trick her into opening the door.

These were dangerous times. Terrible things happened to old women living alone. They were such easy prey. Watch the news any night and it was easy to be frightened. She had many locks on her door, but so what? Life had certainly taught *her* harm comes in any door it wants and doesn't need a key. Yes, she grew quickly worried, but again it was only because she hadn't finished her diary. Her prayer, if she had been a religious woman, would have been, "Please let me finish. Give me the strength and the time to finish. The rest is yours."

Uneasily, she peeked again through the window in the door and saw something odd. The first time she had looked only straight ahead. Now she moved from side to side and saw that the steps leading to her front door were covered with cookies.

"Waa—" bewildered she pressed up closer for a better view. Cookies. That's right. From the sidewalk across the small but perfectly kept front yard to the door were sixteen octagonal paving stones. She had liked those stones the moment she first saw them. They reminded her of an English country cottage or a magical path in a fairy tale. Zoe had liked them too, and when it was necessary to dig up the entire yard years ago to repair the septic tank, both women insisted the workers replace the stones exactly where they'd been.

Now cookies covered each one. Well, not exactly covered. With her bad eyes, she could clearly see five of the stones leading to the house. On each stone were four? Yes, four cookies, big ones, like the kind Mrs. Fields and Dave's sold in their stores. Miranda loved them. Chocolate chips. With dark or light chocolate chunks, macadamia nuts . . . it didn't matter. She loved big chocolate chip cookies and here they were on her *front walk*!

An unfamiliar dalmatian loped onto her lawn in a hurry to get somewhere. But he must have caught their scent because, slamming on his brakes, he started gobbling. Dogs don't eat when they're excited, they inhale, and this guy was no exception. He ate so fast, jumping from stone to stone, that Miranda began to giggle. She didn't know who'd put them there but she doubted they meant the cookies for this fellow.

"Follow the yellow brick cookie. They're your favorites, right?"

She froze. The voice came from directly behind her. She didn't know this voice, but it was a man's and it was definitely right behind her, *near* her.

"Don't you recognize him? It's Bob the dalmatian. Hugh and Charlotte's dog. Say hi to Bob."

He spoke calmly, his voice quiet but amused. She had to turn around because there was nothing else she could do.

Shumda stood five feet away wearing a gray sweatshirt with "Skidmore" printed across the front, jeans, and elaborate blue running shoes. He had not aged at all from the last time she had seen him, decades ago.

"I had a whole little scene planned out with a follow-the-yellow-brick motif but it didn't include old Bob. Cause I know you loves dem cookies."

What could she say? It was all over. The time had come for her to die. Why else would Shumda have come? How many years had it been? How many thousands of days had passed since she last saw this handsome bad man on the porch of the house in Crane's View, New York?

"What do you want?"

He touched both hands to his chest and put on a wounded expression. "Me? I don't want anything. I'm here on assignment. I've been given orders."

"You've come for me?"

"Voilà. *Es muss sein.*"

"Where . . . What are you going to do?"

"I've come to take you for a ride in my new car. It's a Dodge! I asked for a Mercedes but they gave me a Dodge."

She hated his voice. It was a nice one, deep and low, but the tone was mocking and arrogant. He spoke to her as if she were a stupid child who knew nothing.

"You don't have to address me like that. I'll do what you say." It came out hard, steely.

He didn't like that. His eyes widened and lips tightened. Something between them had shifted and he hadn't been prepared for that. He'd probably expected her to whine or beg, but that wasn't her way. His unsure expression changed to a leer and suddenly he was back in charge. "I told you I was coming, Miranda. A long time ago. Don't you remember that dog you liked that was set on fire?"

"That was *you*?"

"Yes. I thought for sure you'd know that it was I with *that* one. What bigger hint did you need? Don't you remember that Frances saved me by burning a dog?"

"You killed a dog just to tell me you were coming?"

"It was dramatic but obviously not very effective. Anyway, we have to go now. You won't need to take anything. We're not going far."

The fear came. It rushed up through her like water and she immediately began to tremble. She hated herself for it. Despite the staggering fear, she hated herself for letting this appalling man see her shake. She started a deep breath that stopped halfway down her throat because she was so afraid. Still she managed to say "May I take something with me?"

"You want to *pack*?"

"No, I want to take one thing with me. It's in the other room."

He looked at her a long tormenting moment, then smirked. "Do I get three guesses? Is it bigger than a breadbox? Go on, but hurry up."

Somehow she mustered her meager energy and shuffled toward the back of the house. Thank God she had the cane, because her body now felt like stone. It did not want to move; it did not know how to walk anymore. But she moved. She walked slowly and unsteadily down the hall to her workroom.

She went in and for several seconds stared at the desk and on it the open diary. She would never finish. She would never be able to complete it and put it away in a safe place where one day they would find it and know the whole story. Never. All over. Finished.

"All right. It's okay. Just walk away." She said it out loud as she walked over to a dresser pushed up against a wall. She slid the top drawer out and reached in for the piece of wood. The silver piece of wood Hugh had given her the last time she saw him. She had since collected other pieces over her long life, but they would have to stay here. She didn't know what she would do with it wherever she was going but she needed to have it with her. Closing her fingers over it, she left the room.

Shumda was waiting by the front door. When he saw her he opened it. Bending forward at the waist, he gestured with an exaggerated sweep of his arm for her to go first. She shuffled forward, leaning hard on her cane. She was so scared. Her knees ached. Where were they going? She heard him close the door. Gently taking her arm, he helped her down the one step to the front yard. The dog was gone and so were the cookies. A few minutes ago it was all strange and funny—chocolate chip cookies on her footpath—but now funny was gone. Soon everything would be gone.

They walked to the street, where he told her to wait. He strode away and around the corner. She looked at the sky. An airplane had left a thin white contrail across the blue. A car peeled out somewhere, its long screech filling her ears. Then it was silent, and soon some birds began singing.

A shiny green van drove up and stopped in front of her. Shumda was at the wheel wearing a San Diego Padres baseball cap. He got out, opened the passenger's door, and helped her in. She had trouble getting into cars but rode in them so rarely now that it made no difference.

"Where are we going?"

"It's a surprise."

"I don't want a surprise. Just tell me. At least give me that."

"Be quiet, Miranda. Sit back and enjoy the ride. You haven't been outside in a long time."

Folding her hands in her lap she looked out the window. When Shumda spoke again she ignored him, wouldn't even turn to look. As soon as he realized she wouldn't respond, he chattered on non-stop. Told her what he had been doing all these years, told her what *she* had been doing all these years ("They said to keep tabs on you"), told her everything she didn't want to hear. She looked out the window and tried with all her might to ignore him. If this was to be her last ride, she didn't want his voice nattering in her ear. A hamburger stand, a gas station. Why had it come so abruptly? Couldn't they have given her some warning? A day. If they had given her one more day she could have finished everything and been waiting at the door when he arrived. A yellow convertible driven by a beautiful brunett passed them. Then a Volkswagen that looked as though it had been driven around the world six times. The driver was a man with a shaved head. His hands danced back and forth across the top of the steering wheel. A used book store. One day would have been enough. Today while she was working, her stomach had knotted up several times because she knew in her secret self that she would be finished soon, and then what would she do with her days? Why had Shumda been watching her for years? She was no threat. She had never been a threat. Besides, all *that* had been so long ago. Soon after it was over she'd started forgetting things and despite having written this diary, so many memories of that time were like Greek ruins to her by now.

She had never planned to reread her account, but riding along now she grew furious that she would never even have the choice. All that work, but now she could not go back to relive for a while certain experiences that she might already have forgotten. How much can an old brain hold before it begins to spring leaks from the weight of so many years?

Honey-cooked hams, discount sunglasses, Mansfield Avenue, street signs all flew by the car window. He was driving faster now. Where were they going? She remembered Frances Hatch in her hospital room surrounded by flowers.

Maybe Shumda would drive her someplace but then drive her home again. A flutter, a hummingbird's heartbeat of hope raced through her but was gone just as quickly. It was over. Whatever he had waiting for her would be appropriate and terrible, she was sure. She remembered walking back into Frances's room and seeing her crying.

He turned left on La Brea and accelerated. Evening was beginning. The sky was still bright but when they walked to the car from her house the air had been cool and still, already starting to settle for the night. Down La Brea past the cheap furniture stores, cheap drugstores, cheap fast-food places. More people stood out on the sidewalks here waiting for buses, waiting for friends, waiting for some kind of luck or change that would never come.

Miranda had been lucky and she knew it. She had traveled, she'd had an interesting job and been her own boss. She'd made money. For a short time she knew and was loved by a remarkable man. Hugh. If this was the end, she wanted to spend it thinking about Hugh Oakley. As if he knew what she was trying to do, Shumda interrupted her.

"Why did you do it?"

"Why did I do *what*?" Her voice came out cranky—she wasn't interested in answering his questions, especially not now when there was so little time left.

264 / Jonathan Carroll

He lifted a hand off the wheel and let it fall back again.

"You're not alone, you know. There were others who did what you did. But I'm just interested, you know? What would possess anyone to voluntarily give up the life you had for this one?" His hand rose again off the wheel and batted the air as if flicking away a fly. "And you didn't even know who you were giving it to! That's incredible. You handed over your immortality to a stranger. Someone you never even met!"

Coming to a red traffic light they slowed to a stop. He glanced at her and made a face. She ignored him and looked straight ahead. The light changed but instead of accelerating, Shumda continued watching her.

Eventually she said, more to herself than to him, "I never really thought about it. The moment came and it had to be. That's all. Isn't that *interesting*? I was always fighting with myself—my head, my heart. Sometimes one won, sometimes the other. But with that there was no fight. There wasn't even a question." The old woman beamed. Her whole demeanor changed, as if whatever inner storms had been raging had now passed and she was at peace. Shumda had never seen anyone in her position at peace, and he had seen his share. Oh yes, he had seen quite a few.

"Life is about to spit in your face, Miranda. I wouldn't be too smiley about that."

They were silent the rest of the ride. To her great satisfaction, out of the corner of her eye she observed that he kept looking at her to see if her expression would change—if the enormity of whatever terrible thing was about to happen to her had finally sunk in. Why *hadn't* the great final fear wrapped her in its arms as it always did with the people he had escorted to their destruction?

It took another ten minutes. He kept looking over but her pleased expression never changed. All right, so it didn't change. Wait till she got there. Wait till she saw what waited!

The road suddenly became hilly and there were oil wells all up and down those hills doing their slow work. The land was khaki-colored, sun-parched. It was a strange part of Los Angeles, neither here nor there, a kind of oddly empty no-man's land between downtown and the airport.

Signaling with his blinker, Shumda slowly merged into the right lane and then pulled off the road onto the shoulder. He cut the engine and sat there, savoring what came next. He grinned at her. "Remember this spot?"

Miranda looked around. "No."

"You will." He opened his door and got out of the van. It was all she could do not to watch him. He walked around to the back and opened the two rear doors. She heard him push and slide something metallic.

"Be with you in just a sec. Sit tight."

Slowly reaching up, she twisted the rearview mirror so she could look out the back. He was fooling around with something and it took her a moment to realize what it was. He did something and the thing went pop and suddenly unfolded into a wheelchair.

Cars zoomed by, some close, others far away, all of them loud and smooth, rushing and dangerous. And then of course it dawned on her.

So many years ago she was in one of these speeding cars on her way to Los Angeles airport. She had been in bed with Doug Auerbach that day and afterwards they went to a big drugstore together. Afterwards she rode to the airport in a taxicab and the driver, like Shumda now, wore a San Diego Padres baseball cap. She was so young then, so young and busy, and she hadn't met Hugh Oakley yet. She hadn't met Hugh Oakley and she hadn't seen dead James Stillman alive again. She was flying back to New York that night and only days later her entire life changed forever. So long ago. All of it so long ago, but now all of that day and what followed was crushing her and she couldn't stop the memories and the results, all of them crystal clear.

Shumda pushed the wheelchair around to her side of the car and stood there waiting.

When they drove to the airport that night so long ago, it was just about this time. She remembered the woman sitting in a wheelchair by the side of the road.

"Let's go, Miranda. Time to watch the traffic."

But there was no traffic. Unbelievably, all of the cars had disappeared from the road, every last one of them. A strange silence surrounded them, as if the sounds of the world had simply vanished.

"I can open the door and pull you out, or you can get out and make things easier for both of us."

"What are you going to do?"

"Nothing. I'm going to put you in this chair and I'm going to leave. And you'll be alone. To tell you the truth, I have absolutely no idea what'll happen next. But I'm sure it won't be pleasant. It never is."

"Shumda, was it me? Was it me that night, here, in the wheelchair?"

"I don't know. I just do what I'm told. Let's go, get out."

To her great surprise, the only thought she had was, Do whatever is in front of you and do it fully. Commit yourself to the moment and if you are lucky—

Her door was flung open. He took her roughly by the arm. "Don't touch me!" She pulled away from him and slowly heaved herself out of the van.

The road was empty. Up on a hill an oil well pumped, and now she could hear the roll and heave of the machine. A flock of sparrows fled across the sky cheeping loudly. Those were the only sounds— the machine and the sparrows. She made it over to the wheelchair and, taking hold of the two arms, lowered herself into it. The seat was much too narrow for her wide bottom. She tried to move into a more comfortable position but there wasn't one. She gave up trying and looked up into the evening sky again. What if that night years ago they *had* stopped to help the woman? Would it have changed anything? Had it been she that night? If they had stopped and she had seen the other woman, would she have recognized her?

Shumda pushed the chair closer to the road. "I'd love to stay and see what happens next to you, but I've got things to do." He looked at his wristwatch. "Enjoy the silence. The cars will be back in a couple of minutes."

He looked at her and his face showed nothing. He turned to leave.

"Shumda!"

"What?"

"Did you love her? Did you ever love Frances?"

For a moment it appeared he was about to respond. Instead he turned around and went back the van. The door was open and he reached in for something. He pulled out a red book, her red book, the diary. When had he gotten it? When had he taken it? He pretended to skim through the pages. His face grew serious and he rubbed his chin. In a perfect imitation of the silly lisp of Daffy Duck he said, "Fath-sin-atin'!" and then in a pitying voice he asked, "Did you really think *this* would change anything?" He flung the book back into the car. He got in, the engine came to life, and he was gone. She watched the van climb a hill and disappear.

Everything seemed to be holding its breath. She looked up, but the birds were gone. When she looked toward the oil pump it had stopped moving. Silence. Gripping the arms of the chair, she shut her eyes. She remembered that Hugh's piece of wood was in her pocket, so she took it out. Everything that had ever mattered to her lived in that wood. She gripped it tightly in both hands. How smooth it was. Smooth and warm and the last thing she would ever hold.

How would they do it? Would they come from behind, or from over the hill, or the other side of the road? What would it be?

She could have tried to get up and move away from there—but what was the use? If they wanted it to be tonight then it would happen tonight no matter where she was. And how far could she get on her old legs?

She thought of her diary and what she might have said to finish it. An intriguing question that might have comforted her, or taken her mind away from what was imminent. But then she heard it: the deep rumble of many cars coming her way that grew louder every second. It would be the cars. Something to do with these cars would be her end.

She wanted to close her eyes but knew she mustn't. A moment more and it would all be over. The rushing sound grew and then she saw them. She saw them coming and had never heard anything like it. An eruption of noise so impossibly loud that it filled the world. *Wham thump wham wham thump!* They slashed by her at astonishing speeds: trucks, cars, motorcycles. All of them beating her down into her chair with their power and threat until she felt there was no more air to breathe.

Close. They came closer by the second. Was this it? Was this the second? Or the next? The next? *Whump! Wham! Whump! Whump!* The draft off their speed slammed her face, pushed her body back into the chair. She started to hyperventilate. She wanted to stick her fingers in her ears and make the sounds go away. But how could she? How could anyone block out the end of the world? She tried to swallow but there was no liquid in her mouth.

Because there were so many, she didn't notice the blue car until it veered from its path and came right at her. Headlights straight on her face, it still didn't really register until it flew up to within feet of her—and stopped. There was a wild shush and scrabble of sand, gravel, and dirt flying into the air all around it. Cars on the road hammered by. But now there was this one, so close. Was *this* it? Time passed—seconds? And then the door opened and first she heard a shrill ting-ting-ting of a bell inside telling the passenger something was wrong.

The overhead light came on and she saw the driver inside. A man. He was staring straight at her and did not move. But then he was getting out of the car, careful to look behind so he would not be hit by the slam of oncoming traffic. He pushed the door closed but not enough to stop the 'ting' inside.

He walked slowly toward her. A middle-aged man. There was something in his face, something familiar but so distant and remote that her pounding heart couldn't figure it out. Something . . .

"I didn't know if I'd get here in time."

She said nothing, only stared at him and the noise was brutal and all over but something she knew, something on the tip of her mind said, Look harder, find it. And she did. She recognized him. *"Declan?"*

Only when he smiled did she know for sure it was Hugh's son, because he wore his father's smile. She would have recognized it if she had lived to be a million years old.

"We have to hurry, Miranda. They're coming and I don't know how much time we have. I've broken every rule in the book—"

"How did you know I was here?"

"You know *everything* when you're one of us. Being immortal has its advantages." He looked worriedly behind him.

"How can you know already that you're immortal? You've only lived one life! That's why I was writing the diary! So you'd find it and know and then you could avoid—"

"We have to go, Miranda! There's no time. Tell me in the car. We have to get out of here right now. They're coming."

"Why, Declan? Why are you doing this?"

He spat out the words. "Because you gave me my life! Because you sacrificed your own daughter so that *I* could live. How could I not at least try to help you?"

A pause. Recognition. Amazement.

All she could do and it was done without thinking was hold out the stick his father had given her. Declan would understand what it was.